Critical acclaim for Wildfire

"I've really enjoyed Scott's in the Lei Crime series KW, as well as his historical novels about WWII, but this one, his first venture into crime/thriller fiction, is really good! Wine country, during the recent fires, a look into real winemaking, well developed characters, California scenery, well, add who done it, did they, who was it? A great read, hopefully working into a great series! Highly recommended!"

— Bonnie Thompson, Amazon reader and reviewer

"This book carries you through the return to the winery after the fire to find the truth. It keeps you guessing until the final pages."

— Kenneth Lingenfelter, Amazon reader

"A great read."

— Anna Russell, Amazon reader

"Great start to a new series. Really looking forward to finding out more about Tara and her new job. It starts out at a run, and keeps you hooked til the end."

— Diane G, Amazon reader

Wildfire

A novel

by Scott Bury

The Written Word

Ottawa

Wildfire

C edition

ISBN 978-1-987846-12-6

Published by The Written Word Communications Company, Ottawa, Ontario, 2018.
An Independent Authors International title.

Cover design by David C. Cassidy
Edited by Gary Henry
Proofread by Joy A. Lorton, Typo-Detective
Quality control by Independent Authors International.

Independent Authors International

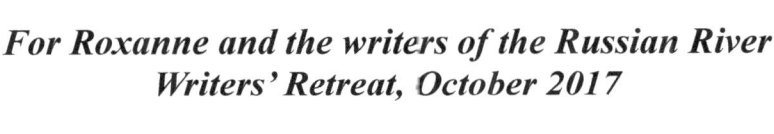

For Roxanne and the writers of the Russian River Writers' Retreat, October 2017

Contents

An open door

Tara's shoulder slammed into the passenger door as the big old pickup flew around a bend. She wanted to tell Roberto to slow down and speed up at the same time, so she clenched her jaws to prevent herself from biting her tongue as the truck bounced on the rough dirt road.

The air in the truck was thick with heat and smoke. Tara tasted ash in her throat. To the west on the left, Tara could see blue sky through the windshield above the scrub-covered, brown slopes. But to the east on her right, grey clouds that faded to black at the horizon blocked the sky. A slope fell away beyond the road's narrow shoulder, smoke obscuring the vineyards she knew grew there. Opening a window would only let in the smoke, and it was already hard to breathe.

Tara clutched the door handle as the truck fishtailed. She heard the crunch of tires on the narrow gravel shoulder. Roberto wrestled the wheel, bringing the truck back on course.

Tara risked a glance at him. His brows drew together in a frown and he pressed his normally full lips into a tight, thin line. But there was determination in his brown eyes.

Roberto's hands were tight on the wheel as he negotiated a sharp bend. The truck didn't fishtail this time, but the turn made

Tara slide across the seat and the seat belt dug into her side. Her hands flew up to the dash just in time to brace herself as Roberto braked hard, then turned sharply to the right onto a paved road.

"Is this—" she said, regretting it as her mouth filled with the taste of smoke.

"The road to the main gate. We got past the roadblocks," Roberto answered without looking at her. He pressed the pedal down and the truck's engine roared. Tara kept one hand braced on the dash, the other holding the door handle to keep herself from sliding across the seat as they rounded the last curve. She knew there was a gate a quarter-mile ahead, but she could barely see a slightly darker tone to the smoke across the road, let alone the brass plate that read "Rocky Creek Winery."

"Think the gate's open?" she asked, moving her left hand to brace against the roof.

"Sure hope so." Roberto coughed, and Tara answered with her own cough, but it did nothing to ease the heat in her throat. Her eyes burned, but there were no more tears to cut through the ash on her cheeks.

Roberto slowed the truck, and Tara moved her left hand to the dash again. The low stone wall, decorative more than functional, slowly materialized behind the billowing smoke.

Seeing it brought a vivid memory to mind, and she saw the wall on a clear late-summer day, the first time she had seen it, with the ornate wrought-iron gates, both wide open. Beyond the wall on a small rise stood a Spanish-style mansion whose terra-cotta roof tiles seemed to glow in the California sunlight. She had parked her old Civic in the last place at the far end of the visitors' parking lot.

She remembered how she had checked her face in the rearview mirror before opening the door, hoping she had not put on too much makeup. She had seen a question in her green eyes—was she really going to apply for a job in a restaurant?

She got out of the car, recoiling from the heat rising from the pavement. She straightened her jacket, pulled the strap of her briefcase higher on her shoulder and flipped her brown hair back as she strode up the front steps with all the confidence she could fake. Even that slipped away when a young, African-American man in a uniform put his hand on her shoulder to direct her back onto the porch of the mansion that had been transformed into a restaurant. He pointed past the manicured lawn and customer parking lot toward a simple barn-like building at the back of the estate. Tara swallowed, pulled her strap up again and strode toward it.

From a distance, the winery looked like a simple barn, but when she got close she could see it was a modern building, painted to match the yellow and orange of the mansion-restaurant. Set into the ersatz stucco front wall was a wide barn door made of solid dark wood. In its center, a human-size door gaped open. When Tara walked close enough, she could feel conditioned, cool air flowing out.

She leaned in and knocked on the open door. No one said anything. She could hear the hum of some kind of machinery. Smooth concrete floors and light grey ducts and pipes gleamed under halogen lights on the high ceiling. To the left, windows in sheetrock walls showed offices, where a man with dark hair sat, writing with a pencil.

Tara took another deep breath of cool air, stepped up to the office interior door and knocked on its frame. The dark-haired man looked up quickly, hazel eyes wide, then relaxing. She could now see a shaggy dog curled up on the floor near his feet.

"Yes? Can I help you?"

His voice was deep and smooth, his tone fast but courteous. *Tinged with sadness? Stop imagining things, Tara. You haven't even met him yet.*

"Mr. DaSilva?" She stepped farther into the office, hand extended. The dog stood up, looking at her. The tail wagged tentatively. Its head was just below the level of the desktop, its light brown fur curly. It had a square nose and the fur at the blunt end of it looked to Tara like a moustache.

"I'm Tara Rezeck."

The dark-haired man stood to shake Tara's hand. He was tall and slim. The sleeves of his open-necked dress shirt were rolled up over his elbows, showing ropy forearms. His hand was rough, his grip firm. On the left hand was a large gold ring with a dark stone. "Rezeck? Oh, yes. Sophia called about you." He indicated a guest chair in front of his desk and sat again. "So you're looking for a job?"

The dog's mouth opened slightly and its tail wagged freely now.

Tara already had a crisp new copy of her résumé out of her briefcase. He took it and leaned back in his chair.

She waited, trying not to look around the office like some kind of thief casing the place. It wasn't much to look at, just the working office of a company that made wine. Messy stacks of paper and notebooks took up most of DaSilva's desk, and on an extension at right angles to the main part sat a large office telephone and a laptop computer. The screen saver was a picture of a vineyard.

On the wall beside DaSilva, over the laptop computer, a large whiteboard hung, covered with a multi-colored chart and acronyms that Tara could not begin to interpret. Behind him was a large window that looked out into the winery. Beyond high tanks, Tara thought she could see people moving around.

A window on the other side looked outside, where trucks were parked on a wide, dusty yard. Behind that was a thick hedge, a fence, and beyond that the vineyards, on south-facing slopes bathed in sunlight.

"You have a law degree?" DaSilva was staring at her, eyebrows high and mouth slightly open.

Tara nodded. "From Vermont Law School. I graduated cum laude last spring."

"Then what are you doing here? Why aren't you applying for jobs with law firms in Vermont?"

I knew this question was coming. I'm ready for it. "After my daughter was born 18 months ago, I decided I needed a change." She kept her voice steady, her words paced. "I finished my law degree and came to California to start fresh."

DaSilva sat forward, a smile growing across his face. "A baby girl? What's her name?"

"Roxanne."

DaSilva nodded. "A beautiful name. And where is she now?"

Tara suppressed the hitch she could feel in her throat. "She's staying with my parents in Burlington for now, until I get established here."

"Oh, that must be hard on a young mother like yourself."

I hope he didn't see me swallow right there. "Yes, I guess it is." She blinked rapidly and looked at the vineyards. A man in jeans and work boots climbed into a dusty pickup truck and started the engine. More dust blew across the road.

"Well, you still haven't explained why you're applying at a vineyard instead of a law office."

You have this answer prepared, too, Tara. "Thousands of people graduate from law schools every year and come to California looking to start their careers at a prestigious firm with a big reputation. I guess it was naive of me to think I would land a job with all that competition."

"Even with a cum laude degree from an eastern college?" DaSilva sat back, twirling a pencil in his hand. Tara tried not to let it distract her.

"Even with a cum laude degree. I guess it's like everything else—it's not what you know, it's who you know. And I don't know anyone in California."

"Except Sophia Vorona."

"I just met Sophia in Sausalito. She's very nice."

"Ah, that's better."

"What's better?"

"You're smiling, finally. You know, they say you should try to smile in job interviews. It helps the prospective employer feel more positive toward you."

Tara did not know how to answer. After waiting for a few seconds, DaSilva chuckled and picked up the résumé again. "Well, I don't have much use for another lawyer. Not just yet, anyway, but you never know. So, what else can you do? Know anything about the wine business?"

A laugh escaped her lips. "No, sorry. I know I like to drink it, and I know a little about grape varieties and about pairing with food. But nothing about the business."

DaSilva laughed, too, and looked directly into her eyes. "That's a good thing. And a smart thing to say in a job interview for a winery, too. That you like the product, that is. Not necessarily that you don't know anything about the business."

Tara felt panic tightening her chest. She leaned forward, hand on the desk. "I do know something about *this* business, Mr. DaSilva."

"Please, call me Alan."

"I know you've won a number of awards over the years. Gold medals, prix d'honneur, more. Yours is one of the smaller wineries in the Sonoma Valley with one of the best reputations. And from what I've read, there are several competitors who are jealous of the piece of land you have for the grapevines. They say it's the most ideal location for a terroir in California—with the best soil, best drainage, and the perfect situation to the sun."

Alan was nodding, a smile playing at the corners of his mouth. He twirled the pencil again. "Do go on."

Tara swallowed. "But apparently, you've been struggling to keep up with demand for your product. There have been some accidents in the ... oh, I forget the technical term ..." *Damn it, Tara, pull yourself together. This is no time for memory lapses.* "In the production area. Damage to some of your larger tanks and bottling lines. They set you back and cost you a lot of money."

Alan continued to nod, but he no longer smiled. "That's true. We had a string of unexplained accidents last year."

Oh, no, now he's not happy anymore. Way to blow the first job interview you've had in California, Tara.

Bring it back to the positive. "But you've also had some good news in the past two years. Your restaurant got a Michelin star, and nothing but great ratings in all the reviews."

A faint smile touched Alan's mouth again. "That's right. The restaurant has done—is doing—very well. Making money. That's mostly due to my wife. She found our new chef, and managed to convince him to come way out here to work. And she managed to get some big-name restaurant reviewers to make the drive up from San Francisco, too." He looked out the window, too, and the smile vanished. "I still don't really know how she managed to do that." He took a deep breath and turned his hazel eyes to Tara again. "All right, your résumé proves you're smart and ambitious, and Sophia said you were a hard worker. What did you do for her?"

Tara shrugged. "Nothing much. We just sort of met by accident. I needed a place to stay. She needed some help around the house and diner she owns. I helped her and stayed in her guest bedroom for a few days. I said I was looking for some steadier work, and she mentioned you."

"So, you've worked in Sophia's restaurant?"

"Yes, just helping with some of the food prep."

"Did you study food service?"

"No, but I worked in a restaurant in the summers between college terms. I love to cook." *Talk yourself up, Tara.* "And I'm good at it. Very good."

DaSilva nodded. "Anything else I should know about you?"

"I have a black belt in karate. I got that when I was in high school."

"Wow. A dangerous woman. Remind me never to get into a fight with you. I don't know whether we can use you in the winery, but we do need some help in the kitchen."

The dog came to her and pressed its nose between Tara's knees. "Charlie, down," Alan said. The dog looked at Alan and whined. Alan pointed at the floor where the dog had been sleeping. "Charlie," he repeated.

The dog whined again but sat down where it had been, its eyes fixed on Tara.

"What kind of dog is Charlie?" Tara asked.

"A terrier mix." Alan leaned over and patted its head, and the tail swished back and forth across the floor. "Not the smartest dog in the world, but he does know good people. Everyone who works here has had to pass the Charlie test."

"What's the Charlie test?"

"Charlie has to make friends with you. Well, one person isn't Charlie's friend. But … never mind." Alan sat back in his chair and fixed an intent look on Tara's eyes. "We've had a lot of turnover in the last few months. Chef Donald is great, but he's not exactly the easiest guy in the world to work for. If you've got a thick skin, I can put you to work in the kitchen. The pay's not great, but it's steady, and it comes with room and board. You can start tonight, if that works for you."

"Tonight?"

Alan smiled again and stood up. "Like I said, Chef's not easy to work for. We had a line cook quit last night." He reached a hand across the desk and Charlie got up again, his tail wagging fast. "So, you ready to work?"

Tara looked into Alan's hazel eyes. She noticed the very middle of the iris, a narrow rim around the deep black pupil, was like a ring of green fire.

"You know, it's traditional that when someone offers you a job, you shake their hand." Alan laughed. "Especially when they're holding their hand out to you. Like this."

Tara shut her mouth and took Alan's hand. "Yes. Yes! I can start tonight. I have all my things in my car, right in the parking ..."

Alan laughed, long and deep this time. "That's fine. Come on, let's meet the people you'll be working with, and then I'll show you where you can stay." They went out of the office, Charlie trotting behind.

The sound of grinding gears snapped Tara back to the present. She became aware again of the smoke filling her nostrils as Roberto eased the big pickup through the space left by one open gate. They went slowly past the old mansion that housed the restaurant, and Tara almost sighed with relief when she saw her Civic in the parking lot.

They both gasped when they passed the corner of the mansion to see a lurid red glow and thick black clouds from the back of the property. "The guest house," Tara said at the same moment that Roberto exclaimed "The winery!"

Smoke and ash

As Roberto drove past the restaurant mansion toward the source of the billowing black smoke, Tara saw a form kneeling in the dust beside the winery, its back to them.

"It's not the winery; it's the garage," Roberto said. One wall blazed and the roof was gone. Black clouds rose to join the smoke the wind pushed into the valley.

Roberto stopped the truck with a lurch and threw the door open. "That's Nicole!" He jumped out and ran toward the kneeling woman.

The smoke assaulted Tara as soon as she opened her door. Tears blurred her vision, but she could see Nicole's shoulders shaking. Ash flakes turned her dark brown hair grey and covered her shoulders and back. Beside her was a blurred shape that could only be Charlie, his nose to the ground.

There was something in front of the dog, something long and dark and covered in grey ash. *No, no, don't let it be ...*

Roberto bent beside Nicole, his hand going to her shoulder for a moment. Then he turned and stepped away, doubled over and vomited onto the dust and ash.

Tara fell to her knees beside Nicole. *Oh, my god, it is, it is, I can see his ring.*

It's Alan. Alan's dead. He's burned. I can't even recognize him.

Charlie whined, licking Alan's burned face, pawing his shoulder. Tara felt her stomach heave as black flakes came off on the dog's tongue.

His clothes are burned, they've—don't let yourself think it, Tara. Help Nicole.

Nicole sobbed silently, her body shaking, her mouth wide open. Fresh ash stained her cheeks where tears had temporarily cleaned them. She took a shuddering breath, then choked on the smoke and ash she inhaled.

From somewhere, Tara found the strength to stand. She pulled Nicole to her feet. "Come on, we have to get out of here." Nicole shook her head. A thin whine came from her and she pulled her arm from Tara's grip to reach for her husband's body. When her hand touched him, though, it made a crispy, cracking sound. The black outer layer, whether cloth or skin, crinkled and broke. Blood stained Nicole's hand, bright red as a traffic light. She recoiled, coughing and crying.

Gagging on the smoke, Roberto lifted Nicole from under her arms, practically dragging her to the truck. Tara followed, pushing on the woman who would have been shrieking if she could stop coughing. "There's nothing you can do for him now, Nicole," he said, pushing her into the back seat and buckling the seat belt around her.

Nicole's face was streaked black, grey and red. She shook her head, her mouth a wide, trembling hole, and she tried to reach out. Tara climbed in, kneeling backwards on the front seat so she could push Nicole's arms out of the way to shut the door. "There's nothing more we can do, Mrs. DaSilva. You have to save yourself. There's no point in both of you ..." She could not bring herself to say *dying*.

Nicole breathed in audibly again and found the desiccated remains of her voice. "We can't just leave him there."

Roberto stood outside the driver's side, his hand on the wheel and one foot in the truck. He exchanged a look with Tara and nodded toward Alan's body. Tara swallowed and nodded back.

"I'll take his shoulders," Roberto said in a voice dry as the falling ash. "Let me open the tailgate first."

Tara bent at Alan's feet, hesitating before she touched the blackened ankles. Charlie pressed his nose into her leg, looking up at her and whining.

Please hold it together, Tara. Please don't let his body break or bleed on me. If he does, I'll fall apart, I just know it. Keep it together.

Roberto lifted Alan from the shoulders, much as he had taken Nicole, and Tara lifted by the ankles. She did not let herself look at the way soot spread black across Roberto's t-shirt as they lugged the body behind the truck.

Roberto grunted as he lifted the body over the edge of the tailgate. It rolled onto its side, but together, Tara and Roberto managed to push it beyond the gate.

Charlie jumped up beside the body, whining, before Roberto could lift the tailgate. He had to drag the dog by the collar, until Tara could gather him into her arms and carry him to the cab. He sat in the back seat beside Nicole, who held her face in her hands. Charlie whined and put his head on her thigh, looking up at her blood- and ash-smeared hair.

I hope she wasn't looking at us putting Alan's body into the truck. God, that was awful. So undignified.

Roberto threw the truck into gear and gunned the engine. They flew through the gate and down the road, now barely recognizable through the smoke and under the ash.

Tara looked down. Black soot streaked her shirt and pants, and her running shoes were grey. She did not dare look into the vanity mirror in the sun visor.

Roberto was even sootier, a black smear across his chest and reaching up his throat and chin. His hands spread soot across the steering wheel and gear shift.

Tara found her water bottle, now nearly empty, and passed it to Nicole. *Now's not the time to worry about germs.* Nicole looked up barely long enough to see the bottle and shook her head.

"Take some. You need it," Tara urged. "Go on." As if to urge her to comply, Charlie poked his nose into her shoulder.

Nicole took the bottle, gulped, choked, and spat water on her knees and the back of the seat. She coughed twice, then drained the bottle. Tara took it back as gently as she could.

She rocked to the side as the truck negotiated a tight turn, but the main road toward the highway was much smoother than the back roads they had navigated to the winery.

Tara was still kneeling backwards, and she and Charlie nearly slid to the floor when Roberto braked suddenly. "What the—"

She recovered and turned. Red and blue lights flashed in the smoke ahead, and then they could see a police car, parked across the intersection with the highway. A highway patrolman in a reflective vest climbed out and waved his arms, indicating they should stop.

"It's not like I was going to smash right into his car," Roberto growled.

"Where the hell did you come from?" the cop yelled. "Didn't you hear all the roads into the valley are closed?"

"We have a body in the back," Roberto answered, nodding toward the back seat. "Her husband."

The cop was fresh-faced, young and nervous. Even in the dimness and ash, his face shone with sweat. Fear or heat? Both, Tara decided. He looked at Nicole, who was sobbing quietly, shoulders still heaving.

The cop moved his light to the truck bed. "Oh, my god." Tara could see him shaking. "I—you—oh, my god." He turned away, bending over, trying to breathe—which was not easy in the smoke. Finally, he turned back to them. His eyes were rimmed red. "You better go to the evac center in Barnestown. There's medical help there." He leaned closer and lowered his voice. "And a morgue, too."

"Okay. Thanks."

The cop hustled to move his car and Roberto turned onto the highway, driving away from the smoke. Tara could no longer see any blue sky, even to the west. A bilious yellow spot in the smoke showed where the sun was sinking below the horizon.

She turned to look past Nicole out the rear window, and saw one of Alan's legs at the back of the truck bed. She only realized then that the shoe was missing. She thought of the first day she had met Alan.

After having Tara fill out the paperwork to become a full-time employee at Cyrano's, Rocky Creek Winery's upscale restaurant, Alan took Tara to the big old Spanish-California style mansion, Charlie trailing at Alan's heel. "When we bought the place, this old house was falling apart," he said. "We took almost a year converting it into this restaurant."

Alan pointed at the deck behind the back door. Charlie whined, but sat, licking his chops. Alan led Tara into a gleaming, modern kitchen. White tiles covered the walls, terra-cotta the floor. Stainless steel refrigerators took up most of the back wall. The front was only a half-wall, giving a clear view of the cooking area, where a gas range stretched across a wide counter. Beyond it was the dining room.

In between were counters, sinks, two stainless steel ovens and a wide gas range. A tall, thin man in a dark kitchen uniform and hat stood at the counter, stirring something in a bowl, and a shorter man in the same uniform rinsed dishes in the sink.

Standing at the range was a short blond man with an angry expression on his face. Alan rapped on the counter to get their attention. "I'd like you all to meet Tara Rezeck, your new line cook. Tara, meet our Chef, Donald Bailey. This is Antonio, sous chef. Miguel, plongeur."

"New line cook? Great," Chef Donald growled. "About time you got someone to replace that useless what's-his-name. Jerk quit without notice yesterday," he said to Tara. "You're a lot easier on the eyes than him, too," he leered. "Get a uniform on. We've got plenty for you to do before the supper rush starts."

"Just a minute, Donald," Alan said. "We have some formalities to complete, first."

"Formalities? I have a kitchen to run."

"Then keep running it. Come with me, Tara."

Donald scowled, but Alan ignored him, leading the way to the dining room.

A tall, curvy woman came down a staircase near the front door. Her long, black hair and facial features spoke of a mixed Asian heritage, and she was wearing a loose top and black yoga pants that hugged generous curves. "Tara, meet my wife and the manager of the restaurant, Nicole."

They shook hands, but Nicole looked puzzled. "Nice to meet you."

"I've just hired Tara to be our new line cook, to help Chef Donald in the kitchen."

Nicole's eyes flashed. She forced a smile. "Oh? Don't you think that the restaurant manager should have a say in that?"

Alan nodded, looking sheepish. "You're right. I'm sorry, dear. But we really need someone, and Tara is the only qualified applicant we've had all week."

"Qualified?"

"She's worked in a restaurant kitchen before."

"Where?"

"Back east."

"Three consecutive summers, between college terms," said Tara. "Don't worry. I know my way around a kitchen."

"She's also worked for a few weeks for Sophia's restaurant in Sausalito."

"That's just a diner, Alan. It doesn't compare to a restaurant like this."

"Still ... she comes highly recommended."

"By Sophia Vorona." It was not quite a sneer.

"Sophia knows people. And Tara here graduated this spring cum laude."

"Cum laude? From the Cordon Bleu?"

"Vermont Law School, actually," Tara said, forcing a laugh.

"Law school?" Nicole looked from Tara to Alan and back.

"Send her back here, already!" Donald hollered from the kitchen. "We've got three hours before the rush starts."

"You heard the man," Alan said to his wife, who opened her mouth, then closed it tightly.

"Fine. We'll take her on a probationary basis. Good luck, Miss Rezeck. You're going to need it. Now I need to get ready." She stomped out the front door.

Alan led Tara out again, across the lot to a long bungalow that was out of sight of the restaurant. "These are your quarters until you want to move into your own place. You have two housemates: Alex—Alexandra, that is—and Greg are both on the wait staff. You each have your own bedroom, and you can work out the bathroom and kitchen cleaning duties with them. They're at work right now. As I said, rent is included with the job, and you can have all the meals you like from the restaurant, but any food you want here is up to you to buy."

He showed her a small bedroom, furnished with a single bed, a dresser and a nightstand. The window looked out onto part of Rocky Creek vineyard, and in the distance, she could see people moving along the rows of vines. Folded sheets sat on the foot of a bare mattress. "It's not much, but it's clean. And we'll trust you to keep it that way."

"It's wonderful! Thank you so much." *Maybe my luck is finally changing.*

"There are a few kitchen uniforms in the hall closet. Find one that fits, then come and meet me at the kitchen door."

After an exhausting, stress-filled supper shift, Tara set up her laptop, connected to the wifi network and opened a video call. Her mother answered on the sixth trill. "Tara. It's after midnight, you know." Her mother wore a houseccat over a nightie, and her dark hair, sprinkled with graying strands, was tied behind her head. She did not look like she had been sleeping. Tara knew she usually stayed up past midnight, reading. Usually, historical fiction, occasionally a mystery.

"Sorry—time difference. I couldn't call earlier. I just got off work."

"You got a job? Wonderful." Marie Rezeck turned, momentarily going out of focus. "John!" she called. "Tara's on Skype." Tara heard a distant reply. "Tara! Come up here and talk to your daughter."

"How is Roxanne?" Tara asked.

"Sleeping like an angel. She's such a dear."

"I miss her so much."

"She misses you, too. But don't worry. She ate all her supper, and she had a bath before bed. And she's getting better at using a sippy cup."

The screen seemed to brighter as her father's head reflected light into his computer's camera. Tufts of white hair stuck out on the very top and from the sides, but the goatee and moustache were, as always, perfectly trimmed and groomed. "Hey, sweetie. How's California treating you?"

"Tara got a job, dear," Mom said.

"You did? Great. With some fancy San Francisco law firm?"

Tara laughed. "No, actually, with a winery in Sonoma County."

"A winery needs legal help?"

"No, I'm working in the kitchen. They have a restaurant called Cyrano's."

Both her parents said, "Oh" at the same time.

"What kind of work are you doing?" Dad asked.

"Chef put me to work as a line cook. It was good—I made a cake."

"Oh, good, you get to do something you like," Mom said. "How did it go?"

"Chef's kind of a grump. Not friendly, but then, none of them are. Likes to give orders."

"Sounds like a typical chef," Dad said.

"He tasted a cake I made and didn't complain about it, and Nicole—she's the restaurant owner and manager—said that was a very good sign."

"What's she like?" Mom asked.

"She seems nice. I didn't get much of a chance to talk with her. She's busy. Actually, she seems kind of preoccupied."

"Didn't she talk to you when she hired you?"

"She didn't hire me, her husband did."

Dad's eyebrows rose, making ripples in his forehead.

"He's the co-owner. Alan DaSilva. He runs the winery part, and Nicole runs the restaurant.

"But he hired you to work in the part of the business his wife runs," said Dad.

"Yup." *I know where this is going.*

"Man hires a beautiful young woman to work at something he's not responsible for ... Are you certain about why he hired you?"

"I'm sure. He's not like that."

"You don't know anything about him, Tara."

"I can look after myself, Dad."

"I know, I know," Dad said, backing away from the camera. "All I'm saying is, be careful."

"Yes, Dad." *Dad, oh Dad. I'm an adult. I think I know how to live in the world.*

But I had an unplanned child, and now I'm a single mother. Okay, I'm not perfect. I make mistakes.

Mom broke her reverie. "So do you like the job?"

"Sure. It's good to be working in a kitchen again."

"Working in a restaurant is not like cooking at home, honey. I know all about that."

"I do, too, remember? Working at Fratelli's three summers in a row and a full year before law school?"

"I remember. It wasn't that long ago."

"But you're going to keep looking for something in your field, right?" Dad said.

"Of course. It will probably take some time. Like I said yesterday. And the day I left for California."

"But you won't give up, right?"

"Sure. Listen, I better go. It's been a long day, and it's later over there, right?" She forced a yawn.

"Just a minute," Mom said. "Where are you staying now? Still with that lady in Sausalito?"

"Oh, yeah, that's the best part! The job comes with room and board in the guest house."

"Guest house?" Dad frowned. "What kind of restaurant is this?"

"It's a very high-end place that's part of a winery way up in Sonoma County. I guess it used to be a farm or a ranch or something. The main house is now the restaurant, and there's a smaller house with three bedrooms for some of the staff who don't have homes close by. It's two hours' drive from San Francisco."

"And where do the owners live?" Dad asked.

"I'm ... not sure. I think there's another house on the property. Obviously, they didn't give me a tour."

Dad put on his ironic face. "So this man who hired you for a job he's not responsible for, also has a key to your house?"

"We just had this conversation, Dad. A minute ago. I told you, I can take care of myself."

Dad held up his hands. "I know, I know. Okay. I won't bring it up again."

"All right, honey. Call again, but earlier if you can, okay?" Mom said. "Maybe before Roxanne's bedtime?"

"For sure, Mom. Love you."

"Love you," Mom and Dad said together. She closed her laptop, stretched and yawned for real this time.

Then she remembered the bed. The sheets were still folded neatly at the foot. She listened as she made up the bed, and decided that Greg and Alex, her housemates, had gone to bed. She pulled on a housecoat and went for a shower.

An hour later, Tara gave up on sleeping. *I can never sleep the first night in a new place. It was the same at Sophia Vorona's in Sausalito.*

She got out of bed to look out the window at the vineyard, leaning her elbows on the sill. A faint, bluish gleam moved beside the winery, which was only a deeper shadow in the dark. *Is someone out there with a cell phone? Sending messages after midnight?*

The old song "Walking After Midnight" started playing somewhere at the back of her mind.

Then she heard a deep murmur. More shadows moved near the winery, coming together, merging, falling silent for a moment, then parting with more murmurs.

Who's out there?

She cracked the window open, letting hot, dry air flood into the room. She held her breath, listening as hard as she could.

Murmuring. A woman's stifled cry. A rhythmic rustling.

Are two people doing it out there?

A low, long groan, and the rustling ceased. Silence.

Crickets chirped.

Then more murmurs. Then a man's voice: "Damn it, I love this ass." A smack and a soft squeal. Whispered words that Tara could not make out.

Wow. Two people just did it, almost under my window.

I knew I would love California.

Orientation

Tara sipped from a steaming mug and stepped out the door. Greg and Alex were still sleeping, or at least quiet behind their closed bedroom doors.

They don't have to start work until afternoon. I guess I'll have to adjust to a later schedule if I'm going to work until 11 p.m.

She strolled toward the winery barn, trying to get a better idea of the layout of the place.

Nine o'clock and it's already hot. Maybe I should switch to iced coffee in the morning. At least until the weather changes.

She decided to call her parents before noon, so that she could at least see Roxanne and hear her little voice. The thought of her baby daughter kindled an ache deep inside.

I'll have to get my own place soon. This guest house is nice, but it's no place for a baby. Then I'll have to find day care. So I'll need a job that pays more than this. Dad's right. Keep looking at law firms. Maybe the state. Or a municipality.

She passed the winery as Alan DaSilva came out the door, Charlie at his heel. "Good morning, Tara. Hot enough for you?"

Tail wagging fast, Charlie nosed Tara's thigh. She bent to pat his wooly head. "You could say that. Is it normally this warm here, this time of the year?"

30

"Not at all," Alan said, his eyes sweeping across the grounds. "This is the hottest late summer or early fall I can remember in Sonoma. Not to mention the driest. But it's good for the grapes." Charlie flopped to the ground, tongue lolling. "So, did you sleep well?"

Is Dad right about this guy, she wondered. "I never sleep well the first night in a new place."

Alan nodded. "Neither do I. I hope you're feeling okay. Not too tired?"

No, I'm just being paranoid. "I guess I've gotten used to moving around a lot over the past couple of months."

"First day on the job went okay? I hope Chef wasn't too tough on you."

Tara laughed. "No, it was fine."

"I heard you made a good impression on him."

That puzzled Tara. "You heard that?"

"Well, he didn't yell at you, and he told Nicole you made a good cake."

"He said that? He looked to me like he barely tolerated it."

Alan laughed. "That's high praise from Chef Donald. Don't get used to it. He's a tough taskmaster."

"So, where is Mrs. DaSilva? Nicole? I barely had a chance to talk to her last night before she went out."

Tara thought a dark cloud passed over Alan's face. "Oh, she just went to ... visit a friend of hers." He clapped Tara on the shoulder. "Look, I gotta go up to the vineyard. But if there's anything you need, you just let me or Nicole know. Ciao."

He strode to a dusty, battered old pickup. Charlie jumped inside as he opened the door, crossing to sit in the passenger seat. Alan slammed the door and drove out a gate behind the winery that Tara had not noticed before. It led to a dirt road that went down a slope. In the distance, Tara saw rows of grapevines.

But where is Nicole?

She tried a sip of coffee. It was finally cool enough to drink, but the sun was cruelly hot on her forehead. She walked around the winery into the shade and nearly stepped on a dark-haired man who was crouching against the wall, smoking a cigarette. "Oh, I'm sorry."

The man rose to full height of about six feet, flicking the half-smoked cigarette into the dust. "That's all right. You must be Tara."

"You already know who I am. People sure talk about other people around here."

The man's smile was like a movie star's, full and bright white against his dark skin. He had thick black hair with one full wave over his forehead, thick eyebrows and large, dark eyes.

Wow—this guy is hot. Those eyes, and that full mouth—

Focus, Tara. Thinking like that cost you a year's delay in your education.

But it gave me Roxanne.

"My name is Roberto Gonsalves." He held out his hand. Tara shook, and his grip was gentle. "I am the manager of the winery."

"I thought that was Alan's job."

Roberto flashed that smile again. "He is the boss, yes, of the whole place. I am in charge of only the winery—where we make the wine. Not of the vineyards, or the restaurant."

"That's where I work."

"I know. You did well on your first day."

"I heard that, too. So how is it people know so much about me before I know anything about them?"

"Alan holds a daily briefing with key managers first thing in the morning. New employees are always on the agenda. It's important that we know what's happening in every department. Are you always this paranoid?"

"Only around handsome California men." She smiled and flipped her hair back over her shoulder.

Roberto laughed, flashing his white teeth again. "Funny *and* a good cook. My mother would tell me to marry you. So, can I show you around?"

You can show me anything you like.

Stop it, Tara. "Sure. All I've seen really is the kitchen and the guest house."

Roberto led the way around the building again. Tara regretted stepping into the hot sunlight again. "This, of course, is the winery," he said, pointing toward the building of the faux Spanish-style barn. "Where we crush the grapes, ferment the wine and bottle it. Over there," he pointed to the back of the winery, "is the garage, where we keep the trucks and other vehicles."

"Hence the name, 'garage.'"

"Smart. You know your English." He turned around to face the mansion. "That's the restaurant, of course. It was the original owners' house. Built in the 1920s, I think. Upstairs are offices."

A pickup truck, a new Ford F-350, turned from the road into the parking lot, then went past and stopped in front of Tara and Roberto. A man with white hair and a florid face climbed out. He buttoned a blazer to hide a sizeable belly and smiled as he took a good look at Tara. "Morning, Roberto." His voice was deep, gravelly, projecting self-assurance that sounded to Tara a lot like arrogance.

"Buenos dias, Steven. What brings you here this morning?"

"Aren't you going to introduce me to your friend?" He had not taken his eyes off Tara.

"Of course. Tara, this is Steven Harris. He owns Harris Estates down the road. Steven, this is Tara Rezeck, our new line cook."

He shook Tara's hand, exerting just enough pressure to let her know he could, and looked into her eyes. "Charmed. Line cook, huh? I hope you last longer than the last one. What was his name, Roberto?"

"Danny. No, he did not last very long," Roberto said.

"Chef Donald can be rough on his employees," Steven Harris said. He still had not taken his eyes from Tara. "You can't let him get under your skin, Miss."

Miss?

"Guys like him like to throw their weight around. You just have to stand up to them. And you tell Nicole if he's bothering you. Or better yet, tell Alan. Or Roberto, here." Harris leaned closer. He still had not released Tara's hand. "Just between us, Nicole is intimidated by Chef Donald."

"Thanks," Tara said, and extricated her hand from Harris' grip.

"What brings you out here this morning, Steven?" Roberto asked again.

Harris finally looked at Roberto. "I was just wondering if Cameron was here. I need him at the crusher, and I can't find him anywhere at home."

"Cameron is Steven's son," Roberto said to Tara. "And a good friend of mine." Tara noticed Roberto put a weird emphasis on the word *good*. "No, sorry. I haven't seen Cameron today—or yesterday, in fact."

"Hmmm," Harris grunted, looking around as if Cameron might be hiding on the property. "Well, if you see him ..."

"Have you tried calling his cell?" Tara asked.

"That kid never answers. I don't know why I pay for a cell phone for him. All he uses it for is sending texts." Harris pulled a new phone from his inner jacket pocket. "But I guess I could try again. If you do see him, tell him to at least call me, will you, Roberto?"

"Of course."

Phone to ear, Harris climbed back into his truck. Tara saw him shake his head and put the phone down before he started the engine and drove away.

Tara sipped her coffee, which was now getting too cool to enjoy. "Are all your neighbors this friendly?"

"Not all," Roberto said. "Steven acts friendly, but to tell you the truth, he's been trying to buy out the DaSilvas for years. He's a corporate guy more than a vintner. He's the CEO of a corporation that owns a lot of vineyards and wineries across the state."

Tara decided to bring the conversation back to Rocky Creek. "I read about how this vineyard is the envy of the county."

Roberto's eyes took on an intense earnestness. "Absolutely." He waved toward the slopes behind the winery. "It's not the largest vineyard in the valley, not by a long shot, but it's the most ideally situated in the whole state of California. The way the slope faces mostly south, the way the hills protect it from the worst of the storms from the west, the soil composition, the excellent drainage—it's like God decided to make one perfect place to grow the ideal grapes to make the best wine."

"But there's more to making wine than just the grapes, right? You have to know how to do it."

Roberto smiled his supernova smile again. "That's my job."

Tara took one last sip of her coffee, then poured the last of it onto the ground. "So, I see the winery, the garage and the restaurant. Where do the DaSilvas live?"

Roberto touched the back of Tara's shoulder to encourage her to turn. He pointed across the parking lot in front of the restaurant mansion. "There's another, newer house over there. Come on."

Tara followed him across the parking lot. When they were in front of the restaurant-mansion, Tara could see a modern bungalow nestled under a stand of trees beyond it. "That's the DaSilvas' house. Built around the 80s, I think. Anyway, it's a lot more modern and comfortable to live in than the mansion would be."

Tara tried to take it in. It looked neat and well maintained, with flowerbeds flanking the front door. As she stared, a red SUV came along the road from behind them, too fast. With tires squealing, it braked and turned hard into the DaSilvas' driveway and screeched to a stop in front of the garage on the far side. A woman jumped out and ran up the front steps.

That's Nicole DaSilva, wearing the same clothes she had on last night.

Nicole's hair was loose and messy, not carefully piled in an updo on top of her head like it had been the night before. *Where was she all night?* Tara wondered. *Did she spend the night somewhere else? Is she having an affair?*

Don't let your imagination get away from you, Tara.

Roberto's hand was on her shoulder again, encouraging her to turn away. "Come on, there's more to show you."

Roberto led Tara back to the gate to the vineyards, and they strolled for a short time between the rows of grapevines. He pointed out different varieties of grapes, some of which Tara had heard of before, like pinots and gamays, and others she hadn't, like cabernet franc and mourvèdre.

Roberto pointed uphill. "That's technically the best part of the vineyard, with the best drainage and the most sun exposure," he said. "But really, the whole place produces the best grapes that I've ever found in this part of California. For that matter, anywhere in the state, and actually, it's better than almost anywhere in the world."

"It's strange that it's owned by a relatively small winery like Rocky Creek," Tara said. "I mean, no offense, but you'd think something this desirable would have been bought up by one of the really big corporations."

Roberto nodded, surveying the vineyard. "Yeah, you'd think so. And there have been a lot of offers on the land over the years. But Alan's pretty determined to hang onto it, pass it on to his children."

"Does he have children?"

Roberto looked at Tara intensely for a moment, then back up the slope. "No. Not yet." He took a deep breath.

After waiting several moments for Roberto to say something else, Tara shrugged inwardly. "We.l, thanks for the tour. I better get to the kitchen. We're going to start soon."

Roberto turned to her again, looking as if he did not understand a single word she was saying. "Okay. Sure. Come on, then."

Tara returned to the guest house to change into her kitchen uniform. Before leaving, she inspected her reflection. *Gotta look good,* she told the mirror. *You're still the new guy on the job. Still making an impression.*

The kitchen uniform, with Rocky Creek embroidered in an elegant style on the left breast, at least looked attractive. *Nice clean white, with these black accent points. They must have had a fashion designer come up with this.*

California.

Tara's housemates, the servers Alex and Greg, were at the corner of the verandah that ran the length of the front of the old mansion. Alex sat on a wooden bench under the shade of the awning, while Greg stood in the corner of the shade, smoking a cigarette.

"You're too close to the entrance," Alex said, holding her long red hair in a bunch over her neck and rubbing her glasses across the front of her restaurant uniform with her free hand. "You know that Nicole hates smoking close to the door."

"Nicole is a pain in the ass," Greg answered. He was a short, stout, young African-American man with a razor-thin beard where he wished his jawline was.

"Morning, Greg, Alex," Tara said.

"Good morning," Alex answered, her voice high and bright. Greg just nodded.

Before Tara could say anything else, a hatchback came from the road, through the parking lot and stopped behind the restaurant. Chef Donald, a heavy, middle-aged man with short light-brown hair got out, opened the hatch and hefted a big box. Green leaves hung over the edges of the box. Tara could see more produce in the back of the car.

"Miguel! Antonio!" the Chef barked. The two kitchen staff ran down the back steps.

Antonio was an Italian immigrant, skinny with brown hair and large eyes. He was the main assistant in the kitchen, with professional training in Italy. Miguel, as far as Tara knew, was from California. Short, with short black hair and muscular forearms, he washed dishes and mopped the floor, fetched pots when Chef yelled for them and took the brunt of Donald's abuse.

They grabbed bags and boxes of produce and hustled them into the kitchen.

"Guess it's time to get to work," said Tara. *I wish I had time for one more cup of coffee.*

"Guess so," Greg said, grinding his cigarette into the dust.

She entered the kitchen to find Chef Donald inside the walk-in cooler, counting inventory.

"Good morning, Chef," Tara said.

Donald grunted. "Start making pasta."

Tara did a little tour around the kitchen to remind herself of the layout. She took a closer look at the gas stoves, wondering what she expected to see that was different from any other commercial gas stove. The serving counter, where she would put completed dishes for Greg and Alex to take to the customers, was at a comfortable height for her.

"Don't think that just because you made an edible dessert yesterday, you're a professional cook," Donald growled. "I'm keeping my eyes on you. You can bake the bread today. Dinner rolls, Italian style. And I want you to start roasting the chickens, too. And you can start making Bolognese sauce."

My specialty.

Midafternoon is typically a lull in a restaurant's daily activities. The lunchtime crowd has left, and everything that can be prepared ahead of time for the supper crowd is complete.

Greg and Miguel stepped outside to smoke. Alex carried her book out to read in the foyer. From the kitchen window, Tara saw Antonio's car coming out of the parking lot.

She jumped when a hand reached around her to place a tall stem glass on the counter. She turned to see Chef Donald almost nose-to-nose. She leaned back, and he lunged closer, picking up the glass before she knocked it over. He smiled and put the glass in her hand. He held another in his other hand. "Take it easy, there. It would be a shame to spill wine this good."

"You startled me."

"I didn't mean to. I just thought you deserved a little glass of wine for your hard work today."

What is this about? The Chef who berates and belittles the rest of the staff is praising me?

"The sauce is especially good—almost as though I made it myself," he continued. He smiled even more. "Talented, and gorgeous, to boot. This is a trend that I hope Alan continues. Drink up." He drank half his wine.

"Uh, is it ... I mean, are staff allowed to—"

"I run this kitchen. Staff do whatever I say."

"Oh. Oooh—kay."

Donald put his hand on the counter, bringing his face even closer to Tara's. "*Whatever* I say." His hand came up to her face then, to move a stray lock of hair away from her eyes. His touch was light and so gentle.

Now I know what this is about. She squirmed away from the trap between Donald and the counter. "Good to know. I have to do something on my break. Thanks for the wine." She strode out the back door and forced herself not to walk too quickly to the guest house.

At last, it's over. A full day of Chef Donald's abuse. Not to mention harassment. Oh, yes, and working my ass off in a kitchen. Now I remember why I decided against being a chef as a career. Tomorrow, I am definitely going to look for a job in a law office.

She stepped off the restaurant's back steps to see a man walking across the lot near the winery. "Roberto! Do you always work this late?"

The winery manager turned fast, and his teeth gleamed in the light over the winery door as he smiled. "Tara. You startled me." He came close. "All too often, I'm afraid. We had another breakdown of some bottling equipment. I've been working since afternoon to fix it."

"By yourself?"

"Alan was here, too. He just went home." He pointed with his chin toward the DaSilvas' house, beyond the restaurant mansion.

"Did you fix it?"

"Yeah. I hope so, anyway. We won't know for sure 'til we run it at production speed, though. How was your day?"

"Okay," she lied. "Chef Donald is ... demanding."

"He's a total jerk." Roberto opened the door to the winery. "Would you like to sample some wine before the night's over?"

Way to a girl's heart. "Sure."

Roberto led the way inside the winery, flipping on a single light in the office where Tara had met Alan the day before. "Have a seat," he said and disappeared into the winery's shadows. He returned with an unlabeled bottle. "We just tested the line with some chardonnay, so we're not gonna sell this, anyway," he explained as he filled two stem glasses.

"That's okay." They clinked glasses. "Wow, this is really good."

Roberto beamed his movie star smile at her. "Thanks." He sipped from his own glass. "It's a bit young—not our best vintage, either. But good for testing bottling equipment."

"I think it's excellent." Tara settled as comfortably as she could in the office chair. "So, wine's really your thing, huh?"

"My family's thing, really. My papa was a vintner, and my abuelo, too."

"Abuelo?"

"Granddad." He refilled Tara's glass.

"So, why are you working for Alan?"

Roberto's smile disappeared. "My family doesn't have its own winery anymore. We just had a small vineyard, smaller than this, and it didn't get through the crash in '08."

"I'm sorry."

Roberto leaned back in the desk chair. "S'alright. My folks're okay now. Pop's retired and my brothers all have jobs."

"And you're the manager of a famous winery."

Roberto barked a laugh. "Not that famous. We got a couple of good reviews."

"You make great wine."

Roberto nodded. "We do. But tell me about yourself. Alan tells me you have a law degree from a fancy eastern college."

"Not that it's done me much good. I work in a kitchen, remember?"

"A famous kitchen. Cyrano's has gotten more good reviews than the winery. But why are you working in a kitchen at all, if you have a law degree?"

Tara drained her glass. "I got a law degree. Along with thousands of other graduates this year, when you add up all the colleges in the country. I've wanted to live in California ever since I was a little girl. I actually wanted to study at Berkeley, but my father said, 'no way, I'm not paying for you to go to another university when there's a perfectly good one right here.'"

"Yeah, college is expensive. I hear." Roberto filled her glass again, then emptied the last of the wine into his own.

"Not for him. He's a college professor, so I got my undergrad degree for free."

"Wow. That's great. Just a sec." Roberto jogged into the depths of the winery again, returning with another bottle of wine. "This is something special." He glanced over his shoulder, as if afraid someone else would see him. "It's something I've been working on, on my own. A special blend of grapes I put together last year. I just made a couple of barrels to try. Not even Alan knows about it." He poured a glass half full of a deep purple-red wine for each of them. They toasted each other.

"Wow, this is really good. I've never tasted anything like this. You made it yourself?"

Roberto's smile lit up the office. "Not quite. It's based on my abuelo's recipe, but with some of my own touches, too."

Tara sipped more. "It's … complex. But in a good way. A great way, actually." She drank more. "It's almost as if it has a personality."

Roberto laughed.

"So, go on."

"Go on with what?" Tara's words were a little slurred. *It's late. I'm getting sleepy. And if I have much more wine, I'm going to find myself sitting in his lap.*

"With your life story. You always wanted to come to California. So you did law school, and then you came here to fulfill your dream, or something?"

"Something like that. I did some other stuff in between."

"Stuff?" He would not let her glass get lower than half-full.

"I had a baby."

Roberto froze. "A baby?"

Tara gulped more wine. "Uh-huh. A little girl. She's 18 months old now. Roxanne."

Roberto looked at her intently. "So, where is she now?"

"With my parents. They're looking after her until I get settled here in California. Fine a—I mean, *find* a good place for her to grow up in. Near schools, although I guess I have a couple of years before I have to worry 'bout that."

"I guess. And where's Daddy?"

"My father's in—"

"No, I mean, um, I don't want to pry or anything."

"Oh! Roxanne's daddy. Right." Tara sipped more wine. *Slow down there, girl.* "'Daddy's' not in the picture anymore. Never was, after I told him I was pregnant. Ran for the hills." *Oh-oh. TMI.*

"Too bad. The jerk doesn't know what he's missing," Roberto said, smiling. He sipped his wine.

He doesn't have to get me drunk, Tara thought.

Another part of her brain said, "Slow down."

"No, he doesn't know," she agreed. She leaned forward. "I think we're out of wine."

"I can always get more. For some reason, there always seems to be wine here."

God, that smile could do it by itself.

She put her hand on his knee. "I think I'm a little tipsy. Help me get home?"

"Sure." Roberto helped Tara rise, even though she really did not need it. She held onto his arm as they walked across the lot to the guest house. "We'll have to be quiet," she warned at the door. "I have two roommates. You know Greg and Alex, right?"

"Of course. Here you are. See you tomorrow."

Tara felt herself sway, and not from the wine. "Don't you want to come in?"

That smile again. "I'd love to, but you have two roommates. And you're an employee."

"Oh. Does the company have rules about … dating employees? Employees dating?"

"Not really. But it's late, and I have to get up a lot earlier than you do. And you have had a lot of wine."

He's turning me down? What did I do?

"Good night," he said.

She watched him get into his truck and drive away.

Turned down. Maybe I shouldn't have told him about Roxanne.

If that turns him off, to hell with him.

She went to bed.

Breakdowns

Alan came into the restaurant, wiping his hands on a towel. "Got anything to eat?" he asked Donald, plopping down on a barstool beside the serving window.

"It's a restaurant," Donald growled without looking up.

"Gimme some of that leftover beef stroganoff," Alan said.

Donald nodded vaguely in Tara's direction, so she put down the dough she was kneading and turned an element on under a pot of water. She took out a container of the previous night's stroganoff.

"Just microwave it," Alan said. "Don't make any special effort for me. I'm just the owner."

"It's nothing," Tara answered. The water boiled by the time the microwave beeped. She dropped fresh pasta into the water and fried chopped vegetables while the pasta boiled. She dropped the leftover meat and vegetables into the frypan just long enough to heat it as she drained the pasta, then put the plate in front of an eager Alan.

"Mm. This is good, but it's not stroganoff."

"Call it beef rezeck."

The front door slammed. Nicole crossed the dining room and kissed Alan on the cheek. "What brings you in this time of day?"

"I needed a break, and I was hungry, so I thought I'd find out for myself how good a cook Tara is."

"And?"

"Fantastic. Try." He put a forkful into his wife's mouth, who nodded as she chewed.

"Great," she said with a full mouth.

Tara tried not to notice Donald's scowl. "Okay, now you can quit sucking up to the boss and get going with the bread," he said.

"Everything okay?" Nicole asked, sitting beside Alan and pouring them both a glass of white wine.

Alan sighed. "I don't know what's going on lately. I've invested in high-end equipment. The latest stuff. And it's not cheap."

"Don't I know it," Nicole said.

"And we keep having these breakdowns. It seems we barely finish fixing one thing when the next breaks down."

"What is it this time?"

"Clog in the crush line. I've changed the filters three times in the past four days, changed hoses. And every morning this week, the line is clogged in a different place. I can't figure it out."

"And last week, the power failure. A short in the lighting subpanel, wasn't it?"

"Yup. And the week before, the computer server failed two months after I installed it. It's a good thing I backed everything up."

"Maybe we're cursed," Nicole joked.

"Sometimes I wonder if we're being sabotaged," said Alan, scooping up the last of the pasta.

Everyone in the kitchen turned to look at Alan.

"Who would do that?" Nicole said.

Alan shook his head. "I don't know. I don't know who would have an interest in sabotaging us."

He stood. "I better get back to it. Thanks, Tara, that was terrific. Hey, Chef, maybe you should think about adding beef rezeck to the menu."

Donald grunted, concentrating on a pan in front of him.

Alan left out the back door. Charlie, who had been sitting on the landing outside, stood, tongue hanging and pranced. He went down the steps, Nicole following him, her voice fading.

"Are you done with that bread yet?" Donald barked.

"Almost," said Tara, putting dough into loaf pans.

"Well, hurry up. You need to get those steaks marinated."

"Yes, Chef." *It's going to be another long day.*

Ignition

By her fifth day, Tara felt like she had fallen into a solid routine at the restaurant. In the late morning, dressed in the kitchen staff uniform, she kneaded dough for dinner rolls as Chef Donald checked the inventory, making notes on a clipboard. Antonio chopped vegetables for the soup, Miguel cleaned herbs from the restaurant's garden, and somewhere in the dining room, Greg and Alex polished the cutlery and fussed over the table settings.

Wearing jeans and a t-shirt, Nicole stood out from the others in the kitchen, who were all in uniform. She sat on a barstool at a small counter, typing out the daily menu on her laptop computer, frowning a little.

Those jeans really are too tight for you. Nice shoes, but heels like that won't be comfortable for long.

A radio sat on a shelf over Nicole's head. A song ended, the music replaced by the phony cheer of the announcer. "Strong winds again today across the state, and it'll be another record high temperature for this late in September, folks. No breaks or rain in the forecast for at least another week. The Public Health Department is advising everyone to stay well hydrated, and if you don't have to, don't stay outside for extended periods. But the weather isn't the only thing that's hot. We've got the hottest hits here on …"

Everyone in the kitchen turned as the back door banged open. Roberto stepped in, carrying a heavy cardboard box that bore a logo Tara did not recognize.

Nicole stood up as Roberto deposited his load on the main counter in the middle of the kitchen. "What are you doing? What's with the Harris wines?"

Harris—that's the next winery up the road. What is he up to?

"Relax, Nicole, it's a new—" Roberto began.

Nicole cut him off, stepping close and wobbling a little on her heels. "A new what? Don't you have enough to do in the winery without bringing our competition in?"

The door banged again, and a handsome young man wearing a blue and white plaid shirt entered, carrying another crate of wine. "Hello, everyone. One more crate."

Nicole's open mouth slowly turned into a smile. "Well, good morning, Cameron. What brings you here?"

Wow—he's as good looking as Roberto, but in a completely different way. Tall, athletic. Look at those shoulders. Reddish-blond curly hair, blue eyes. A hottie.

Concentrate on your work, Tara.

She thought about calling her parents at the break and seeing Roxanne.

Nicole twisted her hair around a finger as Cameron put the carton next to Roberto's. "It's an idea my Dad came up with: cross-promotion of the local wines in local restaurants and stores. We're giving you a couple of cases of chardonnay and sauvignon blanc to serve in Cyrano's, and we're putting some of your pinot noir and cabernet sauvignon in our storefront."

Nicole shifted her weight from foot to foot. "Well … but why?"

Cameron shrugged. "You know what Dad's like after he comes back from another business seminar. Cross-promotion with similar businesses is the newest trend, I guess. Don't worry, he talked to Alan about it."

"He did? When?"

Cameron shrugged again, and Tara thought the motion of his chest under his t-shirt was one of the sexiest things she had ever seen. "Dunno."

"I just spoke with Alan," Roberto said. He picked up the case again. "I'll put this in the cellar. Meet you in the winery, Cam?"

"Sure," Cameron answered, watching the winery manager's back as he hefted a case. "I'll start with loading a case from your inventory, okay?"

Nicole stepped closer to Cameron. "I think I'm going to ... have to have a *meeting* with ... Alan about this." She gave the young man an intense look.

Cameron nodded slowly. "Okay. I'll, uh, get the wine. The case of wine."

Tara realized she had ceased kneading the dough, so she started rolling it between her hands. *What am I seeing here?*

"Nicole, if you speak to Alan, remind him about that shipment from L.A. this week, will you?" Donald asked without looking up from his clipboard.

Nicole tapped a shapely fingernail on the counter. "Nicole? Mrs. DaSilva?" Donald prompted.

Nicole shook her head as if she were waking up. "The shipment ... right." She closed the lid of her laptop and picked it up off the counter. "I'll get these menus printed." She practically ran up the back stairs, her heels clicking on the hardwood.

"How are those dinner rolls coming?" Chef demanded.

"Almost done," Tara lied, rolling dough furiously. "How many dozen did you want again?"

"It's a midweek day, so six dozen for now. Remember to have something ready to go on the double if we get a rush. Miguel! What are you doing, watching the sage grow? Get to work. Antonio, is the soup ready yet?"

"Just putting it on the stove, boss," Antonio answered, sweeping a pile of chopped greens into a big stock pot.

"Get on with it then. I need you to get going on dressing those hens."

"Right away, boss."

"And stop calling me 'boss.' It's 'Chef.'"

"Yes, Chef."

Roberto returned from the wine cellar, smiling at Tara. He nodded at Chef Donald, who scowled back, then turned to Tara again and winked. "See you later."

Okay. Last night, he turned me down. Now this. What does this mean?

Chef gave everyone a break at 2:30 in the afternoon, allowing them to rest from the preparation activities of the early afternoon, before the evening customers started to arrive. Greg went outside to smoke again, Alex sat on an antique leather sofa in the front lobby, reading a book. Chef stayed in the kitchen, and Antonio and Miguel left out the back door.

Tara wandered into the dining room, looking closely at the furniture and décor. *It looks old-fashioned, but it's all new. High quality, too. This place must have cost a fortune to set up.*

She turned and saw Cameron standing at the bottom of the main stairs. "Oh, hey. You must be new here," he said, flicking his head to toss a reddish-blond curl out of his eyes. "I'm Cameron."

Tara shook his hand. "Tara Rezeck. Yes, I just started a few days ago. So, you're from the competition?"

Cameron laughed. "I wouldn't say that. All us wineries are more like … colleagues. It's friendly competition. We help each other out. And Roberto—the winery manager here? Have you met him?"

"Yes, I have."

"Yeah, well, he and I are best buds."

"So, friendly competitors in Sonoma just wander around each other's houses randomly?"

Cameron laughed again, shining a bright smile at Tara—much as Roberto had done when she had first met him. *Must be a California thing.* "So where you from, Tara Rezeck?"

He changed the subject without answering my question. He's a California charmer. My Dad warned me against these guys. "From Vermont."

She found herself following Cameron out of the front door. Alex glanced up at them when they came into the lobby, then put her nose back into her book. "So you came to sunny California to seek your fortune, huh?"

"Something like that." She could not help smiling at him.

They stepped outside and started walking toward the winery. "Listen, I promised to help Roberto with something. But maybe you and I could have a coffee sometime?"

"Maybe iced coffee."

Cameron laughed, waved, and trotted to the winery.

There's not much time left to Skype with Mom and Dad.

Mom answered on the second ring. The screen showed the kitchen. Roxanne sat in a high chair beside the table, something green smeared across her chubby cheeks. "Hello, sweetie!" Tara called, hoping her baby would turn toward the screen. But she never did. "Oh, I miss you so much, baby."

"She's having a great day today, aren't you, baby?" Mom said, holding up a spoon and a bowl decorated with a pink kitten. "She's eating up all her peas, and then she's going to have a big bottle of milk."

"She's really eating like a little horse," Dad's voice came from somewhere off-camera. "Hungry little girl." Dad's long fingers appeared to rub Roxanne's round head.

"Is that more hair I see?" Tara asked.

Mom leaned close to the baby. "Oh, yes, her hair is coming in thicker all the time. She's such a little beauty!"

"How's work going?" Dad asked.

"Not bad. It's busy, but the Chef seems to like what I make."

"That's good. Keep up the good work so you can get a good reference."

"Yes, Dad."

"We've heard on the news about fires in northern California," Dad said.

"Yes, there are wildfires in Napa. I can smell smoke."

"Are you safe?" Dad looked alarmed.

"We're fine, so far. Napa is a whole different valley from Sonoma."

"Well, make sure you look after yourself."

"How are the accommodations?" Mom asked as she guided another spoonful of green mush into Roxanne's wide-open, waiting mouth. The baby smacked her lips as she swallowed, then opened her mouth wide again for more.

"Nice. Not big, but clean and comfortable."

"What about something more permanent? Suitable for a family?" Roxanne opened her mouth and spat green mush onto the high chair tray in front of her.

"I think she's had enough for now," Dad said. His hand appeared on the screen again, holding a bottle of milk.

Seeing the baby take the rubber nipple into her mouth made something in Tara's chest hurt. "Oh, I miss her so much," she moaned.

"Well, how about it? Have you found a place for you and her to live?"

"Honestly, Mom, I've just gotten here. I haven't had a chance to look."

"Well, don't let it go too long," said Mom, standing and vanishing from the screen. Tara heard water running. "It's not good for a child to be separated from her mother for too long," she called, her voice hollow with the distance from the microphone.

"I promise, I'll start looking tomorrow morning, before work." She glanced at her watch. "Okay, Mom and Dad, break time's almost over. I have to get back to the kitchen. I'll call again tomorrow, okay?"

Mom and Dad both appeared in the screen. "Okay, sweetie. See you then." Dad picked up Roxanne's hand and made her wave. "Say 'good-bye' to Mama, Roxanne."

Tara managed to close the connection and her laptop before a tear escaped down her cheek.

Tara took a bottle of water from the guest house's refrigerator and returned to the restaurant's backdoor. Greg stood at the bottom of the steps, smoking. Alex stood at the top beside the kitchen door, drinking a soda.

To the west, the sky was blue. Eastward, where Tara knew Napa was, nothing but a dull grey haze. Wind blew her hair in front of her face and a stronger smell of smoke into her throat. She took a gulp of water, and it tasted of ash. "Isn't it smoky enough for you already?" she said. Greg just scowled in answer, taking a deep drag on his cigarette.

"They say the fires are really bad in Napa," Alex said. "They're evacuating some of the towns already."

"What about here in Sonoma?" Tara asked. She gulped down more water, but it did nothing to soothe her throat.

"I haven't heard anything yet." Alex tapped at her smartphone. "They're telling people to be alert and ready to go, but there's nothing official about evacuating. The highways are getting busy, though."

"They're always busy this time of year," said Greg.

"I can't stay out here for long. It's hotter than in the kitchen."

"They say it's the hottest summer on record. Since they started recording temperatures. It's weird, after the floods last summer," Alex said.

They heard muffled yelling through the door. "That'll be Antonio and Miguel. Chef isn't happy with them today."

Alex shook her head. "He never is." She finished her soda and tossed the can into a blue bin beside the steps. "Come on, Greg. Let's start the setup in the dining room. Nicole will be here any minute."

"Nicole is a pain in the ass," Greg said again. "How come we have to be on time if she never is?" He dropped his cigarette and ground the butt out with his toe.

"Because she owns the place, that's why. Come on."

More yelling. "I better get in there before Chef makes Antonio and Miguel quit, too," Tara said.

She stepped inside the kitchen again to see Chef Donald throw a steel bowl at Miguel's head, who ducked. "You call that clean? You're useless!"

He whirled to Antonio at the counter. "And you. How many times have I explained how I want things arranged!"

"But I did it the way you said yesterday, Chef," Antonio protested.

"No." Donald moved a platter to one side of the counter, the knife block to another spot, and a pot onto an unlit element on the stove. "This is how professionals do things in a kitchen. Learn that or get out."

He noticed Tara. "It's about time you got back. No more breaks for you today. We're going to be busy with a big group."

"What do you want me to do now, Chef?" she asked.

Tara endured a long look up and down. *It's like I can feel his eyes moving down my body.* "That dessert you made yesterday," he said, turning away. "It was ... acceptable."

"Thank you, Chef."

"Make it again." His eyes locked on her breasts.

"Yes, Chef." She turned, grateful for the excuse to remove her breasts from his view. *I'll bet he's staring at my ass now.* She quickly went into the walk-in cooler for ingredients.

Tara was whipping batter in a large bowl when the kitchen door swung open, smashing into the wall behind it. Alan stepped in, holding his phone in front of him. "Donald, can you explain this?" he demanded, his voice bouncing off the tiled walls and stainless steel refrigerators.

Chef Donald ignored him, stirring something in a pot. Alan shoved the phone under his eyes. "Well?"

Tara, Miguel and Antonio crowded behind Alan's wide shoulders to look at the screen. "That's the white supremacist rally in Sacramento last week," Antonio whispered. "I saw it on the news."

Greg and Alex stood, frozen, staring in from the dining room.

"Well?" Alan said again.

Donald put down his spoon. "What about it?"

Roberto stepped in through the back door that led out to the lot between the restaurant and the winery.

Alan touched the phone's screen, advancing the action. A "News7" logo flashed onto the bottom corner. He paused at a shot of men carrying placards on the lawn of the State Legislature. They read "White pride," or bore varied crosses. One man waved a Confederate flag.

Alan zoomed in on a man with his mouth wide open, holding a shield with a white cross on a red background. "Is that you?"

"It's pretty small, Alan," Donald said, turning to a pan of water that was starting to boil.

"Is it or is it not you?" Alan demanded, shoving the phone under Donald's face again.

"Do we need to talk about this now? I'm in the middle of getting ready for the evening rush."

"You're damn right we need to talk about this now. Tara, take over the stove. Donald, I want you in my office right damn now."

"I don't answer to you—"

"Goddamn right you answer to me. I'm the co-owner of this restaurant. In my office, now!"

Alan went upstairs. Donald moved from the stove, and Tara stepped in, moving pans off burners. "That's chili pequin peppers for tonight. Fresh steaks are in the walk-in," Donald said, wiping his hands on a towel. He did not meet the eyes of anyone in the kitchen.

Donald followed Alan up the back stairs.

Tara started issuing orders to Antonio and Miguel, anxious to save the preparations that Donald had started. The supper rush would start in just a few hours, and there was barely time to get ready with one less person on the kitchen crew.

"Are you going to be able to handle supper tonight?" Roberto asked Tara.

She looked up from the stove. "What do you mean?"

Nicole entered from the dining room door, straightening her dress. "What's going on?" She adjusted a pin in her hair.

"Alan is firing Chef Donald," Roberto said.

"What? Why?"

"He saw a video of the racist rally in Sacramento yesterday, and Donald was there, carrying a banner that reads 'God hates faggots.'"

Nicole screamed, "Where are they?"

"In Alan's office, upstairs."

Nicole ran up the stairs, her heels clattering.

Five minutes later, as Tara was in the midst of preparing pasta, Chef Donald stomped down the stairs into the kitchen. He took off his apron and threw it onto a stove. Miguel swept it off the stove onto the floor before it caught fire.

Donald wrenched open a drawer and took items from it, stuffing them into his pockets. Alan appeared at the bottom of the back staircase, Nicole behind his shoulder, as Donald took two ceramic knives from the knife block. "Put those back," Alan said.

Donald whirled, brandishing the knives in both hands. "These are mine. I brought them when I started here."

"If you think I'm going to let a nazi walk out of here with big knives in his hands, you're crazy. Put them back or I'll call the cops and charge you with theft."

Donald stood still, holding the knives. "If you keep them, you'll be the thief." His eyes blazed and Tara could see the little muscles behind his jaw moving under the skin.

"Put the knives down, Donald," Roberto said, stepping into the kitchen and reaching for Donald's hands.

Donald took a step back. "Don't you touch me," he snarled. "I know enough about your kind." Roberto flinched as one of the blades came close to his hand.

Antonio stepped between them, and Tara gasped as the blade cut across his arm. Antonio groaned, holding his arm with his other hand, blood seeping bright red between his fingers. Tara rushed a towel to him before more blood could drip onto a surface they used to prepare food.

That was enough to distract Donald, allowing Roberto to take the knives from him.

"You think firing me is some kind of punishment? I'm so glad to be out of here," Donald snarled. His eyes swept across the group in the kitchen. "You people are what's wrong with this country today. You're soft. You're bleeding hearts for every weakness in the country. And none of you knows how to cook."

"Get out, Donald," Alan growled. "Take your poison with you."

"Race traitor," Donald snarled. "Marrying a slant. You're *weak*."

Alan closed the gap between him and the Chef. "Shut the fuck up and get out, or I'll shut you up."

Donald backed away, pushing the door open behind him, forcing Charlie to jump down the stairs. Donald turned to Roberto, near the dining room door. "And you," he sneered. "You make me sick. You shouldn't be allowed in a kitchen to spread disease." He spat on the floor and disappeared out the door. Tara saw Charlie back up, baring his teeth as the Chef stomped across the back lot.

Alan ran after him, but Nicole grabbed his arm before he got out the door. "Stop! Let him go."

Alan pulled his arm away, glaring at Nicole. "You're defending him now?"

"No, of course not!" She moved between him and the door. "But what are you going to do? Beat him up?"

"I should. Or someone should. Beat the crap out of him." He leaned over Nicole's shoulder to push the door open. "You're what's wrong with America, pal! You and your nazi friends. Get off my land and stay off. If I ever see you again, or one of your fascist buddies, I'll kill you all!"

He turned to the kitchen staff. "What the hell is the matter with you? Trying to catch flies? Close your mouths."

"You know, he has a right to his own beliefs," said Miguel.

"He believes you should be deported," Alan snarled. He disappeared up the stairs. Nicole called after him from the bottom landing. "And now what are we going to do without a chef, three hours before opening time?" They heard a door slam.

Miguel brought out the first-aid kit and cleaned Antonio's cut before bandaging it. Tara concentrated on finishing the dish that Donald had been working on. She glanced at the clock.

There's no way we can prepare meals today in time. We're not only short-handed, we're without a chef. I better tell Nicole to close the restaurant today.

She looked to the dining room, where Nicole, Greg and Alex were setting tables. Wiping her hands on a towel, she stepped into the dining room as someone pounded on the front door.

All four in the dining room froze, with one thought: Donald's come back, madder than when he left.

More bangs, and Tara could see the door moving. "Mrs. DaSilva!" said a man's voice, muffled by the door. "I'm Officer Filler from the Highway Patrol. The winds are pushing the wildfires up the valley. You have to evacuate immediately."

Nicole stood frozen, but Tara could already smell the smoke coming through the kitchen door.

Evacuation

Nicole ran up the front stairs from the dining room. The others heard a door slam, something rattle, a closet door sliding and more thumps. Then Nicole was back at the bottom of the stairs, wearing a leather jacket and carrying a briefcase for a laptop computer. The corners of papers stuck out at odd angles from the bag's outer pockets.

In her other hand, she held a paper grocery bag, with more papers, notebooks, a pair of sandals, and other odds and ends. She ran out the front door, and Tara watched her sprint to the bungalow.

"Come on, let's get out of here," said Greg. "I see Alan and Roberto are getting people organized at the winery."

They ran to the guest house. Tara stuffed her laptop into her duffel bag and grabbed a couple of other personal items. As she followed Greg and Alex to the winery, she hit her parents' speed dial on her phone.

Her phone issued a strange tone. She glanced at the screen. *Damn—cell service is out.*

The big Ford F-150 pickup stood outside the winery. Roberto looked up as he put a cardboard box into the back, while the other two winery employees, Mark and Amy, each carried something else.

Alan was on the landline's cordless handset, pacing between the winery and the gate to the vineyard, Charlie following. "Just get them here," Tara heard him say. "We'll all leave together. We're not leaving anyone behind." He shoved the phone back in his pocket as he strode to the garage.

A minute later he drove a smaller Toyota pickup truck out, stopping in front of the winery. "The wait and kitchen staff can go with Nicole—Miguel, Antonio, Tara, Greg ... and Alex."

"Wait a minute, Alan," Roberto interrupted. "Will they all fit in her SUV?"

"Okay, whoever doesn't can go with you and the winery staff. The pickers will go with Rosa, and I'll take whoever's left." As if on cue, a big old flatbed truck with wooden railings around the bed pulled up, emerged from the smoke roiling in the vineyard. "There's Rosa and the picking crew."

The truck halted behind Alan's Toyota. The pickers, men and women that Tara had seen once or twice over the past week, sat in the beds, looking grim but not frightened.

"We should do a head count," Tara suggested. *Like in the Girl Scouts.*

"Good idea," Roberto said. He began counting, finger moving up and down. "Everybody hold still till I'm finished counting," he said as he turned to the two winery staff who were carrying items out to the trucks.

"Never mind any more stuff," Alan growled at Mark and Amy, who were headed back to the winery. "Just people."

"I have 21 people, including you, me and Nicole," Roberto said.

"There are still two of my people to come," said Rosa, stepping out of her truck. "Gabriela and Toby. They were heading to the south end of the vineyard, last I saw them."

"I'll pick them up," said Alan. "Every vehicle have an FRS radio? Tune to channel 7-12." Roberto adjusted dials on his handheld radio, and Rosa held hers up to indicate she was ready.

Nicole's red SUV pulled into the lot. Alan strode to it and opened the backdoor. "Shoes? Really?"

"Just two pairs. Along with the laptop, the backup hard drive and the photo albums. Irreplaceable stuff."

"I told you we should have backed up on the cloud."

"This is not the time for that argument."

Alan sighed. "You're right. Fine, you take Charlie." He pointed at the SUV and bent toward his dog. "Go with Nicole, he said."

Charlie sat on his haunches, tail swishing on the dirt. He sneezed. "No, get into Nicole's car." Alan insisted.

Charlie yipped and rolled onto his back.

"Oh, for crying out loud," Alan groaned. He took Charlie by the collar and pulled him to the SUV. "All right, I think that's everything. You guys get moving. Head to Monte Rio on the Russian River."

"I turned on the water in the irrigation system," said Mark, one of the winery employees. He was short and stout with thick black hair and a neat beard. "There's not much pressure, and it's just coming in a trickle, but it should help a little."

"That's fine, Mark. Thanks," Alan answered, coughing as he got back into his small truck.

"One last sweep," said Roberto. "Greg, check the mansion. Mark, the garage. I'll look in the winery."

Three men ran in three different directions. Mark returned first. "No one in the garage." He coughed.

Is that snow falling? Impossible. Wait—it's ash.

Roberto was next. "No one in the winery."

All eyes went to the mansion. Less than a minute later, Greg appeared on the verandah, pausing to check the door was locked.

He ran across the lot, coughing with the exertion. Tears ran down his face, and his eyes were red. "All clear."

"Get into the trucks as fast as you can," Alan ordered.

Rosa got behind the wheel of her truck and threaded between the others, the first to clear the gate.

Greg slipped into the front passenger seat of Nicole's SUV, while Alex ended up sandwiched between Antonio and Miguel in the back. Tara climbed into the bed of the Ford with Mark and Amy, a middle-aged blond woman who also worked in the winery. She sat between a cardboard box and a stubby steel barrel.

I wonder what's in that?

Alan leaned into the driver's window. "Go ahead, Roberto. We'll meet at the beach parking lot in Monte Rio. Don't stop until you get there."

"When are you coming?" Nicole asked from the driver's seat of her SUV, her voice high and thin. She tried to blink away the smoke, then choked and coughed.

"I'll take the small pickup through the vineyard to pick up the rest of the picking crew."

"Alan, don't take any chances," said Roberto.

"I'm not leaving people behind," he said.

"Alan, come with us now!" Nicole shrieked.

He shook his head. "Go now. I'll be all right. I promise." He coughed. "There's no time left. You two, head for Monte Rio now." He got into the old Toyota pickup, a dwarf next to the Ford. With a spin of the tires, he drove onto the dirt road into the vineyard.

"Alan!" Nicole shrieked again.

"Come on, Nicole, we have to go," said Greg, beside her in the SUV.

"No, no, no ..."

Roberto got out of the Ford, nodding at Greg, who climbed out of the SUV. Together, they coaxed Nicole out of the driver's seat, and led her around the SUV to the passenger side. Greg slid behind the wheel. Wondering where Charlie was sitting, Tara watched it turn onto the road and disappear into the smoke.

"Hang on tight, everyone," said Roberto, climbing back into the big Ford. He drove for the gate, following Nicole's SUV, and turned onto the main road toward the highway.

They were barely past the vineyard when the truck stopped as two women jumped over the fence. Roberto jumped out and called to them. "Gabriela! Toby! Climb in back."

The two pickers ran up, where Tara and Mark reached over to help them in.

We have the missing people. Did Roberto tell Alan? Tara looked into the cab and saw Roberto putting the FRS radio handset down on the seat beside him. *Guess so.*

"Where were you guys?" Mark asked as the truck started rolling again.

Toby, a tall woman with wild red hair and freckles, blinked soot away from her eyes. "We were working our way downhill. Gabriela has a little FM radio, and we heard the evacuation order for the area. So we decided to head straight for the road and hitch a ride." Gabriela, a slight Latina with hair cut short under a sooty baseball cap, held up a little silver square with headphones dangling from it.

Who listens to FM radios these days? "It's a good thing you were. Cell service is out," Tara said.

"Alan is looking for you," Mark said.

"We didn't know that."

"Maybe from now on, the picking crews should have FRS radios all the time," Amy suggested.

This is like one of my nightmares, where I'm driving somewhere but can't see ahead or behind.

The winery, the gate and then the restaurant disappeared into thickening smoke. Ahead, Tara could barely see the taillights of Nicole's vehicle in the white haze.

The smell of smoke was a rasp in her throat and nose. Ash fell like snow, catching in the hair of the three in the back of the truck. Tara watched a large flake land on the top edge of the side of the truck bed, then blow down to the back before falling off as the truck lurched over a bump in the road.

The air started to clear as they drove. Within a half hour, the road had taken them higher up the hills on the valley's western side, and they could see blue sky. Fifteen minutes later, Tara could barely smell smoke. She cracked open a bottle of water and rinsed ash out of her mouth and throat.

But by this time, the road was thick with trucks, each stuffed with people and belongings fleeing the fire. Roberto only stayed on the highway for a few miles before exiting for a much quieter road, still heading west.

Tara kept looking behind them for Alan's truck. *How far back could he be?*

Two hours after leaving the winery, the little convoy constituted the only vehicles moving on a road that wound through the hills. Tall redwoods teased a clear blue sky, and the smell of smoke was almost forgotten.

All the passengers in the back of the truck braced as the truck negotiated a tight turn. Tara saw a blue clapboard house on one side of the road, and a dilapidated building on the other with an ancient gas pump in front.

Then more buildings, and the road split. To the right, it disappeared among more redwoods. The left-hand branch led to a bridge high over a bright blue river, and in the triangle between the branches was a sun-faded sign reading, in big, rounded letters that made Tara think of hippies, "Welcome to Monte Rio."

Nicole's SUV went around the sign onto a wide, empty lot between it and the river. Roberto followed after Rosa's pickup.

Nicole was the first out of the vehicles. "Why didn't we stop for Alan?" she cried at Roberto. "Where is he? Where is his truck?"

"He probably got stuck in all that traffic on the highway," Roberto said. "Don't worry. I told him using the FRS radio when we picked up the missing pickers, and he answered. He said he was coming out of the vineyard right behind us."

"Then why isn't he here now?" Nicole cried.

"Like I said, Nicole," Roberto said in a calm voice. "He won't be long. Don't worry."

"So, what do we do now?" Mark asked.

"First thing is a head count," Roberto answered. He turned slowly, pointing his finger at each person. "I get 22."

"So do I," said Tara. "That's everyone. We had 21 at the winery, then Alan left, and we picked up Gabriela and Toby."

"So, everyone's here, except for Alan," said Mark. "What's the plan from this point?"

"I think that Alan knows someone who owns a hotel here," Roberto said. "It's the off-season now, so maybe we'll be able to get rooms. I'll go ask at that gas station." He strode back up the road from where they had come.

Tara ran after him. When she judged they were out of Nicole's hearing, she asked, "Did you really hear from Alan?"

Roberto glanced over his shoulder before answering. "Yes. He answered me when I radioed him, but it was hard to understand what he was saying with all the static. He said he understood that we had Toby and Gabriela, but then he said something like 'I see something strange.'"

"Do you think something's wrong?"

"I hope not."

A bell jingled when Roberto opened the door to the old gas station. Behind a battered counter and an antique cash register stood an equally antique man. He was short, and so thin Tara wondered if the smoke had affected her sight. His arms were only wide enough to bear wrinkles. Wisps of white hair seemed to float over his speckled scalp, but thick white eyebrows made his large, watery blue eyes look fierce.

"We got no more gas," he said in a voice as thin as his arms. "Fire trucks took the last of it this mornin', and any more deliveries bin cancelled until further notice. Count'a the fires. Lot of highways closed. I hear 101 is closed north of Santa Rosa."

"We're good for now," Roberto said. "Is there anyplace to stay around here? A hotel or something?"

"There's a place across the river, but I hear she's pretty full-up right now."

"Huh. What about a place to eat?"

"There's a store with a counter, also across the river on your right. You can't miss it."

They returned to the group standing beside their trucks. "There's no gas and not much to eat or places to stay here," Roberto said. "And the old-timer at the gas station says the 101 is closed north of Santa Rosa. That explains why Alan's not here— he got caught on the other side of the highway after it closed."

"Then why isn't he calling us to let us know?" Nicole demanded, panic in her voice.

"Cell service is out," said Greg, holding up his phone. "I have no bars."

Nicole had her phone in her hand, and she hit the screen to try calling again. Tears cut through the ash and soot on her face as she paced, waiting for an answer. "Dammit," she muttered when the error tone sounded.

"Let's find somewhere to clean up," Toby suggested. "Maybe get some water, something to eat?"

"Alan told me he knows the owner of a hotel around here," Roberto said. "Nicole, do you know it?"

Nicole did not answer, just shook her head, staring at the phone in her hand.

"The man at the gas station said there was a hotel across the river. There can't be that many in this town," Tara said.

"Let's check it out," Roberto agreed. The two of them set off across the narrow steel bridge. Tara looked at the river flowing below. *Water—that's the key. I wonder if the river is much lower than normal. I can see a lot of rocks. Maybe it is.*

"That must be it there," said Roberto, pointing to a brown wooden building with a big "Hotel" sign on top.

"Wasn't that hard to find after all."

The hotelier was a large man with a white beard and a slight German accent. Wide eyes looked at Roberto and Tara over his reading glasses. "Twenty-three? Well, sure, but you'll have to share. We have a bunch of writers here already, but they're pretty quiet."

"Great," said Roberto. "I'll bring them. I have a business credit card—"

The hotelier held up a hand. "No charge for fire refugees."

"Really? No, we can't—"

"Really. I can't take money for helping out in a disaster."

Tara and Roberto returned to the group, who all looked unhappy and guilty. "Where's Nicole?" Roberto demanded.

"She took off," Rosa answered, looking down the road they had come. "She jumped in her car and went to find Alan."

"What? Why didn't you stop her?"

"We tried," said Toby. "She wouldn't listen. She kept phoning him and crying, and said she couldn't stand waiting any longer. What could we do, tie her up?"

"Yes!" Roberto's face was flushed, his nostrils flaring. "It's way too dangerous to go back." He ran toward the Ford, calling orders over his shoulder. "Go to the hotel—you'll see it from the bridge. It's all arranged."

As he opened the truck door, Tara was at the passenger side. "I'm coming with you." She opened the door and Charlie startled her by jumping in and moving to the back seat.

Roberto did not argue with either of them.

When they had left Monte Rio behind, Tara asked, "If the highways are closed, how are you going to get back to the winery?"

"There's more than one way there. I know a lot of backroads."

"Does Nicole?"

"If she doesn't, she'll end up back at Monte Rio."

"Does Alan know them?"

"Better than I do."

"So he could be on his way there, now, and could miss Nicole."

"Could be." Roberto's eyes remained focused on the winding road, his hands tight on the wheel.

"Do you really think he's okay?"

Roberto did not answer.

Treatment

If the floodlights above the doors of the community center were not enough, there were also the headlights of dozens of cars, trucks and SUVs that crowded the parking lot and pavement in front. Men, women and children walked into and out of the building, carrying boxes and blankets and stretchers, or helping others who limped and staggered.

Roberto stopped the pickup in front of a young woman wearing a reflective yellow vest. "Don't look in the back," he said, so of course, the woman did. Tara could see her face grow pale. Thankfully, they had covered Alan's body with Roberto's jacket and a cardboard box they had collapsed. Still, his feet stuck out.

"We need to find your morgue," said Roberto.

The woman swallowed and pointed, turning away. Roberto drove on.

They came to a large tent, where men wearing gloves and surgical masks took Alan from the truck, laid him on a stretcher and carried him away. Roberto gave information to a cop who also wore a mask. The cop used his phone to take a picture of Alan's driver's license, then pointed them to the community center's main door.

A haggard looking woman in surgical scrubs and Crocs took a look at them. Her eyes widened.

"Take her first. She's in shock," Roberto said. "She found her husband dead."

The woman's expression softened. She called over a slender nurse in burgundy scrubs and led Nicole away. Charlie followed, his tail low.

"We're going to somewhere quiet, where she can talk to someone," said the first nurse.

The slender nurse in burgundy had thick brown hair. A name tag on her chest read "Finigan." She frowned as she held a stethoscope to Roberto's chest, then pointed them to one of hundreds of cots arranged in ranks across the concrete floor of what was normally a double basketball court.

Tara slumped onto a cot. Her lungs burned and her legs felt like lead. Her neck was having trouble holding her head up, which ached in front and behind her ears. She coughed, then did her best to suppress it because it hurt her chest.

All around, people stained with soot lay or sat on the cots, or on mattresses on the floor, coughing and moaning. Children cried, adults called across the space and their voices reverberated off the concrete floor and walls.

Tara lay back. Overhead, banners hanging from the ceiling stretched across the court. "Bobcats Peewee Champs" read one. *I'm glad they won.*

"Gonsalves and Rezeck?" Tara opened her eyes. A heavy-set young man in purple scrubs stood in front of her, holding an oxygen mask. He looked at a clipboard in his other hand. "You Rezeck? Theresa Rezeck?"

"Tara Rezeck," she answered, coughing.

The man in scrubs squinted at the clipboard. "Oh, yeah. Tara. It looks like 'Theresa.' You have smoke inhalation." She flinched back as he put the clear plastic device up to her face. "Relax," he said, and she allowed the man to push the mask against her nose and mouth and stretch a strap behind her head.

He turned to Roberto, and attached a little hose under his nose. "Why is his mask different from mine?" Tara asked, triggering another coughing fit.

"It's what we got left," the man said. He fitted Roberto's tubes into his nostrils, then opened a valve on the tank. "Just relax and breathe for a while. You'll feel better soon, once you get the smoke out of your systems."

"I need to use the john," said Roberto.

The technician removed the hose from Roberto's neck and pointed across the court. "Be right back," said Roberto.

The technician left two water bottles and left to look after others.

Tara breathed through her nose, expecting to cough again, and was surprised when she did not. The air coming through the mask was cool and clean. She imagined clear vapor pushing black clouds from her lungs.

She looked at her hands. They were stained black. Black streaks smeared her pants and shirt. Her once white shoes were dark grey.

She lay back again, closing her eyes. *I wonder how many times the Bobcats won a banner? And what about other ages besides Peewees? Juniors? What are the other ages called? How old are Peewees, anyway?*

I wonder if Roxanne will play basketball. Or maybe this is lacrosse. Or hockey. What do kids play in California, indoors?

The noise of the makeshift clinic faded. *Poor Alan. I can't believe he's gone. Poor Nicole.*

How many other people have died in this?

Then her thoughts turned to herself. *Where can Roxanne and I live now? How many homes have been destroyed already? Besides Alan, how many people killed?*

Maybe coming here was a mistake. Maybe I should go back home to Vermont. Back to Mom and Dad and Bobby.

Bobby. He could be helping. He should be helping. The deadbeat.

That's not fair. He's not a deadbeat. He's paying child support every month.

Roxanne. I miss you, baby.

She sat up suddenly. *Mom and Dad!*

She scrambled the phone out of her pants pocket and hit speed dial. Her mother answered on the second ring. "Tara! Are you safe?"

"Yes, Mom, I'm at an evacuation center. I'm all right."

"What? Tara, I can't hear you."

Stupid, she thought as she pulled the oxygen mask down to rest against her throat. It was annoying, but tolerable. "Sorry. Yes, I'm fine. Just a little smoke inhalation, and I'm getting treated for it now. How is Roxanne? And Dad?"

"Thank god," her mother breathed. "We've been worried sick since we saw the news about the wildfires in Sonoma County. It's awful, just awful. We've heard about houses being burned, and people killed. But are you sure you're all right?"

"Mom—about that. I'm fine, don't worry about me. But my boss was killed in the fire."

She heard a click, and then her father's deep rumble as he picked up the extension. "Sweetie, you're all right?"

"Yes, yes, I'm fine. No problem. We had to evacuate, and everyone is fine, except—except for the boss, the owner, or I guess the co-owner with his wife. Alan DaSilva. He's dead. Burned." To suppress the image of Alan's burned legs under her arms, she focused on breathing clean oxygen.

"You get on the next plane back home. We'll have a ticket waiting for you at—dear, what's the closest airport to you, Tara?"

"There's no need for that, Dad. I'm fine, really, and I think they could use my help right now."

"You worry about yourself first, Tara. If you need to get out of there, just say the word and we'll send you a ticket."

"I appreciate it, Dad. Really. But I'm all right, and I'm going to see what I can do to help out here. Either the DaSilvas, or maybe with disaster relief."

She could almost see her father's chest expand and contract with the huge sigh he let out over the phone. "All right."

"How is Roxanne?"

"Sleeping like an angel. She's an absolute delight. Don't you worry about her. Take care of yourself."

"Okay. I better go, Mom and Dad. I hear the cell networks are really jammed."

They said their good-byes and I-love-yous, and as Tara closed the line, she heard a gravelly voice beside her shoulder. "I'm sorry, did you say something about Alan DaSilva?"

She looked up. Standing beside her cot was a short man with thick, wavy gray hair, a bulbous nose and a full mouth. His deep brown eyes were bloodshot and red-rimmed, and his business suit rumpled and ash-stained. "Did I hear you mention Alan DaSilva?"

Tara put her oxygen mask back in place. *I never knew oxygen could feel so good.* "How do you know Alan DaSilva?"

"He's my friend. Also my client. I'm his lawyer, Paul Rondeau. I just got evacuated here from Sebastopol. How do you know him?"

Tara sucked in another breath through the mask. It's so good. "He's my boss. I work in Cyrano's restaurant."

"Where is he?"

Tara looked past Rondeau's shoulder, where people moved across the arena. Some carried blankets, others cases of bottled water. She took another deep breath. "I'm sorry." She coughed, but there was no moisture in her throat. She lifted the mask to take a drink from the water bottle beside her cot. "We brought ... his body here. The coroner's people took it—took him, I mean." She swallowed more water.

Rondeau closed his eyes and groaned. "Where is Nicole?"

Tara pointed back to the clinic area. "I think they're treating her for shock. Or maybe PTSD."

"What happened?"

Tara closed her eyes. It was strange, how painful this was to retell, now. Almost worse than when it happened. "We all evacuated the winery. Alan stayed behind to look for some of the grape pickers. He was supposed to follow us as soon as he found them. But we found them—I mean, the truck I was in found the missing pickers, and we radioed Alan, and he answered ... I think."

"I'm sorry, I don't understand."

Tara took another breath from the mask. "I'm sorry. Alan stayed behind, but he wasn't supposed to wait too long. We thought he was behind us, and we drove all the way to ... I don't know. Some place called Monte Rio."

"Monte Rio? Why so far?"

Tara shrugged. "I don't know. It was Alan's plan. We went all the way there. Alan didn't show up, so Nicole drove back to the winery. Roberto and I followed her."

"Roberto Gonsalves? From the winery?"

"Right here, dude," said Roberto. Rondeau turned to see that Roberto had returned from the bathroom.

"Roberto!" Rondeau threw his arms around him. "Thank god you're okay. But," he released Roberto and stood back to look at him intensely. "I heard that Alan ..."

Roberto looked down. He picked up the oxygen hose and managed to put it into his nostrils, almost as neatly as the technician had. "He didn't make it."

"How is Nicole?"

"She found the body. Alan's body."

"Oh, my god. Where is she?"

"The nurses took her for some one-on-one counseling, I think. I'm going to look for her soon.

Nurse Finigan returned. "Are you feeling better?"

"I guess …" *How do I feel?* "My lungs still hurt. Everything stinks of smoke and ash."

Nurse Finigan listened to Tara's lungs, then Roberto's. "You could use a few more hours of oxygen, but there are other people who need it more, right away. I'm sorry." With practiced, efficient movements, she took the mask and hoses off of Roberto and Tara, and walked into the crowds of cots.

"What's the state of the winery?" Rondeau asked.

Roberto shrugged and took a sip of water. "It was dark when we got there. The garage was burning. It was mostly gone. But I don't know about the other buildings, or the vineyard."

"These fires are an absolute catastrophe," Rondeau said, shaking his head.

The technician returned carrying a cloth bag. He handed the three of them more water bottles, asking, "Any food allergies?" When they all shook their heads no, he handed them granola bars. "We'll be having more food soon, but if you're really hungry, there's food, more water, coffee and stuff in the canteen."

"Can you tell us about our friend? The woman we came in with?" Roberto asked. "She was in worse shape than us, and her husband died."

"You'll have to ask at the front. But she's probably with a trauma counselor, as well as getting oxygen. We have a separate, quiet place for people who've lost loved ones."

Tara, Roberto and Paul Rondeau went as quickly as they could through the crowded arena to the front. The people at the intake desk were different from the ones they had first met, and they waited while a young, red-haired woman with "McGuire" embroidered on her nurse's uniform scanned a list on a clipboard. "V. Fong?"

"No," Tara began, but Rondeau interrupted her.

"Yes, Nicole Fong."

As they walked in the direction McGuire pointed, Tara asked, "Nicole kept her maiden name? I was introduced to her as 'Mrs. DaSilva.'"

"Her ID shows 'Fong,' so it's the name she uses for dealing with official things, like health services and so on," Rondeau said, his breath getting short.

They reached a door with a scrawled paper sign reading "Trauma Center." It opened on what was normally the community center's administrative office. Computers and phones had been pushed to the sides of desks to make room for medical equipment. About a dozen people sat or stood, speaking in low tones. Some held clipboards. Others sat slumped on office chairs, or wept quietly.

A young man in a t-shirt and jeans came up to them. "Nicole Fong?" Roberto said. The young man pointed at an inner door.

Roberto strode to it and knocked twice gently before opening the door just enough to look in. Through the crack, Tara saw a tall Asian woman in a hoodie, crouching in front of a woman in a chair.

Tara recognized Nicole by her clothes, but could not see her face. She slumped in the chair, arms on her knees, leaning forward. Her long, dark hair, now disheveled by smoke, hung down in front of her face. A thin, keening sound came from her throat and her shoulders rose and fell with shuddering breaths.

Charlie lay on the floor, head resting on his front paws. He stood when he saw Roberto and Tara. His tail swayed slowly, tentatively.

The crouching woman stood. She held a wad of wet tissues in one hand. "Are you Roberto?"

Roberto knelt beside Nicole and put his arm around her shoulders. "I'm here, Nicole. Paul is here, too. And Tara."

Nicole nodded and sniffed, but did not look up.

"She needs to be with loved ones. Is there any family with you?" the counselor asked.

"Her only family around was her husband," said Paul. "The rest of her family are out of state."

"I'm here for you, Nicole," Roberto repeated.

"Take her to the sleeping quarters we have for evacuees," said the counselor. "Talk to her. She needs the support of the people closest to her."

Roberto pulled Nicole out of the chair. Paul embraced her. "I just found out. I'm so sorry, Nicole." She nodded and said something in a voice so low and broken, no one could understand.

They led her back to the basketball court. A teenage girl moved over so they could have four cots together. Charlie curled up on the floor beside Nicole's cot, and Paul went to find food and coffee.

Tara managed to down two granola bars and a cup of foul, old, tepid coffee, but Nicole did not eat anything. She lay down on the cot, curling up on her side in a fetal position.

Paul, Roberto and Tara looked at each other. None of them could think of anything to say. Exhaustion finally overcame them, and they lay down. Roberto kept his hand on Nicole's shoulder even as his eyes closed.

Return to the winery

As soon as they heard that their section of Sonoma was clear of fire danger, Tara, Roberto and Nicole climbed into the F-150. The sun was still low in the sky, tinting clouds to the east a dirty orange.

Tara sat in the back seat beside Nicole, holding her hand. Charlie sat between them, resting his head on Nicole's knee. Nicole pressed her lips together tightly, but other than that, she was expressionless.

Wildfire had swept by one side of the road. The skeletal remains of trees punctuated the ashen ground. What had been houses were now just two or three roofless walls, black, windows shattered. Smoke rose from dead grey cars. Tara choked on a cry and turned away when she saw the blackened body of a dog, its legs stiff, lying beside a charred cinder block wall.

But as they got closer to the winery, the fire damage ended. The road that led to the winery entrance was lined with green bushes and grass on both sides. "Thank god, it looks like the vineyard wasn't touched," Roberto announced when he could see it ahead.

Nicole gave a little cry when they turned the corner and could see her house. To Tara, it appeared untouched. Even the flower bed in front seemed okay.

The restaurant mansion also looked fine as they turned into the parking lot, where Tara's Civic and Roberto's small truck were unscathed. They passed the mansion. As Roberto stopped in beside Nicole's SUV where they had left it the day before, she let out a sob. Tears streamed down her face.

"It's too soon," Tara said. "Let's go back to the evac center."

"No, no, I'll be okay," Nicole gasped. She opened the door, and Roberto took her hand as she got out of the truck. Charlie jumped out, staying by her heel.

"The winery doesn't look like it suffered any damage," Tara said.

Roberto unlocked the door. "Everything looks okay," he said.

"Even the guest house is fine."

"It's just the garage that burned," Nicole said, her voice small and tight. "Everything else is untouched."

"Strange," Tara said.

"Very strange," Roberto agreed, approaching the smoking remains of the garage.

The front wall was completely gone, with only a few blackened timbers standing. The roll-up door lay twisted and buckled on the ground, partly in front of the garage and partly inside what was left of it. The front of the roof appeared to have been obliterated, and the back half had collapsed inside, crushing a four-wheel ATV.

The nose of the small Toyota pickup pressed against a charred timber at the corner of the garage. It was also burned, and the mirror was missing from the passenger side.

This is very strange. Alan's truck is burned, and he was burned, but not inside it. How did that happen?

Charlie trotted up, sniffing the charred walls and ground. He nosed something lying on the ground beside the corner of the burned structure. Roberto crouched to pick it up from the ground. "Looks like someone dropped some pliers here. Must have been Mark or Amy. Probably Amy. She's always dropping stuff." He slipped them into a pocket and looked more closely into the garage. "Yeah, we've lost both ATVs as well as the small truck. Tools, air compressor, ladder ... looks like they'll all have to be replaced."

Nicole sniffed deeply and started for the mansion. Tara followed.

Inside, everything was as they had left it: everything in its place, the tables in the dining room ready for serving.

"The power is out," Nicole said. To prove it, she flicked a light switch up and down.

Tara glanced at the black face of the digital clock on a clock radio behind the bar. "This is also strange. Why is the power out if nothing else is wrong?"

"The wiring here is wonky," Roberto said from the doorway. "Always has been. For some reason, the electrical meter for the whole estate is attached to the garage."

"Don't open the refrigerators," Tara warned. "They should still be cold inside, even if the power was out all night, but you'll let warm air in if you check on them. We don't know how long it will be until we have power." Tara checked her phone. "It looks like there's cell service."

"Call the others in Monte Rio," Nicole said, looking at her hand as it moved over the counter. "Tell them they can come back."

"We'll have to go pick them up," said Roberto. "We took three trucks down there, and we brought two back here with us."

"Then you'd better go do that."

Roberto looked at Nicole, his face blank.

"Call Rosa, tell her to bring the picking crew back as soon as possible," Nicole said. "We have a harvest to bring in and it's already late."

"Ohhh-kay."

"Then tell Antonio that you're coming to get him and the rest of the restaurant staff." Nicole's voice was quiet, distant and devoid of emotion.

"Umm … Okay, Tara, think you can drive Nicole's vehicle?"

"No problem."

"No. Tara is staying with me," said Nicole, her voice still flat. She moved slowly through the dining room toward the front door.

"I don't think we'll have enough room in just one vehicle," Roberto protested. "Rosa's truck is going to be full of the picking crew, and there are," he counted on his fingers, "six more people to bring back. That'll mean four riding in the back, and I don't think the CHPs are going to tolerate that."

"You'll figure something out," Nicole said flatly. She opened the front door. "Come on, Tara."

Tara shrugged at Roberto and followed Nicole outside, then to the house.

Tara had never been in the house before. It was furnished in a modern style, but dark and cool compared to outside. Nicole collapsed onto a leather sofa in the living room. Charlie lay down beside her.

Tara tried to turn on the TV, then remembered the power was out. She wandered to the kitchen, all granite and dark wood cupboards and floors. She opened the stainless steel refrigerator and found a half-full bottle of Rocky Creek Chardonnay.

She found a bowl and filled it with water for Charlie, who lapped it noisily. Then she brought two large stemmed glasses to the living room.

Nicole was now stretched out full-length on the sofa, her arm over her eyes. "Thank you. I just feel so … exhausted. I can't bear to look at the winery again. Not now. And now I suppose I'll have to start making funeral arrangements."

"I can help you with that," Tara said. *How? I don't know the first thing about funeral arrangements. How do you choose a funeral home? Where is Alan's body now?*

"Thank you. And I'll have to start thinking about getting the business going again."

"I think you can wait a few days for that. You've had a shock, and I don't think there will be as many people driving out here for supper, with the fires burning and everything."

"We need to bring in some money, somehow. We still have people to pay, bills to pay … I don't know how I'm going to manage Alan's job," her voice hitching at her husband's name.

"I'm sure Roberto will take care of that."

Nicole grunted at Roberto's name. "I'm sure he will."

"Are you angry with Roberto?"

Nicole lifted her arm, her eyes flashing. "I'm sorry," Tara said. "It's just that … well … sorry. Maybe I've overstepped."

Nicole took a deep breath and looked out the window. Across the road, the fields were green, but the sky to the east was hazy. "Alan hired Roberto as the winery manager. Someone to make the wines. Not to work in the restaurant. And Roberto is someone else who likes to overstep boundaries."

"I'm sorry," Tara repeated. She sipped her wine. *I wonder if there is still ice in the freezer. I know you're not supposed to ice wine, but it's so hot, even in the house.* "How long do you think it will be before the power comes back on?"

Nicole did not answer. She drank some wine, then pulled her phone from her pocket. Ignoring Tara, she hit a speed dial number. "It's me," she said. Tara heard the bubbling buzz of the other person on the line, but could not distinguish the voice. "Have you had much damage at your place?"

She must be speaking with the Harris people.

"I have something to tell you." Nicole's voice choked. "It's bad news. About Alan."

From the cadence of the faint buzz from the phone, Tara knew the other party said, "Oh, my god."

Then more buzzing. Tears ran down Nicole's face again. She held the phone out to Tara and shook her head. "You tell them."

Tara took the phone. "Hello? Who's this?"

"Who is this?" said a familiar voice.

"It's Tara Rezeck from the kitchen at Cyrano's. Mrs. DaSilva asked me to talk to you."

Nicole was lying on her side on the sofa, her face to the back. She made no sound.

"Tell me what?"

"Is this Mr. Harris?"

"Yes, this is Cameron Harris. Tell me what?"

Tara took a deep breath. *This is hard enough for me, and I'm not married to the man.* Wasn't *married to the man.* "Mr. DaSilva. He was killed yesterday."

"*Killed?*" She heard noise on the other end. "In the fire. Somehow the wildfires burned down the garage, and Mr. DaSilva was caught in it. He ... he died."

The voice got distant. "Dad! Come here!" Then it came back to the phone. "How is Ver—Mrs. DaSilva?"

"She found the—she found him. In front of the garage."

There was more confused noise on the other end of the line. Then a deeper voice came on. "This is Steven Harris. What happened?"

Tara repeated the story, and she tasted tears when they reached her lips.

"How is Nicole?"

"She's had a bad shock. I ... well, she's resting now."

"We'll be right over," Steven Harris said, and the line closed.

The Harris family had arrived minutes after their call, carrying baskets and bags of food.

Mrs. Harris was a small woman with thick glasses, thick, wavy brown hair and a wide, bright smile. She wrapped her arms around Nicole as soon as she saw her, rocking the larger woman gently. "Oh, my poor dear. This is just awful. Awful. I feel so badly for you, dear." She stepped back and looked at Nicole carefully. "You are holding up so bravely. Let me tell you that if there's anything you need—absolutely anything—all you have to do is call. We had a little damage, but nothing like your loss."

She carried three big grocery bags into Nicole's kitchen. Tara went to help her unpack. "Thank you, Mrs. Harris. I think this will mean a lot to Nicole."

"Call me Janet. My name isn't 'Harris,' anyway. It's Oakley. Steven and I aren't married, and I'm not Cameron's mother."

"Sorry. I guess I just assumed—"

"Perfectly understandable, dear." Janet began unpacking produce and plastic containers of prepared food into the refrigerator. "Oh! Is the power out?"

"Is it okay at your place?"

"Yes, thankfully. We lost a lot of grapevines, and one of the outbuildings we use for storage is gone. But we have power."

"It's got something to do with weird wiring," Tara explained. Janet gave her a quizzical look. "I'm not sure, but it seems that the power comes in through the garage, so with the garage gone, all the power for every building is out."

"Well, I guess I better not leave the fridge door open, then."

They returned to the living room. Mr. Harris wanted to see the fire damage, so Tara decided to take him and Cameron to look, leaving Nicole in the warmth of Janet Oakley.

"Did you have any damage?" Tara asked Steven Harris.

"Some to one of our outbuildings, and we lost a couple of acres of vineyard," the elder Harris replied. He walked toward the gate that led to the Rocky Creek vineyard.

"What happened to you?" Tara asked, pointing with her eyes at the bandage on Cameron's arm.

"This? Oh, I ah … I fell when we were evacuating."

"You fell on your arm?"

"Sometimes the boy can be clumsy," said the elder Harris. "It's the damnedest thing."

"What is?" Tara asked.

"How this kid can be an athlete, a rock climber, and then fall and damn near break his arm walking from the vineyard to get into the car. And you know what else is damned strange?"

"Uhhh …"

"This vineyard is between mine and the garage. It's untouched. Damnedest thing."

"Flying embers," Cameron said. The other two looked at him. "Embers. That's how wildfires spread. The wind was really strong. They're what started the fires in the first place. Didn't you hear? High winds knocked down a power line, and sparks started a fire. It's been so awfully dry all summer, which made perfect conditions for a fire. Those same winds spread them fast. They blew embers from our vineyards, which are upwind here," As if to prove his point, a gust ruffled Cameron's curly hair. "to the DaSilva property, setting the garage on fire."

"And skipping the vineyard completely? There are acres of property in between," said the elder Harris.

Cameron shrugged. "They were really strong winds, remember?"

"I remember."

"Have you ever had anything like this happen before?" Tara asked.

"Wildfires are a yearly problem in California," the older Harris answered. "If it's not wildfires, it's mudslides."

"Yes, but fires with winds like this? Skipping over large areas?"

"Wildfires are very unpredictable," Cameron interjected. "The news reports are full of stories about how one house is burned to the ground, and the next-door neighbor is untouched."

Cameron strode back to the garage. "Look at these bushes," he said, pointing to a pile of charred wood on the ground between the gate and the garage. "This is where they must have landed. The bushes started burning, and that set the garage on fire. But since the wind was pushing from the east, the fire didn't go back toward the vines. It pushed the fire into the garage. Plus, there's always lots of flammable material in a garage."

"Alan was always very neat and careful," Harris growled. "He wouldn't be one to leave flammable material lying around."

"Could be oil, gasoline …" Cameron shrugged again. "Or someone other than Alan left something out. Or it was just the dry conditions, the heat, the fire—"

"It's still damned strange," said Mr. Harris. He walked around the burned wreck of Alan's small truck. "I suppose Alan was driving fast, and that's why he hit the garage. Maybe that's what started the fire. Still," he bent down to look closer at the truck's bumper where it pressed into the stump of the garage's corner. "It doesn't look like he hit all that hard. Huh." He pointed. "Look—a tire iron. What do you suppose it's doing on the ground, outside the garage?"

"Maybe it fell?" Cameron asked.

"Well, obviously, it fell. But outside the garage? Where did it come from?" He turned to Tara. "Have you called the Sheriff yet?"

"Roberto reported Alan's death to the police last night. They took him—his body, I mean—in the morgue at the evacuation center. He must have told them about the fire, too."

"Where is Roberto?" Cameron asked.

Tara looked at her watch. "On his way to Monte Rio, to pick up the staff. We evacuated to a hotel there that Alan knew about." *Except that Alan never made it there.*

A Lexus pulled off the road and stopped beside them. Paul Rondeau, looking much fresher than he had the night before, climbed out. His hair had been recently styled, and he wore aviator sunglasses, linen pants and a cool, white silk shirt. "Good morning, Tara. Steven. Hello, Cameron."

"What brings you here, Rondeau?" Harris growled.

"Same as you, Steven. My friend has died. I came to see Nicole."

"She's in the house," Tara offered.

"You're also here for business reasons, aren't you?" Steven Harris said.

What's between these guys?

"Not at the moment. I'll go see Nicole now."

"I'll take you," said Tara.

"I know the way. I've been here before." But he did not seem to mind Tara walking beside him to the house. The Harrises came slowly behind.

In the house, Janet Oakley was bustling around the kitchen, while Nicole sat at the table, head resting on one hand. A plate of food lay on the table in front of her, untouched.

Charlie looked up from a corner of the kitchen, but his tail did not wag. He settled down again.

Tara pushed past the others into the kitchen first. "Nicole, Paul Rondeau is here."

Nicole looked confused. "Paul?"

He sat at the table beside her, taking her hand in his. "I just wanted to say, again, how so sorry I am. Diane sends her love, too. We can't imagine how you feel. Alan was our friend. I want you to know that Diane and I are here for you. If there's anything you need, just call my private cell."

Did she hear him? Seconds ticked by before Nicole nodded. "Thank you, Paul. I suppose there is a will and insurance to take care of. Papers to sign. Is that why you're here?"

"No, no," Paul said, patting the back of Nicole's hand. "All that kind of thing can wait a few days. As for anything legal, it looks like the county is going to be preoccupied with the fires for a while."

Does she understand what he's saying? She's still in shock. Is this PTSD? What should I do?

Janet put a glass of water on the table. "Drink this, dear. You need to stay hydrated."

Nicole looked at the glass, then at Janet and finally at Steven Harris. "Maybe I should just sell the winery."

Glimmers of at least three different emotions swept across Steven's face, but not long enough for Tara to interpret them.

Rondeau was looking at Harris intently. *Is he angry?* "Don't make any decisions today, Nicole. You're under stress I cannot even imagine. Take time to ... just take your time."

Nicole nodded.

"I think we should all be going," said Cameron.

"No, please, don't ..." Nicole stammered.

"Cam and I have to get back to work. There's a lot of fire damage to clean up," Steven said, clapping Cameron on the shoulder. "Janet, you can stay, can't you?"

"Of course."

Paul watched the Harris men leave, then stood. "I should go, too, Nicole. But promise me you won't make any major decisions about the future today, and not without talking to me first." Nicole nodded, looking down at the uneaten food.

Tara followed Paul to the front door. "Do you know anything about making funeral arrangements?"

"Some," he said, reaching into a pocket. He gave Tara a business card. "That has my private cell number. Not many people have it, so I answer it immediately."

"Even in court?"

"I'm not a litigator." He looked out the front window as the Harris' truck pulled onto the road. "Just so you know, Steven Harris has been wanting to buy the Rocky Creek vineyard for years. They've always been friendly about it, but they want the land for themselves. Alan always resisted it, even though financially he would've been far better off. But with Nicole in this vulnerable of a state, I'm worried she might just make a rash decision."

"So what should I do?"

"Just keep an eye on her, and if she looks like she's about to do anything rash—about selling, or moving, or anything—you call that number immediately." He pointed to the business card in Tara's hand.

"Okay. But ... about funeral arrangements."

"Thicke's is the biggest one nearby. You call them and tell them what Nicole needs. They'll take care of everything. I'll call the Sheriff's Office about releasing the body. There are also several things to look after, in terms of transferring sole title over the property and assets to Nicole. It's complicated, but we don't need to worry her about it, not in her current state."

Tell him, Tara. "Maybe I can help. I just graduated from law school."

Paul looked at her with an expression Tara could not read. "Good. I'll keep that in mind." He left.

Now I have to call a funeral home. But first, I have to find an electrician to see about getting the power back on.

She dialed Roberto. His voice echoed, and she could hear the sound of an engine. She told him about the Harrises and Paul Rondeau coming to the house.

"Good. Don't leave Nicole alone for any reason."

"Okay. I have to call the funeral home, but first, I want to get the power back on. Do you know any electricians?"

"I'll see what I can find. Gotta go now." He cut the connection.

Rosa's truck, with at least ten pickers riding in the back, rumbled through the parking lot and to the vineyard an hour later. Rosa soon appeared in the house and embraced Nicole. "I'm so sorry," she said.

After Rosa finished giving her sympathies, Tara followed her across the yard. "The vineyard looks like it escaped the fire, so we're going to do the rest of the harvest as fast as we can. The trouble is, the grapes are all covered with ash."

"Can you clean them?"

Rosa shrugged. "That'll be up to Roberto. My crew just picks the grapes and brings them to the crush. The rest is not our job."

"Where's Roberto?"

"He should be here soon. He called me in the morning to come back to the vineyard. And of course, he told me about Alan. He said Nicole wanted us to get back to the harvest. So here we are."

"So, he's bringing everyone else?"

"Guess so. Gotta get to work. I'll come back to see Nicole at sundown."

It was midafternoon before Roberto drove the F-150, Miguel and Mark in the back, into the parking lot. Four people piled out of the cab.

"Where are Greg and Alex?" Tara asked.

"They're going home," said Antonio. "They have families back in San Francisco."

"Actually, Alex is from Berkeley," said Miguel. Antonio shrugged.

"So, we have no servers?" said Tara.

"I don't think we're going to be opening the restaurant today," said Roberto. "But I found an electrician." He pointed at a thin man with dark hair and thick, black whiskers who stood beside the pickup's passenger door. "Mike, here, was also staying at the hotel in Monte Rio. He can't get back to his house or his shop, but luckily he did bring some tools with him when he evacuated." Mike hoisted a heavy tool belt to show Tara. "And he could use the work. It looks like his family lost everything."

"Oh, I'm sorry," Tara said. Mike nodded.

"Come on, Mike. I'll show you where the electrical panel is." He led the thin man toward the remains of the garage.

Tara stood alone beside the truck. *Everyone has a task to do. I guess it's time for me to call the funeral home.*

The electrical panel

Tara came into the house to hear the phone ringing. *Weird that the phone lines work when there's no power.*

"This is Gary Henry, County Fire Marshal," said a hoarse voice. "We're wondering if your restaurant can help feed a crew of hungry volunteer firefighters."

"Uhh ... I don't know, I'm just—"

"Listen, ma'am, I don't want to sound rude, but we've got hundreds of people volunteering to do a very dangerous, very difficult job. Everybody is doing their part. I've gotten a bunch of other restaurants to pitch in, but I've still got more than a hundred people to feed. So, what do you say—can you do your part?"

"I don't know, Mr. Henry. We don't have power here, and—"

"Oh. Sorry. Okay, I'll try somebody else."

"Wait!" Tara glanced into the kitchen. *Where is Nicole? Did she go to bed?* "We have an electrician working on it right now."

"Okay. Then can I count on you for tomorrow?"

"Call me back in an hour and I'll let you know for sure."

"Thanks, Mrs. DaSilva."

"I'm not—" The line clicked. *Damn.* At that moment, Tara heard a loud *clunk,* followed by a fizzing sound. The kitchen light came on, and the microwave started beeping.

Tara put the phone back in the cradle, feeling lucky for the first time in days.

Then the lights flickered and went out. Tara sighed and went across the lot to the stinking remains of the garage.

Roberto and Mike, the electrician, were pulling electrical cables across the lot. "What's going on?" she asked.

"The electrical meter for the estate is attached to the one garage wall that's still standing," Roberto puffed. "We're making a work-around so that the main electrical panel is in the winery."

"We can't move the meter. The utility will charge you if you tamper with it," Mike explained. "Charge you with a crime, I mean. They'll also charge you money."

"The meter looks okay, but with the garage burned down, we can't have the electrical panel there "

Tara watched as Roberto held a big metal box against a bracket on the front wall inside the winery, beside the big roll-up door. Roberto's arms trembled with the weight as Mike quickly screwed the box into brackets. Then she watched the electrician string cable high overhead from the corner of the winery to the only intact corner of the garage. He was sweating by the time the job was done.

Tara looked at her watch. "Damn. I gotta take a call." She ran back to the house, and saw on the call display that the Fire Marshal had called again. She dialed back. "Okay, we have power again. The dining room is rated for 130 at a time. Will that do?"

She heard a *clunk* and a fizz, and the lights came on. The microwave beeped. She heard more clicks and hums as the refrigerators and other appliances came back to life. *Maybe we can get some air conditioning going.*

"That's great. I have a crew of a hundred men and women still to check off. Thank you, Mrs. DaSilva," said a relieved-sounding Henry.

Damn. He hung up again before I could tell him I'm not Mrs. DaSilva.

After setting the clocks and turning the air conditioning on high, Tara found Nicole stretched out on the bed in the spare bedroom, still in her clothes. Her arm covered her eyes, and a glass sat on the nightstand, a drop of red wine staining the bottom. Charlie lay on the floor beside the bed, and his tail wagged when he saw Tara.

"Are you all right?" Tara asked.

"I'll never be all right again," Nicole said, not moving her arm. "I've done something terrible."

Tara sat on the foot of the bed. "You can't blame yourself because you found him."

"It's not that." Nicole shook her head under her arm. "I hurt Alan before. I knew I was hurting him, and he knew I knew, and I kept doing it."

"I'm sure he loved you." *How the hell would I know that?*

"I'm not worth it."

Tara put her hand on Nicole's knee. "Have you eaten anything today?"

"I'm not hungry."

"You have to eat something, Nicole. You won't do Alan, or yourself, or anyone else any good by punishing yourself. You have a business to run."

Nicole did not answer this, so Tara decided to push it further. "The pickers are back at work, and Roberto brought an electrician who's got the power working again. Look, the clock-radio is flashing." 12:34 blinked redly back at her.

"That's good. But I can't face the restaurant today."

"I think it's too late for today, anyway. Oh, but the Fire Marshal asked if we could feed a volunteer firefighting crew tomorrow. He said everyone's pitching in to help in the situation. Is that okay?"

Nicole's arm flopped down onto her chest, but her eyes remained closed. "Whatever."

Tara went back to the kitchen. The light came on when she opened one of the refrigerators, but the inside was not cold. *Not warm, but not cold. I hope the fridges in the restaurant stayed cooler than this.*

Big, commercial grade refrigerators should stay cold longer. I hope.

She took out one of the containers Mrs. Harris had left. Potato salad. *Not the best thing when there's no power in the hottest summer on record, but I guess it's still okay.*

She popped a piece of potato into her mouth.

Not what Nicole's used to with Chef Donald, but it will do.

She brought a plate to Nicole with a glass of cool water and managed to extract a promise to eat. As she went outside again, the heat hit her face like a blow. *I guess the air conditioning is starting to kick in.*

Her stomach growled. *When was the last time I ate?*

She could see Roberto and Mike, still fussing with cables. She went into the restaurant. Light switches did not work, and the clock in the kitchen was dark. She went back outside.

"There's power in the house, but not in the restaurant," she told Roberto and Mike.

"We've got the house and the guest house going so far," Roberto said. His face was shiny and his t-shirt soaked. "We don't need the restaurant tonight."

"There's all sorts of inventory in the refrigerators. If we don't get power going there soon, it'll all be garbage."

Mike looked at Roberto, who looked at Mike. "Whaddaya think?"

"It's going to take running a couple more cables. I just can't figure the way they wired this place. It's totally bizarre."

Roberto sighed. "I guess we'll be here for a while, still."

"If you get the power going in the restaurant, I'll make supper for all of us," said Tara. Her stomach growled again.

Tara took leftovers from the restaurant for supper in the DaSilvas' house. *At least the refrigerators are working. They're not cold enough, but they'll get colder. I don't dare open a freezer.*

Nicole refused to leave the spare bedroom, and she ate no more than a few mouthfuls of the bland potato salad prepared by Janet Oakley. But she did manage to polish off a full bottle of Rocky Creek Pinot Noir.

After they ate in the kitchen, Roberto took Mike to spend the night in the guest house. "He can stay in Greg's room. Then I gotta go check on my own house."

The night stretched long for Tara. Sitting in Nicole's living room, she made a quick Skype call to her parents, assuring them she was okay. "We're glad, dear," said her mother. "Roxanne's tucked in for the night."

Shit. Missed her bedtime again. How can not seeing a person hurt this much?

"I'll call earlier tomorrow."

"Okay, dear. Talk to you then."

She went back to the guest room to find Nicole sprawled on top of the bed covers, eyes closed, Charlie still at her feet. Tara went to the master bedroom and found a nightgown and coaxed Nicole until she agreed to get changed.

Then Tara led Charlie to the kitchen. His tail wagged furiously when she found a can of dog food, opened it and slopped the contents into a bowl on the floor. He attacked it, chewing with the energy of a dog that had not eaten for days. "Sorry, boy," she said. Then she stumbled back to the living room and fell onto the sofa.

Should I watch TV? What for? Lifting the remote would take too much effort.

She put her feet up. *Maybe I should go back to my own room in the guest house. But it's so far away. I'll go in just a minute. Just let me rest here for a minute. I can't believe how much has happened today. It's been such a long day. Such a long, tiring day. Poor Nicole. Poor Alan. Poor Mom and Dad. I miss Roxanne so much. I can almost feel her sitting on my lap. Her chubby little hands. When is her hair going to come in?*

Birds? Why are there birds singing?

She opened her eyes, then closed them immediately against the flood of light. A ball of flame hung over the brown hills, turning the sky beyond the front window pink and yellow.

The bird tweeted again. Tara blinked, rising from the sofa.

That's not a ball of flame. That's sunrise.

Damn. I slept the whole night on this sofa. No wonder my neck is stiff.

She stood. Her lower back decided to join her neck in feeling sore and stiff. She managed to walk down the hall to the DaSilvas' guest bedroom. The door had been pushed up to the frame, but not latched. Tara eased it open until she could see Nicole under the covers. A faint snore made her smile.

It's still too early to wake her up. Tara stretched out on the sofa again, arranging herself comfortably. When she woke again, it was almost eight.

She went to the kitchen and found bread and eggs. *Not too much for Nicole,* she decided. *Seeing a big plate of food will probably just turn her off. But coffee—she won't turn that down.*

Charlie came into the kitchen, tail wagging as he stared at Tara. He whined. "What is it, boy?"

As if to answer, Charlie pressed his nose against the pantry door. Tara opened it to see a large bag of kibble. "Oh, you want breakfast. Sorry." She poured another bowlful under Charlie's happy gaze. When she put the bowl on the floor, Charlie gobbled the contents in less than a minute, then spent the next few minutes chasing stray kibbles across the tiles.

Tara went back to the bedroom. "Wake up, Nicole," she urged.

Nicole turned onto her back. She looked at Tara, but did not argue against getting into the shower.

As the water poured, Tara made coffee and a moderate breakfast. The two women ate in silence. *What can I say to her?*

Nicole took her coffee to the patio behind the house and sat, staring at the brown hills under the hazy sky. Tara cleaned the kitchen, then went to find Roberto.

She stopped first at the restaurant, just to reassure herself everything was all right. She flipped a light switch in the dining room. *Damn. No power here. I hope the fridges stayed cold enough.*

What is Roberto doing?

She looked up the back stairs. *I've never seen the upstairs here.*

On the third step, she felt a familiar tightness across her chest. Her breathing became shallow and quick. *Why am I nervous? I'm just going upstairs. I work here, after all.*

Why do I get the feeling the DaSilvas are hiding something?

Because you've watched too many bad movies, that's why, Tara. There's going to be nothing to see here. In the meantime, you could be Skyping with Roxanne right now.

I will do that. Right after I finish snooping.

Looking around. Just looking around. You work here. You should know where things are, Tara.

The mansion's second floor was decidedly smaller than the first. At the top of the stairs, a hallway opened to a gallery that overlooked the front entrance. *Now that I think of it, I remember looking up at this from the lobby.*

She pushed open a door on the right. Its squeak made her heart thump. *Relax. You're alone in the mansion.*

Just like the girls in all the horror movies.

It was a modest office. Sunlight poured into the tall window. An ancient computer with a big CRT monitor sat on a scratched old wooden desk that looked like it had come from the back of a warehouse. Shelves held stacks of paper, and two filing cabinets flanked the window.

Nothing interesting here, unless you're an accountant.

Or a lawyer. Should I tell Paul Rondeau?

Tell him what? That I've been snooping in the DaSilvas' office?

The next room was probably once intended as a bedroom, but now held shelves of table linens. More shelves held glasses and plastic bins of cutlery.

What else would you expect to find in a restaurant?

The next door opened on a linen closet, stuffed with dish towels, aprons and kitchen uniforms.

So far, this checks out.

Congratulations, super sleuth. You found a restaurant.

There was one last door at the end of the hall, beyond the gallery overlooking the lobby. It opened silently, and Tara had to squint until her eyes adjusted to the gloom inside. She wondered why the room was so dark until she noticed the heavy curtains drawn over the window.

The room did not seem to have any single purpose, other than to hold unmatched furniture. Three stacking chairs stood in the corner. There was a folding table resting on its side against one wall, and opposite that was an old, sagging couch. *This must be a place where Alan or Nicole can come for a rest in the slow times during the day.* Tara picked up a throw pillow from the floor without thinking about it.

Wait—what's this?

She bent down to the floor.

Nothing but a stray sock. A man's black sock.

It's kind of sad when you think of how many socks are single in this world, their mates lost forever.

Well, this was a fruitless search, Tara. She went back downstairs, and out of the restaurant to look for Roberto.

She found Mike, the electrician, instead, standing at the corner of the remains of the garage. It didn't smoke anymore, but it still stank of char and ash and old oil.

Mike was staring at the electrical meter, attached to a metal pipe on the one standing wall of the garage. A heavy steel-encased cable snaked up to the top of another pole, stretching high overhead to the winery. Another led to a battered looking metal electrical box that had obviously been temporarily attached to the wall. Its door was open, hanging at a haphazard angle.

"There's no power in the restaurant," she said.

"Yeah, I know. I disconnected it this morning," Mike replied without taking his eyes from the electrical box.

"Why? We need power."

"I'm tryin' ta figger somethin' out. It's real strange," he said.

"What is?"

"One of the wires is missing."

"Didn't you move the electrical box to the winery yesterday?"

"We moved the main panel. This," he pointed to a round device with a digital readout, encased in a heavy glass bulb, "is the main meter, which we can't move without getting arrested. This is an old subpanel just for the garage, which we left alone. But the wiring here is weird. I don't know what whoever set it up was thinking."

"So, what's wrong with it?"

Mike pointed at the tangle of boxes. "There should be a wire from there," he moved his finger slightly. "to there. And the ground wire is missing, too."

"Maybe the fire destroyed them?"

"Just those two wires and nothing else?" Mike patted the side of the metal box. "Look. There's no fire damage here. Not even soot or smoke on it. Fire did not touch this electrical box. But human hands did."

Tara looked over the electrical box. Mike was right: it bore no fire damage. Painted a boring beige, it had no obvious signs of fire damage. No soot, no scorch marks. "It doesn't look like anyone has touched this for years."

"Except for two missing wires," said Mike.

"Why would someone remove two wires?"

Mike poked at the box and tapped a screwdriver against the breakers at the top of the box. "Unless they were trying to scr— I mean, mess it up, I have no idea."

"Are you saying this electrical box was sabotaged?"

Mike looked at Tara's eyes, then out the window. "Look, I don't know about sabotage—"

"But you know about electrical boxes, right? What does this mean?"

Mike did not answer. After waiting for a full minute, Tara pulled out her phone and took pictures.

"Why are you taking pictures?"

"To send to the police. They need evidence, but right now, the restaurant needs power."

"Police? Should I be touching this?" Mike was holding up his hands.

"Like I said, the restaurant needs power. We have people to feed."

"I thought restaurants cooked with gas."

"Yes, but there are refrigerators, a walk-in cooler, lights ... A lot of things use electricity."

Mike bit his bottom lip and looked out the window. "Maybe I shouldn't touch this. You know, in case the cops wanna dust it for prints."

What has this guy done? "Fine. Tell me what to do."

Tara took the screwdriver and pliers from Mike, and following his directions, connected a black wire from one incoming wire to an empty pole near the bottom of the box, and a white wire between two other poles. Mike donned latex gloves and pushed on one of the connections Tara made, nodding his approval. Finally, he pushed the main breaker open again with the heel of his hand. Tara expected a buzz, but instead heard another deep, solid *clunk.* "Wait a second," she said, and crossed the lot to the restaurant. In the kitchen, she flipped all four switches on the wall, nodding as the lights came on. She heard another clunk from inside the walk-in cooler, followed by a series of beeps as two microwave ovens, a clock radio and one of the refrigerators came on. From upstairs, she heard a series of beeps as Alan's office appliances came back to life.

She went back to the ruin of the garage, giving Mike a thumbs-up. Mike began to pack up his tools.

She took one more look at the electrical box. *It's just a plain, metal box when it's closed.* Her eyes followed a pipe that led down to the ground, where the cables connected to the main power lines for the estate.

Strange that the electricity comes to the garage before the house. Or maybe this was the original structure here. Oh, well, Mike said the wiring here was wonky.

She looked up toward the guest house, then back at the ground near the garage. *What's that?*

Something glinted metallic in the dust. She picked it up.

A bronze bracelet with a broken clasp. She wiped dust off the bauble dangling in the middle. It was a strange shape with an odd design on it. *Unique, handcrafted jewelry. What's it doing here in the dust?*

She carried it into the winery, to find Roberto fussing over a shiny silver tank. "Hey, great job getting the electricity going again."

"It wasn't me, it was that contractor, Mike Donovan. He's going to connect the restaurant today."

"He just did. Now he's acting weird in front of the garage."

Roberto looked at her with a question on his face, but Tara ignored it. She held out the bracelet. "Do you recognize this?"

Roberto's eyes went wide. He looked at Tara, then at the pendant again. "Where did you find ... it?"

"On the ground beside what's left of the garage. Do you know who it belongs to?"

Roberto looked at the fermenting tanks. "Uh ... no. Never saw it before."

He's lying. Why?

She pocketed the jewel. "Oh, well. Finders keepers, I guess."

Feeding the firefighters

Antonio arrived at eleven, finding Tara wearing her kitchen uniform and doing inventory in the walk-in cooler.

"Where's Miguel?" she asked.

"He's not coming in for the next few days. He went to help fight the fires. His uncle's place burned down, and the fires are close to his parents' house, too."

"Damn. I mean, it's great that he's pitching in, but we're supposed to feed a fire crew tonight. Maybe I can convince some of the picking crew to help out."

"We're going to open tonight?" Antonio looked around the spotless, quiet kitchen. "How? What are we going to feed people?"

Tara gave him a sheet of paper. "I've made a list. Can you get enough of this for a hundred people, plus our own? So, I guess about a hundred and thirty?"

Antonio studied the paper. "I'd better get going."

As he left, she went back to the winery. Roberto was working with Amy and Mark. "Can we get some help for the restaurant this evening? We've volunteered to help feed about a hundred firefighters."

The three winery workers stared at her, mouths open. Roberto took a deep breath. "Let me call Rosa. Maybe some of the pickers can help."

Now it's time to get to work. There's going to be about a hundred hungry people here in a few hours.

That means pasta. Lots of pasta Sauce is easy.

She opened the walk-in cooler, pleased to find it was still cool. Good. The power wasn't out so long that the temperature went too high.

Veggies were a little soft, but good enough. *It's not going to be the freshest stuff, but it will do.*

Antonio returned three hours later to carry big boxes into the kitchen. "I know I took a long time. The food terminal is still closed, so I had to go all the way to Santa Rosa," he said.

"That's okay. What do we have?" Tara asked.

"Standard produce here, fresher than the stuff in the cooler. I have another couple of baskets in the truck. Ground beef, some chickens, a side of pork. And I managed to get a lot of eggs." He went back out, banging the door shut.

"Well, at least we can supply hungry firefighters with soufflés," Tara said to no one.

Now, to consider the human resources. With Miguel helping to fight the wildfires, Antonio and I are the only two with professional kitchen experience.

But I've got Toby, Gabriela and Rosa to help. So that means we have to make this as simple as possible, and that means cafeteria style.

Mike, the electrician, came into the kitchen and handed Tara a piece of paper. "There's no rush on paying this. I know how tough things are gonna be until the wildfires are over. But I'd appreciate it if you'd sign my copy," he said.

"Shouldn't Nicole be the one to sign official documents?" Tara asked.

"I just think Mrs. DaSilva doesn't need to deal with this kind of stuff right now."

"Right. Okay." Tara found a pen and scribbled her name across the bottom of the bill.

Mike folded it and tucked the paper into his pocket. He leaned close. "Look, this is just in case. But I'd appreciate it if you didn't broadcast that I was doing this work here, okay?"

Tara looked up at the thin, dark-haired man. "Why? What are you worried about?"

"Nothing. Nothing you need to know about, okay? But unless the cops ask directly, you didn't see me today, okay?"

Tara thought about the request, then nodded. *There's too much going on right now for the cops to worry about whether Mike Donovan has an up-to-date electrician's license.*

"Okay, but before you go, can you help me and Antonio move some furniture? We've got a couple of firefighting crews coming for a meal, and we have to set this place up cafeteria-style."

"Sure thing."

They spent a half hour moving tables into long rows to accommodate as many people as possible in the restaurant. One row along the wall was for serving, and once those were set up, she and Alex hustled between the kitchen and the dining room to set up warmers, platters, stacks of dishes, and cutlery.

After Mike left, Antonio prepared a mountain of fresh pasta as Tara cooked an ocean of Bolognese sauce. With the pasta ready to boil, she set Antonio to chopping veggies, Gabriela to making as much coffee as she could, Toby to slicing bread. *I could use another set of hands with this crowd coming. Even Nicole could help.*

But Nicole was in her house, silent. *I'm glad Roberto is with her.*

Roberto—is he the one she's having the affair with?

No. That makes no sense. Roberto was showing me around when Nicole drove up that morning. And anyway, you don't even know that she is having an affair.

Still—it could be…

Her phone's trill interrupted her thoughts. She glanced at the screen. "Hello, Chief."

"I've got a hungry crew," Henry, the County Fire Marshal said. "Are you ready to stuff a hundred faces?"

"The restaurant's licensed for 130. I hope they like pasta Bolognese."

"If that's spaghetti with meat sauce, yes. We'll be there in twenty."

Twenty minutes.

The first trucks began arriving just as the pots were boiling. As groups of sooty, tired men and women crowded into the dining room, Toby and Rosa from the picking crew sliced all the bread they had been able to find. Tara and Gabriela hustled platters and bowls from the kitchen to the dining room.

Strange how we've all reverted to traditional gender roles in a crisis.

But then there was no time to think philosophy as more trucks stopped in the parking lot or on the road and more men came into the restaurant.

She organized them into shifts. Twenty minutes after the first group arrived, she let the second group go to the food tables. The first group didn't need more of a hint. They wolfed down their last bites, stuffed bread into their mouths and stood. They carried their dishes to the serving window into the kitchen and squeezed out the door, letting the next batch sit in their places.

It's true: we're at our best when things are worst.

A man came in who stood out from the rest because his clothes were not dirty. "Mr. Rondeau. Are you looking for Nicole?"

"Yes. I thought she'd be here, what with the fire crews coming in."

"Sorry. I think she's just not up to it, ever since ... you know. She hasn't been able to do much. She's in her house with Roberto. Can I help you with something?"

"There's something I have to talk to Nicole about. Some news, but if she's not up to coming to her own restaurant, then ... still, this is too important to wait. Maybe you'd better come with me ..."

Tara looked over the dining room. It was noisy, busy, but controlled. She signaled to Toby. "Watch things. I'm going to take Mr. Rondeau here to the house."

Toby nodded and smiled. "Please, call me Paul," said the lawyer.

On the walk over, Tara asked what the news was.

"I think Nicole should be the first to hear this."

The house's front door was not locked, and they found Nicole alone in the living room. A cup sat on a table beside her. Across the room, the TV showed a guide screen, with nothing playing.

Nicole sat slumped forward in a wing chair, her hair undone, hanging limp around her shoulders. As usual, Charlie lay on the floor beside the chair. His tail started to wag when he saw Tara. He rose and came over, and Rondeau rubbed his shaggy head.

"Where's Roberto?" Tara asked.

"I sent him to the winery. There's work to be done," Nicole answered without looking up.

"Nicole it's me. Paul."

"I know."

Paul sat down in the second wing chair beside Nicole, his hands clasped. Charlie sat beside him, looking at Nicole, as well.

"I'll get back to the restaurant," said Tara.

"No, you had better stay. I don't want Nicole to be alone after what I have to say."

Nicole covered her face with her hands. Tara sat on the edge of a sofa and, for something to do, picked up the cup. It was cold.

"Nicole," he began, his voice soft and gentle. "I've come from talking to Henry Ling, the County Coroner." Tara saw Nicole's shoulder tense. "He's pretty overwhelmed, as you can imagine. A lot of people have … have died in the wildfires, and there will probably be more. So he did not have a lot of time … with Alan."

Paul took a deep breath. He looked out the south-facing window, where the low sun lit the brown hills with gold, and tinted the smoke to the east pink and yellow. "Nicole, when you found Alan, did you notice anything strange?"

"You mean other than his body, burned beyond recognition?"

Paul put his hand on her shoulder. "I'm so sorry, Nicole, but I have to ask you this. The police will, later, when they're not so busy."

Nicole looked up then at Paul. Her eyes were rimmed with red, her face puffy, her nose pink. "What the hell would they want? What good are they? Alan's dead, Paul, he's gone, and I'm …" She covered her face again, sniffing wetly.

Tara found a tissue in her pocket and gave it to her. Nicole dabbed her eyes and blew her nose, then held the wet tissue out to Tara again.

Charlie nuzzled Nicole's leg.

"The police are going to want to talk to you and to look at the grounds for evidence, Nicole," Paul continued, his voice still soft and gentle. "That's why I've come. The coroner looked at Alan, and in addition to the burns …" he took another deep breath. "I know how hard this must be for you to hear, Nicole, and it's hard for me to say. Alan was my friend, too. I loved him. But Dr. Ling told me that Alan sustained a severe head wound. Blunt force trauma is what killed him." Paul choked, looking down. A tear left the corner of his eye and trailed slowly down toward his mouth.

Nicole looked up at him again, her eyebrows drawn together. "What—what are you saying? 'Blunt force trauma'? Someone hit him on the head?"

"It's possible. It's also possible that he fell off of something. Where did you find him?"

"On the ground in front of the garage. I told you, and the police, and the coroner this already!"

Paul took another deep breath. "Could he have fallen from the garage?"

"I don't know! It was burned down when I found him."

"Was there a ladder or anything else around?"

"No, there was no goddamn ladder. Are you saying that someone killed Alan?"

Charlie rose to his feet, looking back and forth between Paul and Nicole. His tail and his ears drooped.

Paul held up a hand. "No one is saying that, Nicole. There's no evidence of that. But there was significant head trauma, and the police and the coroner are going to want to account for that. You were the first person to find him, right?"

"Yes, I found him … are you trying to accuse me of something, Paul?"

"No, of course not, Nicole," Paul said. Tara could see he was working to keep his voice gentle. He put his arm around Nicole, but she shrugged it off, glaring at him. "But you need to get ready for these questions. You need to think, Nicole. I know it's hard, but you need to think about that night—"

"I can't think about anything else! Every time I close my eyes, I see Alan lying there, all black, twisted in pain …" She covered her face again, but then dropped her hands and stood up quickly. She walked to the window and turned to Paul. "My husband is dead. He died in the worst imaginable way, burned to death. But now you're saying that someone killed him, hit him over the head and killed him. Who? Who would kill Alan? He had no enemies. Who would want him dead?"

Paul held his hands up in a gesture of surrender. "I can't imagine either, Nicole. Alan did a lot in the community. He was good to his employees. I can't think of anyone who would want him dead. On the contrary, more people would have wanted him to live. His employees, his suppliers, his wife ... but there it is. There's a question. All I'm saying is, you need to be ready for a lot of questions."

"Get out. Get out of my house!"

Tara did not recognize Nicole's face anymore. It was twisted, flushed, her mouth wide, her lips invisible.

Charlie whined. He looked at Rondeau, then at Nicole. Finally, he slunk behind Nicole's chair.

Paul rose from the chair. "Take it easy, Nicole. I'm not your enemy, here. No one is your enemy. We just need to get to the truth about what happened to Alan."

"The truth? The truth? The truth about Alan is that he was married to the winery, not to me, and now he's gone! Get out. Get out now."

Paul looked at Tara, then at Nicole, and back to Tara. "Will you stay with her?"

Tara nodded. She stood, the cold cup in her hand. "I'll make some tea."

"I think you'd better give her a drink."

In the kitchen, she turned on the stove under the kettle and pulled out her phone, dialing Antonio's number. "Send Rosa over here, fast."

"Why? We really need her here."

"How are things going?"

"Good. We've brought in another shift of firefighters. Two to go. We're cooking more pasta and cutting up more bread. I'm making more sauce. These guys really love it, and we can't say 'no' when they want seconds."

"No, don't do that. I'll be back in a few minutes, but I don't want Nicole to be alone."

"I thought Roberto was there."

"No, she sent him away. I think it would be better for a woman to be here. Send Rosa."

"Okay, but we really could use her."

"I said, I'm coming back soon."

"Look, we have things under control here." Antonio's voice was firm. "You stay there, and when the rush is over, I'll send Rosa. Or maybe I'll come, myself. What's going on, anyway?"

"Nicole got some bad news, and she's not taking it well."

"More bad news? Jeez. That sucks. What was it?"

"I'll tell you later. Okay, as long as you're sure things are under control."

"Don't worry, boss."

She clicked the call closed. The kettle began to sing. Tara found a mug and teabags, and brought a steaming cup to the living room.

Nicole was slumped back in the chair, while Paul stood by the front door. Tara put the cup beside Nicole and went to the door.

She followed Paul onto the front steps, digging into her pocket. "You asked about anything unusual. I found this today beside what's left of the garage." She held the tarnished bronze bracelet in front of Paul. "I showed it to Roberto. He said he didn't recognize it, but I think he's lying."

Paul looked closely at the bracelet. "Why do you say that?"

"I can usually tell when people are lying."

"Hmmm. Okay. You couldn't have known this, but if the police are going to investigate, that could be evidence, so you shouldn't have touched it."

Tara's heart pounded. She felt cold. "Should I put it back?"

Paul put his hand on her shoulder, and it amazed her how much calmer she felt suddenly. "No. Just hang onto it for now. When the police come to investigate—and I think that's going to take a few days, given the wildfires—show it to them and tell them exactly what you told me. They'll probably be pissed that you didn't leave it where you found it, and it may mean nothing … but then, it might."

"Do you know anything about it?"

Paul bent down, looking closely. "No, but it kind of looks like something that could have been made by Cheryl Sirkus, down at the Sonoma Art Works. But I don't know. Hang onto it and tell Sheriff Doyle when she asks. Be ready with the details, and keep your story straight."

"What do you mean? What story?"

"You found something that may or may not be evidence of what may or may not be a homicide. You were also one of the first people to find Alan's body. So whether you like it or not, you're deep into this."

"I know. I told you, I graduated law school."

"Look, I gotta go. Thanks for coming with me. But right now, you need to get back to Nicole. She's not in a good place."

He turned and walked under the darkening sky to his car in front of the restaurant.

Nicole was standing at the doorway between the living room and the hall that led to the bedrooms, Charlie, as usual, sitting on the floor beside her. "Can you stay here again, tonight?"

"Of course. Where do you keep your linens? I'll make up the couch."

"No. You can have the guest room. I'll get you fresh sheets. But tonight I want to go back to the bed I used to share with my husband."

"Oh. Okay. Let me get my stuff from the guest house. Oh, by the way," she held out the bracelet, "is this yours? I found it outside."

Nicole frowned. "It looks familiar, but it's not mine. Maybe it's Amy's."

Tara held it up so it dangled. "It's pretty dirty, but it's kind of dressy to wear to work."

Nicole shrugged. "All I know is, it's not mine."

When Tara returned from the now-empty guest house, Nicole was smoothing a sheet onto the bed in the spare bedroom. Tara put her suitcase down beside a dresser and wordlessly, the two women finished making up the bed.

"Care for some wine before bed?" Nicole asked. She led the way to the living room without waiting for an answer and poured two big glasses. "It's our Cabernet. It's my favorite of the wines we make."

Tara sipped. "It's very good."

She sat on the big easy chair, Tara on the sofa. "I want to thank you for everything you've done for me. I know I've been a zombie," Nicole said.

"That's understandable."

"I just can't believe it. Last night, I would just start to fall asleep, and then I'd remember that Alan is … is … gone." Tears leaked from the outer corner of both her eyes.

"I'm so sorry, Nicole."

"I feel so … alone. My family is far away, and I just need another human being close by." She gave a wan smile as she bent over to pat the dog, who responded with a slow wag of the tail. "Charlie is wonderful, but he's not Alan."

"I understand." Tara crouched to join Nicole in patting Charlie. He closed his eyes in pleasure.

They spent a few quiet moments patting the dog. When Nicole stood, Tara did, too, and the women embraced. Charlie stood to push his nose between them, whining. That got a little laugh out of Nicole as she let Tara go.

They went to their respective bedrooms.

A reassuring video call

It took a full day for Internet service to return. Tara set up her laptop in the restaurant dining room to Skype her parents.

Marie Rezeck came into focus, the kitchen behind her. "Oh, my god, Tara. It's such a relief to see you. We were so worried."

Ken appeared behind her, crouching to be level behind his wife. "Are you really all right, Tara?"

"I'm fine. I wasn't hurt at all."

"But you said your boss was killed."

"It was awful." *I don't have to give them all the grisly details.* "He was ... burned. I don't want to talk about it."

"How is his family? Did he have a family?"

"His wife. She's the co-owner of their company."

"Right, you told us," said Dad. "And she runs the restaurant. How is she doing?"

"She's in a bad way, as you can imagine. I think it's PTSD. I'm no psychologist, but that's what it looks like to me. She doesn't talk much, stays in her room playing the same music over and over."

"She shouldn't be alone," Marie said. "That's the worst thing for someone who's lost a husband like that."

"What about your job?" Dad asked. "I don't mean to seem mercenary here, but ... with the owner dead, where does that leave you, employment-wise?"

"I'm not sure. Other than the garage, nothing else was damaged, and none of the employees were hurt. So I think that it could get back to operations, as long as everyone can get here. Anyway, where's Roxanne?"

Dad disappeared from the screen. Tara heard a chair scrape along the kitchen floor and the image blurred as Mom shifted her computer. Then Dad sat down beside Marie, holding baby Roxanne on his lap. "Here she is, fresh from her nap. Say 'hi' to Mama, Roxanne!"

"Hello, baby!" Tara's voice went up an octave as she went into full mommy-mode. She waved at her laptop. "Hi! It's Mama! Oh, I miss you so much."

"Hi," Roxanne sang. Dad grabbed her hand to make her wave at the computer. He must have tickled her, too, because she giggled, her tiny baby teeth flashing.

"I think she misses you, too," Mom said.

"No, she doesn't," Dad argued. "She's having too much fun with Baba and Pops to miss anyone."

"Oh, John, don't say that."

"Well, it's true. Isn't it, Nanya," Dad said, using their nickname for the baby. He tickled her again, making her squeal and squirm.

"Mom, did you curl her hair?"

"No, it's doing that by itself lately. Must be getting humid here, or something."

"That outfit is adorable. Where did you get it?"

"Cute, isn't it? It was on sale at Macy's."

"It was not on sale," Dad argued.

"Well, it wasn't expensive."

"You and I have different definitions of expensive."

Baby Roxanne reached for the computer. The image on the screen swept downward, and Tara was looking at her parents' laptop keyboard and the wooden kitchen table. "No, no, Nanya," Mom said. "Don't touch the computer. That's not for babies."

"Mine!" Roxanne protested.

"No, no," Marie repeated. "Do you want a cookie?" The image came back up, showing Dad holding Roxanne more firmly, his arms around her. She squirmed against him, a determined look on her face. "Cookie, Nanya?" Mom said again.

Roxanne continued squirming. Mom rose and went off the screen, returning a few seconds later with a digestive biscuit. "How about a cookie and some milk?"

"No," Roxanne said and went back to squirming.

"No cookie? Okay. How about applesauce. Baby want applesauce?"

"Is she eating well?" Tara asked.

Roxanne switched from struggling to get down from her grandfather's lap to squirming around and climbing up his shoulders and head. Dad laughed and picked her up under the arms. "Down," she said. "Down, down."

"I think she wants to go play, Dad," said Tara.

"Why don't I put her down in the family room and let her play with her toys?"

"I'd like that."

Mom carried their computer to the family room, and Tara spent a quarter hour, sipping coffee while watching her daughter play with brightly colored toys. She felt happy to see her baby girl playing cheerfully and, at the same time, felt anguished at the distance between them.

"Hey, Tara, I think we'll hang up. It's coming to the end of a beautiful afternoon here, and I'd like to take Roxanne to the park for some fresh air."

"That sounds great, Dad. I'll Skype you again tomorrow, okay?"

"Take care of yourself, Tara," Dad said.

"Love you," said Mom.

"Love you, too." She closed the connection before letting a tear fall.

Forensics

Tara had just hit the Brew button on the coffee maker on the third day after Alan's death when the doorbell rang. Wearing a light grey suit, Paul Rondeau stepped inside without asking. A gold watch glittered on his wrist, matching cuff links and a tie pin. "I hate to do this, but get Nicole up and dressed as quickly as possible. The Sheriff's Department is on the way."

"Why?"

"They're investigating Alan's death. They have to examine the scene, and they have to make a report."

"Do they suspect foul play?"

Paul shook his head. "No, no. This is mostly a formality. But just so you and Nikki—I mean, Nicole—know, the Sheriff herself is coming, too."

"Why?"

"Alan was pretty prominent in the community. Plus, Sheriff Doyle was a friend. Go and get Nikki now."

Nicole was still in bed, but not sleeping. She sat up, staring at the floor when Tara told her about the Sheriff.

Tara returned to the kitchen to see that Paul had poured three cups of coffee. "How do you take yours?" he asked.

"Lots of milk, no sugar."

Nicole came into the kitchen, wearing her signature billowy top over black yoga pants.

That is not a good look for your thighs, Tara thought.

There was no time to change, though, as the doorbell rang again. Paul carried his coffee to answer, Tara following.

A fit black woman and two men in green police uniforms stood on the porch. "Good morning, Paul," said the woman, who had four gold stars on each side of her collar. "Is Nicole Fong available?"

"Come in, Mary."

Does everyone in this county know each other?

Paul led them to the living room as Nicole came in slowly from the kitchen. "Mrs. DaSilva, first, I am so very sorry for your loss," the Sheriff said. "You know Alan was my friend, and it was a shock for me to learn of his death."

Nicole only nodded back.

"I'm sorry, but I need to take your statement." Sheriff Doyle sat slowly when Nicole sat in the same chair she had fallen into two nights earlier. The Sheriff took a notebook from one pocket and a small audio recorder from another. "Can I speak with you in private?"

Still looking at the floor, Nicole shook her head vigorously. Her black hair whipped back and forth. "No. I want Tara here with me."

Tara froze as Sheriff Doyle studied her, grim-faced. "All right. Are you Tara Rezeck? You and Roberto Gonsalves brought the body to the emergency morgue? You had better sit down, then."

Tara sat at the corner of the sofa as close to Nicole as she could.

"I understand you were the first to find the body," Doyle said. Tara winced at the statement, but it seemed to have no effect on Nicole.

"Nikki," Paul prompted after a long silence.

Nicole nodded again, looking at the floor.

"I'm sorry, Nicole," Doyle said again. "You'll have to speak up for the recorder."

"Yes," she said in a low voice. "I found the body."

"Approximately what time?"

"I'm not sure. In the afternoon. Maybe late afternoon."

"It was probably around—" Tara began, but Doyle held up a hand.

"I need to get Ms. Fong's own account. Please, Nicole, in your own words. Where exactly did you find Alan's body?"

"In front of the winery, near the garage."

"All right. What were you doing when you found the body?"

Nicole opened up. In a low, even tone, she calmly described how the winery staff had evacuated when the order came through, how Alan had driven into the vineyard to look for two pickers who were missing, how the rest of them had driven to the rendezvous point in Monte Rio as Alan had instructed, and how Alan did not show up. She told them how she had driven back to the winery as quickly as she could, hoping she would see his small truck coming toward her at any moment, but she had not seen it until she had turned into the gravel lot in front of the winery.

Listening to her quiet description brought vivid memories to Tara of her and Roberto's nightmarish pursuit of Nicole through the redwood forests and Sonoma vineyards. She could smell the smoke again and see the falling ash and the orange glow behind the hills.

"And again, I am sorry to have to ask this, but was Alan dead when you found him?" Doyle asked.

Nicole nodded and said, "Yes." She sniffed and wiped her face with the back of her hand.

"How could you be sure?" Doyle persisted.

Nicole did not raise her eyes. "He was lying still. His clothes were all burned, his skin was black. His mouth and his eyes were open. And when I touched him—" Her voice broke and she shuddered, but Tara did not see any more tears. She took a breath. "When I touched his hand, the skin came off." She covered her face with her hands.

Tara closed her eyes, too, but that did nothing to soften the horror of the memory of Alan's blackened corpse lying in the dirt and ash, or of the blood that ran red around Roberto's hands when he picked Alan up by the shoulders to put him in the truck.

"Did you notice anything else? Again, I'm sorry, but did you notice a wound on his head?"

Nicole shook her head, still in her hands. "No," she murmured.

Sheriff Doyle waited to ask the next question. "What happened then?"

Nicole shook her head again, still without looking up. "I don't know."

"Please, Ms. Fong," Doyle said. "Nicole."

"I can't," came as a harsh whisper. "I cannot remember anything else until Roberto and Tara were taking me out of the truck at the evacuation center. Everything in between ... is just black."

"That's common with trauma," Paul spoke up for the first time.

"All right." The Sheriff turned to Tara. "Tell me how you and Mr. Gonsalves came to find Ms. Fong."

Tara fought down a shudder. "When we found out that Nicole had gone back for Alan, we went to try to stop her. It was too dangerous."

"It was too dangerous for one person to go back, so you thought it was better to endanger two more?" Doyle said.

Tara felt unsteady under the Sheriff's steady gaze. "I never thought of it like that. I guess we just thought we could stop Nicole—Ms. Fong—before she got into a dangerous area."

"Whose idea was it to go after her, yours or Mr. Gonsalves'?"

"Roberto jumped into the truck, and I went with him."

"Why?"

Tara shrugged. "It just seemed the right thing to do. I wanted to help."

Doyle stared at her. Tara could not read her expression. Her mouth felt dry. She took a sip of coffee that was starting to get lukewarm.

"When did you catch up with Ms. Fong?"

"Not until we found her here at the winery."

"What time was that?"

"The sun was setting. It was getting dark."

"What happened then?"

Tara drank more coffee and choked. When she could, she described how she and Roberto had pulled Nicole away, putting her in their truck, and then how they had lifted Alan's burned body into the back of the pickup.

"Did you notice a head wound?" Doyle asked.

"No. I didn't want to look too closely at him," Tara admitted. She thought of a sunset, surf on a sandy beach, anything that wasn't Alan's blackened, bleeding body.

"Then?"

"Then we drove to the evacuation center."

"Straight there? How did you know the way?"

The image of the young highway patrolman flashed into her mind. "We had to stop before we got on the highway because there was a police car blocking the intersection. I guess they didn't want anyone to get off the highway there."

"We certainly did not."

"The policeman told us where to go."

"Did you get the deputy's name or badge number?"

"No."

"And where was this? Where Rocky Creek Road meets Highway 101?"

"I guess so. You'd have to ask Roberto. I was mostly paying attention to Nicole. Ms. Fong."

"And what time did you get to the evac center?"

"I don't know. I didn't look at the time. We went to the emergency morgue and they, the people there, they took Alan's body. Then we went into the emergency center, and they took Nicole for trauma counseling. And they treated us for smoke inhalation. That's where we met Paul. Mr. Rondeau."

Doyle nodded, her eyes going from Tara to Paul to Nicole. "All right." She shut off the recorder and stood. "Where is Mr. Gonsalves?"

"I guess he's in the winery," Tara answered. "I haven't seen him today yet."

"All right. Take me there, Ms. Fong. And to the place where you found the body."

"I can't," Nicole whispered.

Tara stood. "I'll take you."

Rondeau stood behind Nicole, gently rubbing her back. Tara led the three officers past the restaurant. "Here's where we found him," she said. "Between the winery and the burned-out garage."

"So, the winery was not damaged?" Doyle asked.

"No, not at all. Just the garage burned. And the stuff in it was all wrecked."

"Strange. Well, there's probably not much use in a complete forensic examination after all the activity here over the past two days, with people coming in and out. But we'll take a look." She nodded, and the other two cops opened their satchels.

One took out a large camera and started taking pictures, while the other put markers at various spots. Seeing that sparked a memory in Tara's mind. She took out her phone. "I should show you these." She flipped to the images she had taken the day before.

"What's this?"

"The electrical meter." She remembered she had promised not to mention Mike Donovan, the electrician. *This is going to be awkward.* "See? There are wires missing."

"How do you know? Do you know a lot about electricity?"

"No, not really." *Think fast, Tara.* "But the other day, when … Roberto and the others were working to restore power for the winery—when we got back, we found the power was out all over the winery, and Roberto said the wiring was wonky." *Don't talk so fast. She's a cop. She can tell that you're lying.* "So we all pitched in to fix it. Anyway, when … Roberto opened the electrical box here, I looked at the meter, and I thought it looked strange. So I was wondering, if the electrical meter had been tampered with, maybe that was the cause of the fire."

Doyle looked intently into Tara's eyes. "You and Mr. Gonsalves took it upon yourselves to fix the electricity? Don't you think that's best left to a qualified electrician?"

"Oh, yes, Roberto brought in an electrician. A professional."

Doyle had her notebook out. "What was their name?"

You promised to not tell. "I'm … not sure. Um, 'Mitch,' maybe?"

"I'll ask Mr. Gonsalves." Sheriff Doyle slid her notebook back into a pocket. "Take me to him, please."

Doyle followed Tara into the winery, where they found Roberto with Mark and Amy. Doyle and Roberto went into the office and closed the door, leaving Tara wondering what to say to the other two. "I better go see how Nicole is," she muttered, and went back to the house, where Paul was now sitting on the sofa.

"Nikki's gone back to bed," he said. "Reliving the trauma was too much for her."

"Maybe she should get some counseling."

"I'll look into that."

"I should get to the restaurant. I promised to cook for a bunch of firefighters again this evening, and I've gotta start getting ready."

Crossing back to the restaurant, she saw Sheriff Doyle walking toward her. "We're about wrapped up now. There seems to have been a lot of traffic, back and forth."

"We're in the middle of crush, and we've also been feeding the firefighters for the last couple of days."

"I understand that, but that contaminates the site. And I told Mr. Gonsalves not to do anything about fixing the garage, or even moving that truck, until the insurance examiner sees it."

"Do you think it's a crime scene?"

"We have to get going. We're pretty overwhelmed, given the circumstances."

"You mean the wildfires?" Tara asked. She saw the two crime scene investigators carry their satchels to their car.

"We're stretched to the limit. You know, there are looters going into evacuated towns? They say natural disasters bring out the best in people. But from what I've seen, they bring out the worst, too."

She left, and Tara continued to the restaurant. *There's work to be done.*

Funeral

She had not shown any emotion the previous evening either, while mourners shuffled past Alan's closed casket and repeated platitudes as they either held her hand or kissed her cheek.

Alan's parents had flown in from Los Angeles. Mr. DaSilva was tall, slim and elegant, with white hair and moustache. *He even wears cuff links.*

Alan's mother looked older than her husband, especially with the black veil suspended from the little black hat. She barely spoke, dabbing continually at her eyes and nose with a lace handkerchief.

These must be the most old-fashioned people I have ever seen.

Nicole's parents and a sister stood beside her. Her mother was a tiny Asian woman who spoke English with a Midwestern accent, while Anthony Fong was slightly overweight, like his daughter. Tara did not catch Nicole's sister's name, and the willowy, attractive woman largely remained quiet, speaking softly to her sister or parents occasionally.

For reasons that Tara could not guess, Nicole had insisted she stand beside her in the receiving line. People shook her hand, saying "I'm sorry," and Tara could see the question in everyone's eyes.

Who am I? Really. What kind of role am I playing here?

Am I Nicole's new best friend? Her grief counselor? Therapist? Handmaid?

"So sorry for your loss," said a white-haired man in a grey suit with a black band on his arm.

"Thank you," Tara said, and the man moved on, to be replaced by a middle-aged woman in a black dress.

After the last mourner had left the funeral home, Tara sank into a chair beside Roberto. The funeral director, a bland man named Wesley Thicke, closed the main doors. When he turned away, Tara could not remember a single detail of what he looked like.

"There must have been two hundred people through here," she said. She slipped off her shoe and rubbed her foot.

"Alan was well-liked here in the valley," Roberto said, looking at Nicole, who knelt in front of the closed casket, hands clasped, head bowed. "There were former employees, just about all the suppliers who are in the area, other vintners, business people. City Councilors, people from charities ..."

"Wow. A lot of respect."

"He always treated everyone well—employees, suppliers, customers. He supported Little League teams in about four different sports. Boy and Girl Scouts."

"He sounds amazing."

"Too good to be true," Roberto said, eyes fixed on Nicole.

So much bitterness in his voice.

Tara offered to let Nicole's parents stay in the guest room in the main house, but like the elder DaSilvas, they elected to use the rooms in the guest house that had once housed the wait staff.

"Actually, I prefer that you stay in the guest room here," Nicole said after her parents had left the house. "If my parents stayed in the house, my mom would keep me up all night, talking about how wonderful Alan was. She adored him. Sometimes, I think she loved him more than I did." She looked at Tara from under her eyelashes. "And I am just so tired. I cannot stay up late, but I don't want to be in an empty house."

She sat in the living room, opened a bottle of Rocky Creek Pinot Noir and stared out the window at the darkening horizon.

"Maybe you should get some counseling," Tara offered as she sat down on the sofa.

"Counseling?" Nicole's voice was flat.

"Grief counseling. "

"I don't want grief counseling. I just want to grieve for my husband."

"Maybe it would help you deal with things."

"I don't want to talk to a stranger about my feelings. I think that's bullshit."

I am getting myself in too deep here, Tara thought. *I barely know her.*

But that didn't stop her mouth from saying, "You can talk to me about it."

Nicole closed her eyes and took a deep breath. She looked at Tara then and said, "Thank you. That means a lot."

Does she have to look like a puppy when she says that? "Is there anything you—you want to talk about right now?" *What am I doing? I have no idea how to be a grief counselor.*

Nicole was looking out the window. "It's strange. There are so many things that you think you'll say one day, when the time is just right. Things you think you're going to do or change when you get the chance. Then before you know it, it's too late. You never get another chance to do those things because the person you wanted to do them for is gone. Dead."

Nicole's voice was still flat, her face impassive.

"You can't blame yourself, Nicole. It's not your fault. There's nothing you could have done." *Is that the right thing to say?*

"I know Alan's death is not my fault. But other things are. Things between us. They should have been better. I should have made them better."

"I think they call this 'survivor's guilt.' I hear it's pretty common in people who lose someone in a big disaster." *So what? How do I get her—and me—through this?*

Nicole sniffed. "And now, I look around this place … this house, this business, a winery and a restaurant, everything we've worked so hard on. Building up two businesses, do you know what kind of hours that takes? Alan spent so much time in the vineyards and in the winery, talking with suppliers and distributors at all hours. Do you know why we don't have kids, Tara?"

Nicole knocked back half the glass of wine. "Because we were too goddamn busy. Too busy working to take time for kids. Too goddamn busy to make a baby. Too busy to fuck half the time. Too busy and too tired." She drained the glass.

"And now he's gone," Nicole continued, her voice diminishing. "Now it's too late for us to have a family. Now Alan's gone, and I have nothing of him left." Tears flowed down her face.

Tara sat on the wide arm of the chair and put her arms around Nicole, surprised to feel tears on her own face.

Charlie pushed his nose onto Nicole's lap and whined. Tara leaned to pat his head and felt his nose press against her wrist. They stayed like that for a long time. Occasionally, Nicole would make a thin, keening sound, then sniff deeply.

Finally, she lifted her head. "Thank you, Tara. And you, too, Charlie." She patted him, and he stretched to lick the tears from her face. "I need a tissue." She rose to her feet, dug into her pocket, found one, and blew her nose. Then she poured the rest of the wine into their glasses. She drank most of hers. "I'm sorry to unload on you, Tara. I know this isn't what you signed up for."

"That's all right. Sometimes, we all need a shoulder to cry on. Literally." She tried to smile, but failed. She wiped her face dry with her sleeve.

"I'm sorry about the way I acted when Alan hired you. I shouldn't have been surprised. Alan does that kind of thing all the time. I mean, he did that kind of thing all the time."

"What kind of thing?"

"Make decisions about the business without consulting me first. It made me so mad."

"I think he was trying to help you."

Nicole smiled just a little. "I know he was. He always was … but it made me mad. And I shouldn't have taken that out on you."

"That's all right."

"No, it's not." She raised her arms and Tara stepped in for the hug. Charlie leaned in, too, his tail thumping on the floor.

"We should go to bed," Nicole said when she finally released Tara. "The funeral is tomorrow at 10." Charlie followed her down the hall.

The next day dawned bright and clear. *Thank god we don't smell smoke today*, Tara thought as she pulled on a dark grey dress and the one pair of dress shoes she had brought to California.

Nicole insisted Tara ride in the limousine with her and Alan's parents. At the funeral, the sky was a hard blue over the grey-green lawn of the cemetery. A fading wind swept the smoke to the east and made Nicole's hair wave behind her like a maudlin pennant. Her face was a stone mask as she looked at the minister intoning a prayer over the casket.

She read a eulogy in a strong voice, praising her husband's passion for his work, his love for the community and for his family. Roberto and Steven Harris talked, too, about the pleasure it had been to work for, or with, Mr. Alan DaSilva. Another man and a woman, friends of Alan's whom Tara had never met, spoke, too, about the time they had known him.

The elder Mr. DaSilva sat quietly, a deeply sad calm in his eyes. He held his wife's hand throughout the speeches. Mrs. DaSilva cried continually, and quietly.

At least, that's over. Viewing, funeral, burial, reception. Days of dreariness.

I can't blame Nicole for clinginess. How would I be if I lost my husband?

What if it were Bobby? Tara tried to imagine her emotional reaction at the death of the father of her baby.

It's not like I'd be losing support, other than a monthly check. He was never much for emotional support while we were together, and as soon as he found out I was pregnant—zoom. He was outta there faster than ... faster than we ran to the Russian River. Leaving me a single, unemployed, pregnant grad student, who had to ask her parents to take her back in.

What a day that was. Still, it was better than today.

Break-in

The morning after the funeral, Tara left Nicole with her parents and in-laws, drinking coffee and wine in the kitchen, and found Roberto back in the winery, his arms elbow-deep in equipment.

"Another breakdown?" she asked.

"Yeah. The filter, again. Third time this month."

"Isn't that what Alan was fixing last week? Do you think that someone sabotaged it?"

Roberto peered into the filter. "Maybe. That's the only thing that makes sense. On the other hand, who would do it? No one broke in here. There's no other damage."

"Maybe a disgruntled former employee? Someone with a key?" Tara suggested.

"The only disgruntling that I know about is Chef Donald. He's the only one that I ever heard about leaving angry. And he never had a key to the winery."

"I thought there was a lot of turnover in the kitchen. Whose place did I take?"

"I think his name was Danny. Sorry, I never spent a lot of time in the restaurant. I'm busy enough here. But I suppose Chef Donald was part of the reason he left, too."

"Well, Donald's not here anymore. And once we get the restaurant back up to speed, you could spend more time there." She gave him a bright smile. "It would be nice."

Roberto looked up at her from the floor. His lips parted slowly, but he did not say anything.

"When you're not too busy here," she added, her smile fading.

Roberto nodded and looked at his hands again. "Sure. When I'm not too busy. Thanks."

Tara made an excuse and left.

Maybe he's just not into me.

What's wrong with me?

Maybe I should find out more about "Danny."

Nicole's parents left in the morning, followed by Alan's. Tara went to the restaurant early, to start preparing for another day of feeding firefighters. *This should be the last time we do this. We've done our part, especially considering everything that this business has been through. And we should try to get back to normal operations. Crush should be over soon.*

I'm impressed at how everyone has stepped up. Antonio has really gone above and beyond, with no one else but me in the kitchen. Rosa, Gabriela and Toby were really good, too, for non-professionals.

Another hundred tired, sooty and hungry men and women arrived in trucks at six p.m. Tara, Antonio, Gabriela, Rosa and Toby hustled for three hours, slopping chili, chicken, soup and bread onto plates.

At 8:30, the Fire Marshal appeared at the door. Gary Henry was a thin man with a bristly moustache and thick hair that had captured ash. "You're keeping receipts?" he asked.

"Yes, of course," Tara answered.

"Good. The county will reimburse you for any expenses for the food. Thanks very much for this. It's been great. And tell Mrs. DaSilva how grateful we all are. And how sorry I am for her loss."

"I will."

Even after the hours of hustling between the kitchen, dining room and office, and another hour of cleaning up with Antonio and Toby, Tara lay sleepless on her bed.

It's not my bed. It's the DaSilvas' guest bed.

She gave up trying after midnight. Even with the air on high, it was still too hot. Despite the exhaustion she felt, her eyes refused to stay shut.

She leaned on the window sill, staring across the dark winery estate. A blur behind the dark haze in the sky, she guessed, was the moon.

The restaurant mansion was only a jumble of shadows, the winery lost in the murk behind it.

Tara opened the window and leaned out, hoping to catch some of the wind that still whipped California.

Is that a light behind the restaurant?

She straightened up, which brought her head back into the room, and did not see light anymore. But when she leaned out again, she thought she saw a glow, so dim it was at the edge of imagination.

She leaned forward, started to fall and caught the window frame. Pulling herself back in, she decided to see whether she was imagining mysterious lights in the night. She shut the windows, pulled on a t-shirt and a pair of jeans, and shoved her feet into running shoes.

At her bedroom door, she thought: *Should I have a weapon? What if he has a gun?*

You don't know it's a "he." It's probably your imagination, anyway. And these hands are weapons.

They're fast, but not faster than a bullet.

She slipped her smartphone into her pocket and slipped noiselessly out of the house.

The night air was warm and filled with smoke. *The wind must have shifted.*

Crickets chirped. The wind sighed through the dry leaves. Far away, a truck downshifted on the highway.

The hard contours of the winery sharpened when she stepped into the shadows of the restaurant. *There is a definite light at the corner of the winery, moving to the back. Or is it inside, shining through the window?*

She heard a muffled crash. But not from the winery—from inside the restaurant.

Maybe I should have brought Charlie with me. But that would have woken Nicole.

Moving slowly to avoid making noise, she crept up the back stairs and pressed her ear against the kitchen door. She closed her eyes to listen harder.

Nothing. But crickets had been chirping a minute earlier, before the crash, and were now silent.

She turned, looking back toward the winery to see a darker shadow shift along its wall, disappearing where the dirt road led to the vineyard.

She jumped from the steps and ran as quietly as she could as she pulled out her phone. Pausing at the corner of the winery, she set it to camera mode and touched the icon for flash, then jumped onto the path, holding the phone out like it was a weapon as she raced for the vineyard, hitting the shutter button over and over.

Flashes bounced like lightning off the trees at the vineyard's edge and a shadow retreated into it. She ran, vision bouncing between the phone's screen and the real world ahead.

That shadow—is that a man running from me?

She stopped and swiped past a few of the pictures she had taken. Most were only dark blurs, or garish shots of the dirt road.

But the first one showed a shadow in the middle of the road, and the second displayed a slightly more distinct image of what might be a person's back.

Tara turned back to the winery, studying the images. *Maybe I can improve it on the computer. If it is a person, that proves that Alan was right about sabotage. Someone was poking around here in the middle of the night.*

Passing the restaurant, she froze at the unmistakable sound of a door closing.

Shoving the phone into her pocket, she belted around the mansion. In the weak moonlight, she could see someone running toward the road and willed her legs to move faster, pumping her hands like her trainer had told her.

"Stop!" *Why the hell did I say that?*

The figure in the dark did not stop, but turned right when he reached the road.

He's going for a car. "No!"

She caught up as the figure opened the door of a small car. He whirled, his arm extended and Tara jumped back as the tip of a long blade flashed past her midriff. She fell back on her butt on the road. Years of training took control and she rolled on her back, sprang to her feet, fists raised, knees bent, her left shoulder forward to present the narrowest possible target.

A short, broad man stood beside the open door of a hatchback, brandishing something toward her. "Stay away from me, you little bitch," he hissed.

Is that a kitchen knife? "Donald?"

"Stay away. These are mine."

Tara shook her fists. When Donald flinched, she pivoted on her forward foot, sweeping her back foot around. Her toes smashed his wrist, Donald yelped and the knife dropped.

He jumped into his car. Tara hesitated just long enough to allow Donald to start the engine. The headlights flared as Tara grabbed at the open door's frame. The wheels squealed against the pavement and the car tore out of her grasp. Tara stumbled forward, but could only watch the taillights shrink with distance.

She used her smartphone's light to look at the knife on the pavement. *One of the restaurant's ceramic chef's knives. Donald did say they belonged to him when Alan fired him.*

She dialed 911. "This is Tara Rezeck of the Rocky Creek Winery. We've had a break-in at Cyrano's Restaurant. Yes, I'm safe. He's gone now. I know who it is. Yes, twenty-three-eighty-five Rocky Creek Road. Yes, I'll wait. Please tell the officer to come to the restaurant, in the old mansion, not to the house. There's no need for a siren or lights or anything. No, I won't touch anything. Thank you."

Tara sat on the bench on the mansion's verandah to wait for the deputy, looking at the images on her phone.

There was definitely someone on that dirt road. It's too bad I can't tell who it was, though. But does that mean there were two people sabotaging the winery? Was it Donald all along?

That doesn't make sense. Alan was complaining about sabotage before he fired Donald. Why would Donald sabotage the place where he was gainfully employed?

Anyway, Donald isn't fast enough to go through the vineyard, down to the main road and back to the restaurant in the time it took me to walk across the lot. I've seen him run. He's not fast.

But that means there is still someone else sabotaging the winery.

She did not like that conclusion.

The patrol car arrived within ten minutes, and Tara was relieved that the deputy used neither the lights nor siren. *There's no point waking Nicole. She definitely doesn't need any more stress.*

But do I?

The car pulled into the restaurant's parking lot. Then the spotlight flooded the front of the building. Squinting against the glare, Tara stood. "Hello, Officer. I'm Tara Rezeck. I called it in."

More light. Holding her hand between her face and the light, she made out a blurry silhouette striding slowly toward her, left hand holding a flashlight at its shoulder. "I'm Deputy Wells. Not officer. Put down whatever you have in your hand," ordered a young man's voice.

"Oh, for god's sake, it's just a phone."

The deputy halted. "I said, put it down."

Tara put the phone on the bench. "Okay, okay. Relax, will ya? I told you, I'm the one who called 911."

When the deputy stepped onto the verandah, he was no longer between the spotlight and Tara, and she could see he was the young cop at the roadblock the night Alan had died. "Deputy! Remember me from the night we had to evacuate?"

The young cop squinted at her, playing his flashlight up and down her body. He visibly relaxed. "I'm not gonna forget that for a long time. What did you say your name was?"

"Tara Rezeck."

"Can I see some I.D.?"

"I don't have any on me. I didn't take my wallet when I saw an intruder."

"I have to see some I.D., ma'am."

"Stop being such a stickler. What would I be doing here in the middle of the night if I hadn't called this in?"

"Them's the rules, ma'am."

"Bullshit. You and I both know what the rules are. You're here to investigate a break-in that I called the department about. Look," she pointed at the front door. "That's where the intruder came out."

The cop shone his light on the door. He came close, looking carefully. "I don't see signs of forced entry."

"That's probably because he had a key."

The light moved onto Tara again. "Why would the intruder have a key?"

"Because he worked here until a few days ago. Now get that light out of my eyes."

The flash went lower. "Sorry." He turned the light back to the door. "How do you know it was an employee?"

"I saw him. He attacked me with a knife."

The light swept onto her again. "Are you all right?"

"Get that out of my face. Yes, I'm all right. If I had been cut, do you think I'd be calling the cops before an ambulance?"

"Sorry." The light went back to the door. The cop tried the lever. "It's locked."

"I told you, the intruder was a former employee, and he had a key."

"Do you have a key?"

Tara involuntarily felt her pocket. "Umm, not on me. It's in my room."

"Let's go get it, then. And while we're at it, you can get your identification."

He stepped off the verandah.

Tara followed. "Geez, you really are a stickler for the rules, aren't ya?"

"It's part of the job, ma'am."

"Stop calling me 'ma'am.' What are you, seven?"

She led the way to the main house, the cop's flashlight shining on the grass. At the door, she held a finger to her lips. "Stay quiet. I don't want to wake Mrs. DaSilva."

"Isn't this her property? Shouldn't she be awake for this?"

"Keep your voice down. I'll tell her in the morning. She's just buried her husband—she doesn't need more trauma."

Tara ignored his unhappy expression and pushed the door open as softly as she could.

Nicole stood in the foyer, wearing jeans and a long-sleeved shirt. She flipped on the hall light and Tara could see she had brushed her hair. Charlie stood by her side, eying Deputy Wells suspiciously. "What's going on? A break-in?"

Tara could not speak. "Are you Mrs. DaSilva?" said the cop. "The property owner?"

"Nicole Fong. Yes, I'm the owner." She pushed past Tara to hold her driver's license under Deputy Wells' eyes. When he nodded, she pushed past him and out the door. Charlie dashed out between the deputy's legs and jumped off the porch to join her.

"Let's see what the damage is," Nicole said without waiting.

Tara hurried to catch up with her. "How did you know about the break-in? I thought you were sleeping."

"The Sheriff's Department phoned me, saying a break-in had been reported in the restaurant."

"Why did they phone you in the middle of the night?"

"Because I'm the owner, that's why. Someone who was not the owner reported a break-in. They have to check for fraud. Why didn't you tell me before calling the cops?"

"I'm sorry. I thought you've been through so much lately, you didn't need any more—"

"I'm not a child."

Wow. Is this the same woman who's been doing nothing but crying, drinking wine and sleeping since her husband died? Who's too afraid to be alone in her house? Who was too tired to talk to her mother about her dead husband?

Nicole jerked the front door open and Charlie bounded inside, sniffing along the baseboards. Deputy Wells held a hand up to stop Nicole from following and went in. He swept the flashlight across the entrance, then the dining room until Nicole flipped on the lights. "Do you see any damage or anything missing?" he asked.

"Not in here," Nicole said.

"He took the ceramic chef's knives," Tara said.

Nicole strode into the kitchen. "Damn it. He took all of them. Those things are expensive."

"You have insurance, don't you?" Tara asked.

Nicole stood, rigid, in the kitchen, staring at the wooden block that once held the ceramic knives.

"How do you know what's missing?" the cop asked Tara, trying to make his voice sound low and threatening.

"I told you, I saw him. I chased him to the road. He attacked me with one of the knives and dropped it. It's probably still on the road."

"He dropped a knife? And you left it there?" Nicole demanded.

"I didn't want to touch it. It could be evidence," Tara said.

"Your fingerprints are already on it. You've been cooking in here for the past week. Haven't you touched the knives?"

"I guess so," Tara said in a small voice.

"Take another look around for anything else that may be missing," said Deputy Wells. "Then let's go see that knife on the road."

Tara led the cop to the road, leaving Nicole and Charlie in the restaurant. Deputy Wells snapped on latex gloves and took out a smartphone to snap pictures of the knife on the pavement. "Was it broken like this yesterday?" he asked.

Tara bent down, looking at where the deputy pointed to the tip of the blade. "Damn. No, it was not. I guess it broke when Donald dropped it. It's ceramic, not steel."

"A ceramic knife?"

"Chefs like them because they're sharper than steel can ever be. But they're expensive and brittle."

"I better get this evidence off the road before it cuts open somebody's tires." Deputy Wells took another photo, then put the knife into a plastic bag.

They returned to the restaurant. Nicole stood in the door from the dining room to the kitchen, arms crossed, one foot tapping the floor. Charlie sat beside her, looking unhappy.

"This is all Alan's fault," she said.

Tara did not dare question that, but Nicole answered her anyway. "He shouldn't have fired Donald like that. Just throwing him out the door. Those were his knives. He brought them with him when he started here. That was one of the reasons I hired him—he's top-notch. And then Alan just throws him out. No severance, no notice, and steals his knives."

"Do you know where he lives, ma'am?" Deputy Wells asked.

"In Santa Rosa. I'll have to look up the address."

"I'll send a forensics team out here in the morning. Now, I need to take your statements. Maybe we should go back to the house."

Nicole did not have much to say about the night. She had been woken by the Sheriff's Department calling to confirm the break-in report, and she had waited in the dark for the deputy to arrive.

Tara described how she had seen a light near the restaurant, gone to investigate, then heard the front door close. She told the deputy about chasing someone to the road and catching up with him at his car.

"Then he turned and slashed me with the chef's knife."

I won't tell him about chasing someone into the vineyard. I'm not withholding evidence—there's no way Donald could have run through the vineyard, doubled back and got to the restaurant in the time it took me to walk there.

"He slashed you?"

"He slashed *at* me. I dodged. But that was when I recognized him."

"And this was …"

"Donald Bailey. He used to be the Chef here."

"For how long?"

"Two and a half years," Nicole said. "Until Alan—my late husband—fired him."

"That would be Alan DaSilva?" Nicole nodded.

Deputy Wells turned to Tara again. "And when did this happen?"

"The day before we evacuated."

"The eleventh, then?" Tara nodded.

"How many knives did he take?"

Tara looked at Nicole, and they both said, "Four," at the same time.

"And he left behind the big one? So he presumably has three left?"

"I guess so," said Tara.

Deputy Wells stood, tucking his notebook into a breast pocket. "Thank you, Ms. Fong, Ms. Rezeck. If you could find Mr. Bailey's address, Ms. Fong, I'll take a look around the property again, just to check."

"What about Donald?" Nicole asked.

"I'll call into the dispatch about Mr. Bailey."

After Deputy Wells left, Nicole opened a bottle of Rocky Creek Cabernet Sauvignon and poured half of it into two glasses. She gulped down most of hers, looked at the glass with an odd expression on her face, and then she opened a bottle of scotch. After pouring a generous measure into another glass, she held the bottle toward Tara and arched an eyebrow.

"No thanks, I'll stick with wine."

Nicole knocked back the scotch and poured herself another before settling into her chair.

Tara pulled out her phone. "There's something you should know. The reason I went out there is that I saw a light near the winery, not the restaurant." She showed Nicole the picture from the vineyard.

"What's this?"

"When I got to the restaurant, I saw something moving by the winery. I ran around it and saw someone run down the road through the vineyard. See?" She enlarged the image as much as she could.

"It's just a blur."

"No, look—legs, a back."

"Okay, so there was someone there. You can't see who it is."

"You don't recognize that back?"

Nicole looked up at her. "How the hell can you recognize someone's *back*?"

"Look. Whoever it is, is tall, with broad shoulders. Remind you of anyone?"

"There are a lot of tall, broad-shouldered men, Tara. This is California."

Tara ignored Nicole's tone. *She's under a lot of stress.* "Do you think … think it could be Roberto?"

Nicole's eyes widened. Her mouth opened. Her eyes went from the phone to Tara's face, and back to the phone. "Roberto? Why would he be in the vineyard in the middle of the night?"

"I don't know. But someone was there."

"And it's not Donald?"

"Donald was in the restaurant, stealing the knives. He could not have run through the vineyard, somehow double around, and gone back to the restaurant to close the front door again in the time it took me to jog from the vineyard to the mansion."

"But why would it be Roberto?"

Tara sat on the edge of the sofa, leaning close to Nicole. "I think that whoever that was, was responsible for all the sabotage at the winery."

"Sabotage? What sabotage?"

"Alan thought someone was sabotaging the place. Damaging equipment, trying to drive you out of business."

Nicole fell back into the chair, waving her free hand. "Alan was paranoid." She gulped down more scotch.

Weird way to respond about your recently dead husband. "Alan was perplexed about all the problems you've been having. Even the magazine article about you mentioned the accidents. And tonight, I saw someone around the winery. I'll bet in the morning you'll find some damage again, that'll cost you a fortune to fix and put production behind by at least a couple of days."

Nicole glared at nothing in the middle distance. "Thanks a lot," she growled. She tossed back the last of the scotch, poured herself another generous shot, and strode to her bedroom without another word.

At least I have half a bottle of red wine to myself tonight. It's the only way I'll get to sleep.

Legacy

Tara did sleep, waking to bright sunlight again. The clock on the nightstand read 9:03. She listened, but the only sound she heard from inside the house was the soft rush of air conditioning.

Which means Nicole is still sleeping. Good. What a night.

Tara was making coffee when the doorbell rang. She opened the door to see Paul Rondeau. This time, he wore a blue suit that looked like it had been poured over his shoulders. There was a silver pin in his tie and jeweled cuff links that matched the watch on his wrist. The cuffs of his sleeves were the precise shade of white as his pocket square.

Tara glanced down. *If those shoes were any softer, they'd moo.*

Charlie trotted to the vestibule, tail wagging. "Good morning, Tara. I'm back again. You'll have to wake Nicole." He bent to scratch behind Charlie's ears.

"I really think she needs rest, Paul. Last night was pretty rough."

"I'm not made of glass, Tara," said a voice behind her.

Tara whirled, her hand to her chest. Nicole stood in the hall, dressed in jeans and a loose, light green top. "What brings you here today, Paul?"

"Sheriff Doyle called me first thing this morning. Donald Bailey is in jail now. Deputies picked him up at his home."

"He went home after last night?" Tara said. "What an idiot."

"I don't think that he thought he could get away," Paul answered. "He gave up readily, Mary said. Sheriff Doyle, that is."

"I don't want to press charges," Nicole said, sitting in the living room. "He was only taking his own knives. They're his property, and he didn't damage anything in the restaurant."

"I'm afraid that's not an option," Paul said, sighing. "Even if the law doesn't prosecute for break and enter, he is facing assault charges for taking a swipe at Tara."

Nicole closed her eyes. "Oh, god, like I don't have enough trouble." She glared briefly at Tara.

This is my fault?

"There is something else," Paul sighed. He looked out the window. "Ah. Right on time." A pickup truck pulled up on the shoulder of the road in front of the house. A wide-jawed man with dark skin and thick, black hair climbed out and jogged up the steps. Paul opened the door before he could ring the bell. "Come in, Richard. Thanks for coming. Nicole DaSilva, I'd like you to meet Richard Sarris, counsel for the Wappo Tribe in Barnestown."

Charlie stood in front of Nicole, staring at Sarris. His tail stuck out straight behind him.

Richard Sarris wore a light grey suit, a white shirt with western-style pockets, a string tie and cowboy boots. "Good morning, Mrs. DaSilva. Paul," he said, his voice a deep rumble.

Nicole sat, staring at him, mouth open.

Paul went on. "Mr. Sarris has something important to tell you. I'm sorry—I know this is a difficult time, but Alan's passing triggers a number of provisions related to the inheritance of the property."

Nicole still said nothing, so Tara said, "Why don't you sit down, Mr. Sarris?"

Sarris sat at the end of the sofa, across from Nicole. "I'm very sorry for your loss, Mrs. DaSilva. Alan was a friend of mine, too."

Nicole's eyes sank. "Thank you," she whispered.

"Would anyone like anything to drink? Coffee, tea?" Tara asked. Paul and Sarris both said no, but Nicole did not answer, so Tara went into the kitchen.

She could hear Paul talking in his gentlest voice. *This is going to be bad.*

Paul's arrival had interrupted her making coffee, so she added more grounds to the basket and filled the pot to the top. Then she leaned against the door frame to the living room to listen to the conversation in the living room.

Paul was sitting on the sofa, between Sarris at the far end and Nicole in her usual chair. "There probably is no good time for ... this. And I want you to know that there's no pressure on you to make a quick decision. Mr. Sarris and the Wappo Council are willing to give you time to make a decision."

"Decide what?"

"Mrs. DaSilva, you remember how Alan and I spent a lot of time together in his office last year?" Sarris said.

"I ..."

"We were talking about his long-term plans for the winery."

"It's in his will, Nicole," Paul said.

"His will? We prepared our wills together."

"Alan added a codicil—that's an addition to a will—last year. Now don't worry, it doesn't leave you any worse off—"

"Just spit it out, Paul," Nicole exclaimed.

Paul sighed, looked at Sarris, and went on. "I don't know whether you know this, but the Wappo nation has land claims on much of Sonoma County, including the area that's now your vineyard."

"And the Harris vineyard, next door," Sarris added.

"You're claiming my land?" Nicole asked, her eyes flashing.

"No, no, nothing like that," Paul said quickly.

"The Wappo Tribe is not interested in pushing you out of your home," Sarris said.

I knew it would be bad. I never thought it would be this bad.

The coffee maker gurgled. Tara poured three cups, arranged a tray with milk and sugar and put it on the coffee table. Nicole was looking from Sarris to Paul and back again. She seemed to shrink into the chair. She wrapped her hands around the mug of coffee, decided it was too hot and set it down quickly. "I don't understand."

Paul leaned forward, his elbows on his knees. "Alan was negotiating with the Wappo Tribe for transfer of ownership after his death to the Tribe, in case he died without heirs. Now, you're his inheritor, of course, but you and he had no children. Which means that, right now, if you were to decide to sell, the Wappo Tribe has the right of first refusal."

Nicole stared at her coffee, frozen.

"What does that mean?" Tara asked. *Someone has to tease the details out.*

Paul looked surprised at the question. "It means that if Ms. Fong decides to sell the winery, the Wappo Tribe can make a reasonable offer before anyone else. And if there is a competing offer, the Wappo Tribe can make a matching offer which would be deemed preferable."

"Please understand, Nicole, we have no interest in taking over your business," Sarris said. "We would prefer that you continue to operate the winery. And Cyrano's Restaurant." He chuckled. *That was phony,* Tara thought. "You know how much I love your steaks. Best in the county."

"I don't understand," Nicole said. "How could he add that to the will without telling me?"

"It has to do with the corporate structure, with Alan the majority shareholder of the winery, and you the majority owner of the restaurant. And that won't change."

"Why would he do that?"

"He believed it was the right thing to do," Sarris said. "All the Native people in California were disenfranchised fifty years ago, when the state terminated recognition of 42 tribes and illegally transferred their land. Our people have been fighting since the 1960s to restore our rights and some of our land. Alan understood our position, and he believed in supporting our efforts."

Nicole sat up straight. "No," she said in that strange, flat tone. Tara put her hand on Nicole's shoulder, trying to project calmness.

"I know this is a bad time, but you needed to know about this," Paul said. "Particularly in light of Harris Estates' continued interest in Rocky Creek."

"I am not selling the winery. Nor the restaurant. Not to the Harrises and not to the Wappos either. This is a business that my husband and I built up together, and no one is going to take it from me, just because Alan is gone now."

"Nicole, nothing will happen until you sell. *If* you sell."

"I think you should go." Nicole stood.

Tara followed Rondeau and Sarris to the door. Paul looked shocked, but Sarris' face was inscrutable. As he stepped out the door, Paul turned to Tara. "Call me this afternoon, at the office," he said in a low voice. "I'm really concerned about Nicole's state of mind."

In the living room, Nicole drummed her fingers on the arm of her chair.

"Are you all right?" Tara asked.

Nicole ignored her, staring at nothing, her fingernails tapping.

After what felt like a year, Tara went to her room and changed into her restaurant uniform. Today was the day she had planned to reopen, and she had to beat the staff to the door.

Nicole

Antonio and Toby, who had agreed to stay for a few days to work, were shocked as Tara told them about the break-in. Antonio checked all the drawers for the missing ceramic knives, muttering in Italian.

"I sure hope nothing else goes wrong for Nicole," Toby said, tucking her wild red hair into a pony tail. "You'd think losing your husband like that would be enough, but it's been one thing after another."

Toby swept the floor while Tara checked inventory and made a list for Antonio to take to the markets.

Tara was concentrating on the restaurant's recipe book, trying to work out a menu based on the items they would likely be able to get. A knock on the kitchen door frame made her jump.

"Nicole!" She stood in the entrance, back straight, her hair arranged on top of her head in a neat bun. She wore a smart blue suit, golden earrings and low-rise heels. Her make-up was simple and perfect. Even her nails were freshly polished.

"I own this place, remember?" she said without inflection. "Where is everyone else?"

"Antonio's gone to the markets, and Miguel is volunteering with the firefighters. So it's just me and Toby from the picking staff who's offered to be a server tonight." Tara tried to laugh, and failed. "You look really good, Nicole. How are you feeling?"

Nicole took out a phone. "Please, stop what you're doing. I'm calling a full staff meeting. Let's get together in the dining room. Get Roberto and the winery staff, too." She went upstairs.

An hour later, when Antonio had returned with groceries, he joined Tara, Roberto, Mark, Amy, Rosa, Gabriela, Toby and the other pickers in the dining room, looking expectantly as Nicole came down the stairs, her heels clicking on the hardwood. Her eyes scanned the room, her face impassive.

"I've made some decisions about the future," she said. "We need to be realistic, now that Alan is gone."

Wow, Tara thought, sitting alone at a table for four. *What a difference from the past couple of days. Is this a woman who's getting better, or is this whole ice queen thing another sign of PTSD?*

"We have no wait staff anymore, and with Miguel having joined the volunteer firefighters, and Chef Donald in jail, it's impossible to keep the restaurant going. No offense," she said, looking at Tara. "But we just don't have the human resources, and I don't foresee getting replacements until the fires are over. Even then, finding a new chef is not something you can do overnight."

Okay, time to move on and find a new job.

"So, the restaurant is closing until further notice. I'm sorry, Antonio, I have to lay you off."

"But, if I don't have a job, my visa will not be valid," Antonio protested.

"I'm sorry, but I just can't use you now."

"I only have a few days to find a new job, or I'll be deported." He was almost whining.

"I'll give you an excellent reference. I'm sure you'll find something."

Antonio stood, glaring at Nicole. He stomped out the front door, slamming it on his way.

Nicole stood still, one hand on the back of a chair, her eyes closed until the commotion died down. She took a deep breath and continued. "We are going to concentrate on the winery. We have a harvest to finish bringing in, a crush to complete, orders to fill. We are going to make this winery succeed. That was always Alan's dream, and we are going to make it happen, no matter what."

Silence. Then Roberto started clapping, slowly, and others joined him. Tara picked up the applause. *Weird that I'm applauding my own firing. Still, it's the right thing to do.*

As Tara opened the back door, heading to the guest house to start packing, she felt a hand on her shoulder.

"I feel like I didn't explain myself enough," Nicole said.

Tara turned. "I get it. I'll pack up. Is it okay if I stay one more day?"

"I want you to stay."

Tara felt adrift. "To do what?"

Nicole leaned in and wrapped her arms around Tara. "I need another woman here. I need you here. Someone I can talk to."

"Oh." Tara raised her arms and hugged Nicole back. "Sure." *How did I get in so deep?*

Nicole pulled away. "Unless you don't want to?"

Why does she have to look so much like a puppy when she does that? "No, of course … I mean, yes I would be," What's the right word? "Honored. Happy to." *Oh, shit, I am really fucking this up.* "What do you want me to do?"

"I have some work for you to do, but it's just good to have someone else around who knows how to put the toilet seat down." She stepped to the back stairs. "Come upstairs with me to the office."

I guess I shouldn't tell her that I've been up here before, by myself.

In the office, Nicole put two banker's boxes on the desk. "Here are the last two years of financial records. I'm sorry, but Alan really wasn't one for paperwork. Nothing was more important to him than the winery. He paid more attention to wine and the employees of his winery than he did to his wife."

Wow. That's bitter.

"Anyway, you're a lawyer. Organize these papers as best you can. I don't know whether it will matter to the probate, but I want to be prepared. I want this to go as smoothly as possible."

"Okay, but just to be clear, I'm not—"

"I have to go out now. Errands to run, people to see. I'm going to drop in on Paul Rondeau, too. And then I'll buy some groceries—for us, not the restaurant. I probably won't be back till suppertime, so be ready to cook something."

"Okay. What are you getting?"

"I don't know yet," Nicole said as she went down the stairs. "It'll be a surprise for both of us."

Both boxes were filled with papers and folders stacked, as opposed to standing, in files. Tara put the contents of one in a pile and shuffled through it. As far as she could tell, there was a rough chronological order to them. She started separating them into categories: invoices, statements, inventories, letters.

An hour later, she surveyed the documents she had sorted and compared the stacks to the boxes she had not touched yet. Something close to despair settled into her. *I thought I could learn something about Alan, whether he had any enemies, or maybe something about Nicole. But about all I can get out of this is a history of the cost of wine-making supplies.*

An old CRT TV sat on an older table. Tara found the remote in the desk drawer. The screen came to life with an image of a blackened, branchless tree standing on a field of ash. Behind it, smoke rose from the foundation of a house. Behind it, two jagged, charred walls testified to the former presence of a neighborhood.

The image changed to a lurid night scene of flames engulfing trees. The crawl across the bottom of the screen described high winds spreading fires across Napa and Sonoma counties, while the announcer breathlessly talked about the numbers of homes destroyed. Her voice dropped. "And even more tragically, more than a dozen people have lost their lives in the fires."

The screen changed again, focusing on a pretty man and woman in suits, sitting behind a desk, wearing their grimmest, most concerned faces. "All our hearts and prayers go out to the families of those people," the man said. "Winds are not forecast to let up any time soon, Astrid."

She turned off the set, then realized she was still in her kitchen uniform. She went to the guest house and put on shorts, a tank top and sandals.

Much better. Much cooler. God, will this heat ever end?

She didn't go straight back to the restaurant, but following an impulse she did not want to define, went to the winery. Amy was at the computer in the office, and she smiled, the sides of her eyes crinkling happily, when Tara walked in.

"Hey, Amy. Where's Roberto?"

"Oh, he had to run some errands," she said. "I think he's gone into Santa Rosa. Is there anything I can help you with? Or Mark?"

"No, thanks." Tara left.

So Nicole's not the only one off "running errands," Tara thought. *It's time for me to do some forensics of my own.*

The jewelry store

Tara left early the next morning, arriving in the town of Sebastopol just after 10, when she figured the stores would open.

She parked in front of Adorna Fashion and Home on the main street of the town. A bell tinkled overhead as Tara pushed the door open. The shop was what she had expected: slate grey floors, soft lighting that accentuated the display cases, shelves made of cedar, glass-topped tables, all crowded with objects that were undeniably beautiful, and just as undeniably useless.

A woman with mid-length gray hair and deep brown eyes stood behind a glass counter, the light from inside it accenting the underside of her chin. "Good morning," she said, her voice bright and cheerful as the sun outside.

"Hello," Tara answered, putting her purse on the counter. She took out the bracelet and laid it smooth on the glass display case. Dull and blackened, it looked out of place over the shiny baubles in the case below. "I found this, and someone told me it might have come from this shop. Is that true?"

The woman looked carefully, pulling the chain on the glass so that it described a smoother curve. "Well, it could have. Just a minute. I'll get the owner." She stepped quickly to the back of the store, leaned through a doorway and called "Autumn! Can you come to the front?"

A tall, slim woman with wavy brown hair emerged, wiping her hands on a towel. She wore glasses and a long grey apron over a t-shirt and blue jeans. "What is it, Diane?"

"A customer has a question." Diane turned to Tara. "This is the owner, Autumn Birt.

The tall woman turned to Tara. "Can I help you?"

"She has a bracelet that she thinks came from here," said Diane.

"I found it on the ground, and I'm trying to reunite it with its owner." *It's not a lie.*

Autumn walked around to the front of the counter so that she stood looking down at Tara. She peered at the necklace and tried uselessly to brush off some of the soot. Then she held out a long, muscular hand. "Hello. I'm Autumn Birt, owner of Adorna."

Tara shook. Autumn's hand was firm and cool. "I'm Tara Rezeck. I'm the ... well, I work at the Rocky Creek Winery. I found this on the ground, and someone told me it looks like it might have come from here."

Autumn bent over the counter, and Tara realized it was higher than most display cases she had ever seen. Must have been custom-made for this tall woman.

"Well, we do carry this jeweler's products. This piece was made by Cheryl Sirkus. She's a jewelry designer near Sonoma."

She turned the bracelet over, and rubbed soot off a spot on the clasp. "That's the Sonoma Art Works brand. Let me see ..." She went behind the counter and from a drawer, took out a loupe, a small bottle of jewelry cleanser, a cloth and a pad. She rubbed the clasp in a circular motion until it shone, bright against the dirt and soot of the rest of the bracelet. "See this? That's the Sonoma Art Works brand, and under it is a serial number. I can use that to check whether we sold it."

Tara had to bend close and squint, but there was a tiny logo, a capital letter A with a swoop on the left leg. Under that, even smaller, six digits. "Well, that helps."

Autumn turned to a laptop computer on a counter behind the display case. "What's this all about? This piece looks like it was in a fire."

"It was. Our garage burned down."

Autumn looked at Tara. "In the wildfires? I'm so sorry. We've been so lucky here in Sebastopol. Most of the fires were on the far side of the valley, from what I understand."

"Yes, it seems so."

"I hope no one was hurt."

Tara took a deep breath. "Actually, the owner died."

Autumn's eyes grew wide behind the lenses. "Oh, my god. Was that the … oh, the name of the place …"

"Rocky Creek Winery. Yes."

"I should have realized that when you told me where you work! I am so sorry."

"Thanks."

"It's just terrible, this wildfire situation. But what more can we expect on such a dry, hot summer? Sure, California has had wildfires before, but this year … so many homes and businesses destroyed, so many people killed. It just breaks your heart."

"Yes, it does."

Autumn dabbed her eyes with a tissue and wiped her nose, then concentrated on the computer. "Yes, here it is. We sold this a year ago in February. It was to be a Valentine's Day gift."

"How do you know that?"

"Because we gave the customer a gift receipt, in case the person they gave it to didn't like it."

"Do you do that normally?"

"For unusual pieces like this, and for special occasions, it comes up pretty often."

"Can you tell me who the purchaser was?"

Autumn leaned her head to one side. Her eyes narrowed. "Are you with the police or something? A private investigator?"

"No, no. I told you, I just work at the winery. I started a couple weeks ago, and kind of ... took over the kitchen after the chef quit."

"Oh, so you're a chef."

"Not quite. I don't have the qualifications or experience, but I was the person on the spot at the time. And actually, I haven't worked as a real chef yet, because the previous chef quit on the same day that we had to evacuate from the fires. And since then, we've just been working as a cafeteria for the firefighting crews."

Autumn nodded. "So, why are you asking about this bracelet?"

You've prepared this story, Tara. Tell it smoothly. "I found it on the ground next to what's left of the garage. It looks expensive—"

"It is."

"—and I thought I would like to reunite it with its owner. I thought it might be Mrs. DaSilva. She's the widow of the owner who died in the fire. But if it wasn't hers, I didn't want to bother her with useless questions. She's taking the loss really hard."

Autumn shook her head in sympathy. "Poor woman. To lose a husband like that ... terrible." She clicked the mouse. "Here it is. Well, it wasn't sold to anyone named DaSilva. The buyer was someone named R. Gonsalves."

Roberto! I knew he was lying about not recognizing the bracelet. "Gonsalves? You're sure?"

"That's what it says here. Buying as a Valentine's Day gift. Do you know a Gonsalves?"

"Maybe." Tara gathered up the bracelet and dropped it into her purse. "Thanks for all your help."

"A pleasure. Can I interest you in anything in the store?"

"I don't think I can afford anything in here, thanks." Tara moved toward the door.

"Just a moment," Autumn said, holding up a hand. She went to a shelf and picked up a ceramic vase, painted with lilies. "Diane!" she called, and the grey-haired woman came in. "Get me a gift box."

In a few minutes, they had packed up the vase in a colorful box, and attached a "With Sympathy" card under a ribbon. "Please, give this to Mrs. DaSilva as a small gesture for her loss."

"I don't think … I mean, we don't even know you."

"Please. It's the least we can do in this terrible time."

Tara, carrying the gift box gingerly, pushed the door open, wondering how she should feel, and she bumped into a man coming in.

Cameron

She looked up from the package in her hands to see a tall man with broad shoulders, curly blond hair and a wide smile.

"Well, this is the most pleasant collision I've had all week," he said, and beamed a bright smile at her.

"Cameron!" Tara adjusted the vase in her hands. "What are— I mean, I'm surprised to see you here."

"Me, too," he said, still beaming. He held his place, way too close, for about three seconds too long, then stepped back. "What brings you to Sebastopol?"

"Just trying to find the owner of something I found. You?"

He looked down the street. "Oh, nothing important. Hey, wanna get a coffee?"

"Sorry?"

"You have coffee back east, don't you? You know, hot, dark, milky, sweet?"

"Uhh … yeah."

He beamed at her again.

Jeez, he has really broad shoulders. And those teeth. Are they real?

"Come on. Sebastopol has the best coffee in Sonoma County. My treat."

What could go wrong? "Okay. But weren't you going to get something in the jewelry store?"

Cameron shrugged. "Nah, it's not important. Come on." He put his hand on her shoulder and she felt a thrill pass down her spine.

They walked down the main street to a place called Quitters, all warm colors and brick walls. Cameron apparently knew the entire staff, greeting them by name and asking for his "usual" as he settled into a chair by the window. "What do you want?" he asked Tara.

"An iced skim latte, unsweetened," she answered, stressing "unsweetened."

"So, how are you liking Sonoma so far?" Cameron asked, still smiling.

"Other than the wildfires that destroyed a building where I work, killed my boss and left a constant smell of smoke in the air, it's great."

Cameron's smile faded briefly. "Yeah, that sucks. Poor Alan. Ya know, I really feel for Nicole."

"Oh?"

"Well, sure. She's a friend of the family. Both the DaSilvas are. Or were. You know what I mean."

"Sure. How long have you known them?"

Cameron looked up, waggling his head. "Oh, I dunno. Years. Since they bought the vineyard, I guess. It's been a long time."

"You seem to be good friends with Roberto."

His eyes widened momentarily, and then he seemed to be fascinated by the storefront across the street. "Oh, yeah. We're best buds. We have a lot in common. We both make wine, we both like to be active, go rock climbing, white water canoeing. And we have similar tastes in music." He fixed his eyes on Tara's and smiled with one side of his mouth. "And women."

What a cheesy thing to say, Tara thought. Even so, she felt her face warm. *Goddammit, why am I blushing?*

A young man with a hipster beard brought their coffees. Cameron leaned back in his chair to sip his, his eyes fixed on Tara. "So, tell me about yourself, Tara Rezeck."

"What do you want to know?"

His eyes never left hers. "I want to know the most intimate details. What do you love?"

Her face got even warmer. *Damn it, Tara!* "The thing I love most is my daughter."

A smile spread slowly across both sides of Cameron's face. "A daughter? How old is she?"

"Eighteen months."

"Cute! What's her name?"

Tara took a long drink of her iced coffee, which sparked a headache. "Roxanne."

"A beautiful name. Like Cyrano's love?"

Tara felt as if the legs of her chair had broken at once. "Yes— exactly." *He read Cyrano de Bergerac? Cameron Harris read Cyrano de Bergerac?* "But also Alexander the Great's wife."

"True. She was supposed to be a great beauty, too." Cameron leaned close over the table. "I bet your Roxanne is absolutely gorgeous."

"Oh, god—I know every mother says their kid is the most beautiful in the world, but she's so pretty. So delicate, and she's getting this dark blond, curly hair now ..." She dug her phone out of her pocket and opened the screen capture she had taken from her last Skype call.

Cameron leaned even closer to look at the phone. "Oh, wow, she's a cutie, all right." His eyes fixed on Tara's again. "Like her mom."

Tara felt warm all over. *What is it about this guy?* She flipped through other pictures on her phone, and Cameron made oo-ing sounds, clicks with this tongue and lots of smiles. When she ran out of pictures, Cameron looked at his watch.

Oh, is this over now, whatever this is?

"You know what's really great about this place? On Fridays, they have a 'Gypsy Friday Night' with great food and wine, including Harris Estates' Cabernet Sauvignon and Pinot Noir."

Tara looked at her own watch. "Oh, I don't know. I should really be getting back."

Cameron's eyebrows rose. *Geez, even that looks sexy on him.* "Getting back to what? I thought Nicole had closed Cyrano's."

How does he know that? "Well, yes, but I don't like to leave Nicole alone right now."

"I'm sure she'll be okay for a little while. You deserve some time off. I think she's been making you do a lot of really shitty chores."

How does he know so much about Nicole?

Cameron waved a waitress over and ordered a bottle of Harris Estates' Pinot Noir, then aimed his movie star smile at Tara again. "You'll love this. I think it's even better than Rocky Creek. Of course, I'm biased, but still …"

The waitress showed Cameron a bottle with the Harris Estates' logo. Cameron beamed his smile at her, and she made a little show of uncorking it. She poured some into Cameron's glass for him to taste, but he said, "Not necessary. I know it's good." He passed the glass to Tara. "Try it. I promise, it's fantastic."

She drank and more warmth spread through her body. "Oh, my god … yes, this is good."

The movie star smile shone full force on Tara. "Told you."

The waitress poured two big glasses, and Tara raised hers to toast Cameron's. "To Harris Estates," he said.

Tara took a gulp. "It's not quite as good as Rocky Creek's," she said.

"Oh, come on."

"No, really. It's very good, and I'm not just being a faithful employee, but Rocky Creek Pinot is, well, it's very, very good."

"I know, it's the perfect vineyard."

"And I think it's also that Roberto is a great vintner."

Cameron nodded slowly. "Yes. Roberto is truly an expert. One of a kind, really. He's taught me a lot about making wine. But still, isn't this vintage excellent?"

"Yes. I have to give you that. It's an excellent vintage."

They drank and chatted more, until Cameron said, "You know, I'm getting kind of hungry. And they have live music here on Fridays. You wanna get something to eat? Soak up the wine?"

"Well, it's a little early …"

"Did you have lunch?"

"No."

"So let's have supper."

The hours melted away.

The band came on at nine, two middle-aged men with grey ponytails and two young women with their hair dyed in multiple colors. They launched into an eclectic mix of rock, jazz and other styles that lay beyond Tara's musical knowledge. After finishing the bottle of pinot, Cameron ordered a bottle of chardonnay. Before it arrived, he pulled Tara off her chair and danced her across the floor.

He's a really good dancer. She looked up into his bright blue eyes, and could not help answering his smile with her own.

More wine, more dancing, and when he leaned forward to kiss her, she responded. She heard a small voice somewhere in the back of her mind, but it was drowning in a flood of long unfulfilled desire flavored with California wine.

As the last of her orgasm radiated out of her body, Tara looked down at Cameron's face, gripped in his own orgasm, and knew: *This was a mistake.*

His hands on her hips felt hot, thrilling even as her breathing returned to normal. When he let go and collapsed, chest heaving, she felt disappointed. *Even so ... This has to stop, now.*

Tara rolled off him onto her back. He slid one arm under her shoulders, cuddling and kissed her cheek. "Oh, wow," he panted.

Naked skin on skin always feels great, and he's really good looking, but ...

"Was that as good for you as it was for me?" Cameron managed to say.

Oh, god. This guy is so cheesy. "Yes, it was great."

It was great sex, but I cannot stand this guy.

She savored the feeling of his warm skin on hers for another minute, then rolled out of bed.

"Where are you going?" he asked.

"I should get back to Nicole."

"Nicole? What do you mean?" Propped up on one elbow, his naked body was spectacular. *Yeah, he's hot. And he knows it.*

She found her clothes scattered on the bedroom floor. *How many days has it been since I slept in this guest house?*

How long has it been since the last time I slept with a man? Months.

She leaned over to kiss him one last time on the mouth. His hand rose to cup her breast gently. *Mmm. He even tastes good.* "You should go."

He stared at her, mouth open as she pulled a shirt on. "What did I do?"

"Nothing wrong. It was great, and I really needed that. But Nicole is still fragile and I don't like leaving her alone all night."

"Wait—you've been sleeping in her house all this time?"

"Since the day we came back from the fire, yes."

He stared at her for a long moment, until she said, "Look, I don't want to be rude, but you have to go."

Shaking his head, Cameron got up and untangled his clothes. Pulling on his pants, he said, "Wham, bam, thank you, sir?"

"Not exactly. But—yes. Thank you. That was great. Tantric. Now go."

He left. Tara watched the taillights of his pickup truck shrinking until he turned onto the road. Then she crossed the yard, careful in the dark, to the DaSilva house. She turned the key and pushed the door open as quietly as she could, but Nicole was sitting in the living room, looking toward the door. "Where were you?"

Tara jumped and flipped on a light. "Oh, god. You scared me."

Nicole wore a flowered housecoat that looked like silk. She held a long-stemmed glass with an inch of red wine sloshing around the bottom. An empty bottle of Rocky Creek Pinot Noir stood on the coffee table.

Charlie rose from beside the chair and walked to Tara for a head-scratch.

"Did you drink that whole bottle this evening?" Tara asked.

"What if I did? You didn't answer my question."

"I went into Sebastopol … to do some shopping."

"Shopping? What did you buy?"

"Uhh … nothing, actually. I was at a jewelry store where they make their own stuff, but it was pretty expensive." *Damn. I left that vase in Cameron's truck. And my car is still in Sebastopol. Maybe Roberto can drive me there tomorrow.*

"So you went shopping but didn't buy anything?"

"Well, actually, I met Cameron Harris there. He invited me to coffee, and then we had supper, and listened to music, and …"

"Cameron Harris?" There was an edge in Nicole's voice that Tara had never heard before.

"Uh, yeah. I guess I drank too much wine to drive, so Cameron drove me home."

Nicole drained her wine glass. She looked hard at Tara.

I guess I shouldn't tell her I just slept with him.

But Nicole didn't look angry anymore. She shrugged. "Okay. I guess I can't expect you to hang around here all the time. Good night." She went down the hall to her bedroom, Charlie trotting behind as usual. Tara heard the door close, but not slam.

Am I fired? Then again, I've never been paid since that first day. I guess I'll find out in the morning.

Documentation

Tara's second day of sorting through Alan's documents stretched ahead of her. Yesterday, she had sorted the first box into piles that made sense to her: invoices, receipts, statements, inventory lists, all arranged chronologically.

This morning, she opened the second box which seemed to be filled with tax filings for the past several years, out of order. *Does Nicole know I'll be looking at their income?*

After half an hour, Tara had organized the statements by date, and learned that Alan did not live large. The winery paid him a good salary, but not a lavish one. From what Tara could tell, Alan had put nearly every dollar of profit back into the business: new equipment, training for employees, promotion campaigns. The business grew, but on the thinnest of margins.

Halfway down the stack, she found a folded bundle of legal-size paper that she recognized as a contract. Statement of Understanding was printed in large letters on the outside.

She unfolded it, curiosity trumping propriety.

This is the legal statement that Paul Rondeau mentioned: the agreement between the Wappo Nation and Alan DaSilva. She skimmed through it, and it was just as Paul had explained: in the event that the DaSilvas decided to sell the vineyard and winery, the

Wappo Nation had the right of first refusal to purchase it. Other clauses excluded the restaurant, but not the land it was located on. And one stated that the Wappo Nation pledged to retain Roberto Gonsalves as the General Manager of the winery, should he choose to stay.

If both DaSilvas were to die without children or other heirs stated in their wills, the Wappo Nation would again have the right of first refusal to purchase the property from their estates.

Interesting: it's signed by Alan DaSilva and Richard Sarris of the Wappo Nation, and Roberto Gonsalves. But not by Nicole.

Why would Alan make this agreement, which includes his employee, but not his co-owner and wife? Was he planning to split up with her? If he suspected that Nicole was cheating on him, then he obviously did not suspect it was with Roberto.

On the other hand, Roberto and Nicole could have been playing Alan, so that Roberto would replace him as the General Manager of the winery, as well as in Nicole's bed.

Tara re-folded the contract and put it on a corner of the desk, in its own pile. She returned to sorting tax statements by year. Then she found another interesting document.

Life Insurance Policy in a shiny, stiff folder printed with a local broker's logo. Taken out and signed less than a year ago, five million dollars in the event of death by accident or misadventure of either Nicole or Alan DaSilva.

That's a nice chunk of change. I'm sure it would do a lot for the winery's capital position.

Another interesting thing: it lists Nicole Fong-DaSilva as both an insured party and beneficiary, but it's not signed by her.

Does she even know about this?

Now what should I do? Do I tell Paul Rondeau about this?

She put the insurance policy on top of the agreement with the Wappo Nation. Looking at her watch, Tara was surprised to see it was nearly noon.

I need a break. She stretched and went downstairs to the restaurant kitchen. Through the window, she saw Roberto going into the winery. She paused to admire his shoulders. *Nice butt, too. But right now, I need information.*

She found him in Alan's old office, flipping through a pile of papers. "Hungry?" she asked.

He looked up, eyes wide. "Uh, I guess. Sure."

"Come to the restaurant in about ten minutes." She left, smiling, hoping Roberto watched her walk away.

In the restaurant, she quickly made two sandwiches, binding them together with toothpicks and garnishing them with parsley.

Roberto came in, carrying an unlabeled bottle. His mouth spread into a smile. "Well, to what do I owe this?"

"Would I be right in thinking you'd have the right wine to go with a BLT?"

He brandished the bottle. "Just the thing. It's our cabernet sauvignon. A little young, but uninhibited. Free-spirited, you might say. Perfect to complement the saltiness and tang of a BLT." He uncorked the bottle and filled red wine glasses from the bar.

They sat side-by-side on barstools at the counter where Nicole had worked on the menus. Roberto clinked her glass and they took big bites at the same time. "Mmm. This is one good BLT," he mumbled, his cheek protruding.

"Thanks," Tara said. She swallowed and tried the wine. "You're right. Free-spirited. And it does go well with the tomato and bacon."

"I know my wine."

"You do. But," Tara swallowed another bite, "after all the time we've spent together, all that we've gone through together, I really don't know a lot about you. Tell me about yourself."

Roberto frowned as he sipped more wine. "I told you about me and my pop and abuelo."

"Sure, you come from a wine-making family. But what about you? What do you do when you're not working here? I don't even know if you're married or involved or anything like that."

Roberto looked at his hand. His smile faded. "No, I'm not married. But I am ... involved, if you know what I mean."

Tara sat back, feeling satisfied. "Aha! I thought so."

Roberto frowned even more, looking at her. "Why?"

"Because you were such a gentleman that second night I was here. You got me drunk, but didn't make a move." *Which makes him the opposite of Cameron Harris.*

Roberto laughed. "I didn't think of it as being a gentleman."

"I was afraid I was losing my touch."

"What?"

"Nothing. Just a joke." *Maybe I went too far there.* She sipped more wine. *Careful. That's what got you in trouble with Bobby. And with Cameron, too.*

"It's also not always a good idea to date people you work with."

"Really? From what I know, work is where most people first hook up."

Roberto laughed. "That doesn't make it a good idea. If the relationship goes south, so can the workplace. I prefer to keep things simple."

"So, which is it? You try to avoid workplace hookups, or you're already involved?"

"Both." Roberto looked away, into the dining room. Tara followed his eyes to the stairs. *What's he looking at?*

"So, what's her name?"

Roberto looked at Tara, then away again, this time to the back of the kitchen. He hesitated. "We ... have nicknames for each other. I'm 'Bo-Bo.'"

"And she's?"

Roberto hesitated again. "Uh . . 'Cee-Cee.'" He laughed and looked down.

He's lying. Why? "Cee-Cee"? Or is it "Vee-Vee"?

"Is it serious?"

Roberto drained his wine. As he refilled their glasses, he said, "I thought it was. Lately, I'm not sure."

"That's too bad. What happened?"

"The wildfires, for one. We both have ... complicated family lives. Now with everything that's going on, it's put a strain on our relationship."

"I guess it would."

"We haven't really seen each other—not alone, not like a couple would, you know? Not since before the wildfires. And Alan's death ... well, I guess you'd expect that to change a lot."

"I guess," she repeated.

Roberto took a deep breath and looked at Tara directly for the first time in a long time. "Look, enough about me. Tell me more about you. How's your little girl doing?"

Tara could not help smiling at the thought of Roxanne, even though it also brought a pang to her chest. "She's great. I Skype with her and my parents nearly every day. It's really the highlight of my day right now. My parents are planning to come out here for a visit next week, as soon as the situation is safer and there are some accommodations to be found."

"Yeah, I guess that would be tough." He laughed a little. "Maybe they could stay in Monte Rio."

"They want to help me find a permanent place to live, something suitable for a child."

"So you're still determined to settle down out here? Even after everything that's happened?"

"I told you, living in California has always been my dream."

"You'll have to find another job."

"Well, I'm still working for Nicole."

"What do you mean? There's no restaurant."

"She has me going through a lot of papers for the probate."

"Really? Have you found anything interesting?"

"What do you mean?"

Roberto shrugged. "I dunno. I used to get the feeling, sometimes, that Alan and Nicole both had something secret."

"Why do you say that?"

"Little things, like Alan would start talking about his great plans, then suddenly change the subject."

"Nicole, too?"

"Well, no, but she definitely was keeping something hidden. She's away from the place a lot. Not overnight or anything, but there are times when I wonder where she's been all day. Until the fire, that is. By the way, has she paid you yet?"

"Um ... no. Alan gave me an advance on the first day, but nothing since then. Nicole hasn't even mentioned pay."

Roberto laughed. "That's Nicole. She criticized Alan for being sloppy and late with paperwork, but she's not much better. She's great with ordering supplies and paying suppliers, but when it comes to things like payroll and taxes, she's hopeless. Keep on top of her about that."

Tara thought a moment. "Do you think she'll change? Rise to the challenge?"

Roberto shrugged and ate the last bite of BLT.

"Do you think she *has* changed? Since the fire ... and Alan?"

Roberto looked Tara in the eyes. "Big time."

He stood, drinking the last of his wine. He picked up the empty bottle. "Thanks for lunch, Tara. It was great, but I gotta get back to work. Her Majesty made a task list for me a mile long. But let's do this again, sometime. I enjoyed it."

As she rinsed the dishes, Tara reviewed the conversation.

So both Nicole and Alan had secrets.

You have secrets, too, Mr. Gonsalves Just who is "Cee-Cee"? Or is it actually "Vee-Vee"?

The offer

Tara was in the restaurant office, finishing organizing Alan's paperwork for the probate when the phone rang at nine. She hesitated, wondering whether Nicole might pick up an extension somewhere, before answering the third ring.

"It's Steven Harris," said the gravelly voice. "Who is this?"

"Tara Rezeck."

"Why are you still there? I thought you were a cook."

"How can I help you, Mr. Harris?" *You jerk.*

"I'd like to speak with Nicole DaSilva."

"Her name is Nicole Fong."

"What are you talking about?"

"And she's not available right now."

"So you're her secretary now, is that it?"

I cannot believe what a jerk this guy is. "I'm helping her as a friend."

"Well, you tell your friend that I'd like to come over this morning and present an offer to purchase the Rocky Creek Winery."

"Today? Can't this wait? Nicole's been through an awful lot. She just buried her husband."

"That's the point. I want to take it off her hands and give her some relief."

"I don't think now is the right—"

"You tell her I'll be there at eleven." The line clicked and Tara heard the dial tone.

Yup—Steven Harris wins the prize for biggest jerk in Sonoma. She took out Paul Rondeau's card and dialed his personal cell.

By 11, Nicole was sitting on the big upholstered chair at the end of the coffee table, staring at papers that Paul Rondeau arranged for her. Tara could tell she did not really see them.

Paul sat on the sofa, closed his soft leather briefcase and put it on the floor beside him.

Tara put three cups of coffee on the table and sat beside Paul. *Is no one going to say anything?*

The doorbell rang. Tara opened the door on Steven Harris in a suit and tie, holding a leather case under his arm. A perfectly clear blue sky seemed to deliberately frame his thick white hair. The smell of smoke was gone.

"Good morning, Tara," Harris said, smiling like a movie star. *So that's where Cameron learned it.* "I hope you're well?"

Jerk. Tara stood aside to let him in. Harris went into the living room. "Good morning, Nicole. I hope you're feeling well today. Hello, Rondeau." He held out his hand to the lawyer, who shook, but not before hesitating as if wondering what the man was up to.

There's a lot of tension here. Tara leaned against the wall at the entrance to the living room, unnoticed by the rest.

Harris undid his jacket button and sat across the coffee table from Nicole. He pulled a zipper around three sides of his briefcase and pulled out two stapled bundles of legal-size paper. He gave one to Nicole and the other to Rondeau.

"This, as you no doubt guessed, is my formal offer to purchase the Rocky Creek Winery. There are no financial conditions. All the financing is in place, and the purchase will be for cash. The plan is to keep the winery operating as a separate entity from the Harris Winery, and we'll keep all the staff on for at least the first year. However, because the two vineyards are adjacent, those operations will be merged for reasons of operational efficiency."

"But mostly because your vineyard suffered pretty severe fire damage, and you desperately need more grapes," Rondeau said.

"We'll do fine this year, with or without the Rocky Creek vineyard," Harris said.

"But if you combine the vineyards, what about Rocky Creek Chardonnay?" Nicole asked.

"It's a good seller. We plan to keep bottling it."

"But will it be the same?" Nicole pressed.

Harris smiled. "Once you sell, my dear, that won't be your worry, will it?"

Rondeau flipped to the last page of the bundle. His eyes widened, and he looked at Harris, then at Nicole.

Before he could say anything, Nicole said, "That's not what Alan would have wanted."

"I'm sorry, but Alan was the only thing that made this winery profitable," Steven said. "He put way too much sweat equity into this operation, and that's just not justifiable from a business point of view."

Nicole's face flushed. Her jaw clenched and her hands trembled. *She looks like she's going to explode.*

Rondeau shifted forward on the sofa, pointing to a spot on the last page of Harris' offer. "Harris, this price is thirty percent lower than what we've been talking about."

"That is Harris Winery's best offer," he countered.

"This is almost fifty percent less than the price you offered Alan just three months ago."

Nicole's eyes widened. She flipped to the last page of her copy of the offer and gasped. Tara went behind her and looked over

Nicole's shoulder. The number meant nothing to her. *How much does it cost to operate this place all year?*

"Does this include Cyrano's?" Nicole asked.

"What restaurant? It's closed, and it will take a significant investment to get it going again."

"What are you talking about? It's only been closed for a few days. It's ready to open again as soon as—"

"As soon as you hire all new staff," Harris interrupted. "You don't have a chef, or a sous chef. You have one partly-trained line cook. You don't have wait staff or a dishwasher. And personally, I have no interest in running a restaurant."

Rondeau stood. "Mr. Harris, this offer is not acceptable. We asked you to present an offer to purchase in good faith, based on the understanding of the offers you have made in the past."

"The market value of this winery has significantly decreased since then."

"What are you talking about?" Nicole almost screamed. "We've almost finished the harvest, we're about to crush, we're able to operate at full production—"

"You've had significant fire damage. That decreases the value of this asset."

"We only lost the stupid garage and an old truck!"

Steven's voice continued, smooth and even as oil spreading slowly across granite. "I hate to bring this up again, Nicole, but Alan was the driving force behind the success of this winery. And you don't have him at this crucial time in the crush."

"The harvest is done, and Roberto is in charge of the crush. He's still here. And then there's the matter of the Wappo Tribe having the right of first refusal on any sale of the winery," Nicole said.

Harris waited, looking intently at Nicole. "You're worried about what Alan would have wanted? The Indians will just turn this into a casino. And as for Mr. Gonsalves, I have it on good authority that he will not be here to oversee this year's bottling. He plans to move on."

Nicole seemed to freeze. She did not even breathe. She looked at Harris, then at her lawyer, then at the wall, in the direction of the winery. "What are you talking about? Roberto is ... he's been the manager since ... How do you know this before I do?"

"Perhaps you don't know your employees as well as you thought, Nicole," Harris said.

Rondeau stood. "I think you'd better leave, Mr. Harris."

Harris stood, too. "To answer your question, Mr. Rondeau, I did come in good faith. That is my best offer. It's the best you're going to get in today's market."

Tara saw tears on Nicole's face. She bent down to put her arms around her shoulders.

"I need that money," Nicole said in a high, thin voice. "This offer is barely more than what we owe the banks. It will leave me with nothing."

Harris zipped his briefcase closed and went to the door. "I'm sorry, Nicole. Business is business. I'll wait for your call."

He left, closing the front door with a gentle click.

Nicole stood. "I have to lie down," she said, and went down the hall to her bedroom.

Now what do I do? "Is it really that bad of an offer?" Tara asked Rondeau.

He shrugged. "It's not generous, but Harris is right. She's not likely to get much more if she puts the winery on the market now. No one around here is going to be interested in investing in a winery for some time. That's what Harris is banking on. He's a shrewd businessman, and he's never let friendship get in the way."

"Couldn't she just hang on until things get better?"

"I don't think her heart is in it. She's really depressed. Losing Alan hit her hard. She wants to get out, but with the debts the business has, she won't be left with much to start over with. It's going to be a tough decision."

"So what do we do now?"

Rondeau looked at her intently. "It's Nicole's decision to make. We'll just have to give her time. In the meantime, I'm grateful that you've been such a good friend to her."

Tara pulled the bracelet from her pocket. "Speaking of which—remember that bracelet I showed you? You were right. It came from Adorna in Sebastopol. They checked their records, and told me it was bought by Roberto Gonsalves."

"Can you be sure that it's the same Roberto Gonsalves?"

"Seems pretty coincidental, considering that I found it on the winery managed by Roberto Gonsalves."

Rondeau nodded. He looked closely at Tara for a long moment. Then: "You still have my card?"

"Your business card? Yes."

"Great. Come by my office tomorrow. In the morning, when Nicole is busy with the winery. We need to talk."

The law office

Paul Rondeau's office was in a strip mall off the highway, between a shawarma restaurant and a store that sold supplies for swimming pools. The backlit sign over the awning read Paul Rondeau, Attorney at Law. *Not much to look at*, Tara thought as she climbed out of her car. Maybe I'm overdressed for this visit.

She was glad she wore shoes with closed toes for the oppressive heat on the parking lot asphalt.

Opening the door rang a gentle bell that sounded almost exactly like the one in the jewelry store. A thin, young dark-haired man in a cheap suit stood and smiled as Tara walked in. A name plate on the desk in front of him read "Tyler Patel."

"Can I help you?" Patel asked.

"I'm Tara Rezeck. Mr. Rondeau told me to come in today."

Patel smiled even more broadly and held his hand out to the side. "Won't you sit down? Mr. Rondeau is in a meeting now, but I will tell him you're here." Tara heard a slight trace of a South Asian accent.

She sat down on a surprisingly comfortable sofa and picked up a magazine. Tyler Patel opened a door behind his desk and leaned in. He turned to her and closed the door, saying, "Mr. Rondeau won't be long."

Tara flipped through a six-month-old edition of *Sonoma Outdoors*, tapping her foot on the floor. She picked up a year-old, tattered copy of *Field and Stream*, and threw it down again.

Eventually, the door at the back of the office opened. Tara heard two voices, one of them Paul Rondeau's. Richard Sarris, the counsel for the Wappo Tribe, stepped out, wearing a linen suit and cowboy boots.

Paul Rondeau emerged behind him and walked him to the front door. This time, he wore a tan suit, gold watch glittering on his wrist. Today, his shirt and shoes seemed a little less formal than before, more like California to Tara. "Thanks for coming in, Richard," he said, shaking hands. "I'll explain the situation to Ms. Fong, and we'll be in touch."

The Native man left, and Paul turned to Tara. "Thanks for coming in. Do you want anything? Coffee, water?"

"Water would be good."

Paul nodded at Tyler Patel, who jumped to his feet.

Tara followed Paul into the inner office. *Wow. This place is ... sumptuous.*

The far wall was all glass, looking across a brown and green valley dotted with luxury houses. She could see the terraced surfaces of a vineyard, and glints off a blue river. At one side, a road leaped on the back of a long bridge across the valley.

She heard the gentle whisper of air conditioning, felt a tickle on her face. The temperature in the inner office was perfect. The air even smelled fresh and clean.

One wall of the office was covered in shelves holding even rows of leather-bound legal volumes. Across the back, partly blocking the window, was a wide desk of dark wood. A high-backed chair stood behind it, a smaller one in front.

There was nothing on the desk but smooth, grained surface.

A huge abstract painting hung on the wall opposite the bookcases, over a dark leather sofa. A flat-screen TV hung over the counter. On a small table near the desk was a coffee maker, with a neat arrangement of cups, saucers, tumblers and containers for milk and sugar.

Tyler Patel swept past them. He opened a low door in a cabinet beside the desk, revealing a bar refrigerator, and took out a tall glass bottle and decanted clear water into two tumblers. He reached into the fridge, again using a pair of small metal tongs, and dropped two ice cubes into each glass.

Paul indicated a soft leather chair facing the sofa, on which he sat, spreading his arms across its back and crossing one ankle over the other knee. Tyler carried the two water glasses on a tray and sat it on a low coffee table between Tara and Paul.

"Thanks, Tyler. Pull the file you prepared for Tara, will you?" Tyler nodded and swept out, closing the door behind him.

Why did he prepare a file on me? Tara gulped down half the water to hide her surprise. "Thanks. It's another hot one out there."

"They're saying it's supposed to be hot for at least another week. No rain in sight. Fortunately, the fires have moved out of our region, but they're spreading farther north. It's also really bad in Napa," Paul said.

"So, what did you want to see me about?"

Paul smiled. "I'm fine, Tara. How are you? Did you have any trouble finding the place?"

"No." *Damn. My parents taught me better than that.* "Sorry. How are you?"

Paul waved his hand. "I'm just playing with you. Don't worry about it." He sipped his own water. "The reason I called you here is, first, to tell you that I'm impressed with the detective work you did, chasing down that bracelet."

"Thanks."

"Yes. That was impressive. And dangerous. Not physically dangerous, but you went asking questions that only the police or licensed private investigators are allowed to ask in this state. Or in just about every other state, for that matter. The police generally take a pretty dim view of people who try to move in on their turf."

"Oh. I didn't think ..."

"No. Most people don't. And frankly, I'm surprised the jewelry store gave you that information. They could be opening themselves up to a claim of breach of privacy. They really ought to know better. And so should you."

"Excuse me?"

"You graduated cum laude from a prestigious eastern law school. You know about privacy laws."

"How do you know this?" *Does everyone associated with the Rocky Creek Winery know everything about me?*

"Alan told me. He wanted me to check out his new employee."

"Oh. I see."

"What—did you think he would take nothing but the word of Sophia Vorona?"

"Uhh ...."

"I did a quick reference check Your school loves you. Don't worry—everything is clean."

"Well, duh."

"So, that being said, you should have known about privacy laws. Why did you do that? Why break the law? You could be disbarred."

"I haven't been called to the bar yet."

"You still took a huge chance. You'll probably get away with it—but don't do it again."

"Again?"

"Right now, the police are still overwhelmed with the fire situation. That's consuming all their resources at this point. But eventually, they are going to have to investigate a suspicious death. And they're not likely to take kindly to a private party contaminating the evidence."

"So Alan's death *is* suspicious."

Paul sighed. "It's complicated. It's not officially suspicious yet because there's been no investigation. The coroner, as you can imagine, is extremely busy right now. Unfortunately, there have been a large number of deaths because of the fires. Given the state of resources, there's a certain amount of pressure to close files as quickly as possible."

"So they want to just sweep it under the rug?"

"Not really. Alan was a popular man, well known to the community, and especially the officials of the county. But these people are facing something they've never faced before. And no one likes to think about unpleasant things. So if they can plausibly find Alan's death accidental, they'll be inclined to do so."

"What do you think?" Tara felt her pulse throbbing in her upper arm.

Paul looked out the window. "I don't have enough information. But some things look very strange. The fact that the only damage on the property was the garage. Nothing else burned, even though there were powerful winds that night, and there was plenty of damage to other properties—including the place next door. The fact that Alan was alone is another."

"That was Alan's decision. Nicole didn't want him to stay behind. She just about had a breakdown when he said he was going to wait for two pickers. Greg and Roberto had to force her into the passenger seat of her car to get her out of there."

Paul looked at Tara intently. "They forced her?"

"Well, it wasn't violent or anything. But yes, they pulled her out of the driver's seat and put her on the passenger side. She more or less let them do it."

"You say he was waiting for two pickers. Are they still missing?"

"No, no, we found them. They got into the truck I was in at the main road."

"Why didn't anyone tell Alan he didn't have to wait?"

"We did! Roberto radioed him."

"Roberto radioed him," Paul repeated, nodding. "Then why didn't he leave?"

"I don't know ... I thought he was coming right behind us."

"But he wasn't?"

Tara heard a roaring sound. *That's my heartbeat.* "Are you saying ... *Roberto* killed Alan? That's impossible."

"Why?"

"He couldn't have. He was with me the whole night through. He drove to Monte Rio. I walked with him to the hotel to see if they had room. Then I went with him to follow Nicole, to try to catch up with her. And I was with Roberto when we found Nicole ... and Alan."

Paul nodded again. "Okay, so it couldn't have been Roberto ... if, indeed, there was anything other than a tragic accident. There might be nothing else to it. Still, it leaves Nicole in a complex situation."

"Who would have a motive for killing Alan?"

"There's no evidence that anyone killed him. In fact, the weight of evidence is that he died accidentally."

"Hear me out." *I cannot believe I'm saying this.* "Nicole asked me to sort out Alan's legal papers. They're a real jumble."

"I'm glad it's you instead of me. Alan was terrible with paperwork. And Nicole's not much better. By the way, has she paid you yet?"

"I only got a two-week advance when I started. From Alan. So, technically, Nicole has not paid me anything."

"Don't let her forget. So, you were saying, you're sorting through Alan's paperwork."

"I found that agreement between Alan and the Wappo Tribe."

"I'm glad you found that contract. I have a copy, and of course, the Wappo Tribe has another, but it's good that we know where Alan's copy is."

"Did you know about the insurance policy he took out about ten months ago?"

"What kind of insurance?"

"Life insurance. Five million dollars to the survivor if either he or Nicole die in an accident or misadventure."

"That's not a lot of money for a business the size of Rocky Creek Winery. Don't forget, that restaurant has a lot of overhead."

"That I could understand. What I don't get is why it's made out only to Alan, and has only his signature."

"So Nicole, presumably, knows no more about it than I do? That's ... interesting."

"Now, about the bracelet from Artisana. I showed it to Nicole. She doesn't recognize it. But when I showed it to Roberto, he said he didn't recognize it either."

"So, he's lying."

"Okay, another thing: the first night I was here, staying in the guest house at Rocky Creek, I mean, I heard two people having sex outside in the vineyard."

"You heard them? Did you see them, too?" Paul leaned forward, smiling.

"No. It was dark. But there were definitely at least two people having sex between the grapevines."

"Sounds uncomfortable, if romantic. How can you be sure it was sex?"

"Moaning, groaning, that one-of-a-kind rhythm of fucking. And at the end, a smack and a man saying 'I love that ass.'"

Paul laughed. "Okay, so two people were screwing in the vineyard at night."

"Before the fire, Nicole seemed to act very distant toward Alan. Like they were always having a fight. But she seemed alternately nasty toward Roberto, and sweet, too."

Paul's eyes narrowed, but he said nothing.

"She would be away from the restaurant at odd times, then come running in. In the morning of my second day there, she drove in from somewhere and ran into the house, wearing the same clothes she had been wearing the night before.

"Then after we got back from the evac center, she told me that she had hurt Alan before. Deeply."

"That could be survivor's guilt."

"That's what I thought, but later she told me that Alan paid more attention to his winery than to his wife. And now, she seems to have even more animosity toward Roberto."

"So, where are you going with this?"

"I think ... that Nicole has been having an affair."

Rondeau nodded and sipped his coffee. "I know she has."

"You *know*? How do you know?"

"Alan told me."

"Alan *knew*? Why didn't he leave her?"

"Don't talk so loud. He loved her."

"But he tolerated her affair?"

"He loved her," Rondeau repeated. "He told me a year ago that he thought Nicole was cheating on him. I offered to investigate, but he told me not to."

"So, who is it?"

"You tell me."

"You don't know?"

"Like I said, Alan didn't want me to investigate."

"And you didn't? Just because he asked you not to?"

"He's the client. So if he says no, who would pay for it?"

"So do you know who it was or not?"

"No. Do you?"

Tara sat back on the sofa and looked out the window at the brown and dull green hills of Sonoma. "Maybe."

"Tell me," Paul urged.

"Yesterday, when I was leaving the restaurant, I saw Roberto coming out of the house at around 5:00 p.m., when he was supposed to be in the winery, doing his job. He adjusted his clothing, as if he had just put it on."

Rondeau looked doubtful. "You're saying Nicole was having an affair with Roberto?"

"I've been thinking about it. I spoke to him today at lunch. He told me he thinks Nicole and Alan kept secrets from one another. The agreement with the Wappo Tribe and the new insurance policy bear out that he was keeping secrets from her. An affair would be a secret she's keeping from him. Or thought she was, if he knew about it. Also, when I asked Roberto if he's involved with anyone, he says he is, but won't tell me who."

"That doesn't mean it's Nicole."

"When I asked her name, he made up some ridiculous story about how they have nauseatingly cute nicknames for each other: 'Bo-bo' and 'Cee-Cee.'"

Paul leaned back. "Well, you have a fair amount of circumstantial evidence. And it looks pretty good, given that we've already established that Nicole is, or was, having an affair with someone. But do you really think it's Roberto?"

"I think it fits. There's something between them. They act like they hate each other. But it's a bit too much, you know what I mean? Like they want everyone to know they hate each other."

"What are you saying?"

"I think it's an act. I think she was sleeping with Roberto, and they came up with this charade to hide it."

Rondeau nodded. "Okay. Maybe. But there are problems with that theory. First, if Roberto were having a secret affair with Nicole, he wouldn't be likely to tell anyone that he thought she was hiding something. Second, if he bought the bracelet as a gift, he didn't give it to Nicole.

"And third, Roberto adored Alan. I really find it a stretch to believe he'd betray him. On the other hand, men are stupid when it comes to sex. If they're offered, they'll take it."

Tara smiled. "Speaking from personal experience?"

"Personal experience as the attorney of couples who have shredded their own relationships. In my experience, there are more examples of both sides of a couple having affairs. It gets messy. Very messy."

"Are you saying Alan was having an affair?"

Rondeau laughed, long and hard. "Alan? Mr. Straight-as-an-Arrow? No way. He loved two things: his winery and his wife. Between those two, he didn't have a spare second for an affair."

"So ... if Alan was too busy to have an affair ... why wasn't Nicole?"

"Oh, no. You're not going to pull me into the rabbit hole of analyzing women's psychology."

Tara decided to change tack. "What was Richard Sarris doing here? You said you would talk to Mrs. DaSilva and get back to him."

"That's not exactly what I said, and you should know better than to ask a lawyer what he spoke to someone about."

Paul smiled. *Why is he smiling?* "But in this case ... since Nicole seems to treat you as a confidante ... I can tell you that the Wappo Tribe has decided not to pursue their claim to the Rocky Creek real estate for at least three more years."

"That's a relief."

"It's not that much of a concession. If you were to look up the term 'long shot' in the dictionary, the definition would be the Wappos' claim's chance of success."

"Do you think that the Wappos have a motive for killing Alan? That would seem to be greater than Roberto?"

"Hold on, Detective Rezeck," Paul laughed. "We're really getting ahead of ourselves. We don't know Alan's death was anything but an accident. But we do need to start moving on untangling the legal issues. I know Nicole's been devastated, but we can't put these things off any longer."

"What do you want me to do?"

Paul leaned forward, elbows on knees. "Like I said, I was impressed by your detective work. Now, you're not a detective. That takes time. But besides police and detectives, there are some other people who are entitled to snoop around and ask questions, like lawyers and legal representatives.

"This is what I'd like you to do. Continue to be Nicole's friend. Look out for her interests, and call me immediately if she's about to make some rash decisions."

"I already do that."

"Good. Keep it up. Keep looking into this bracelet business. Be careful, be subtle, and don't arouse Roberto's suspicions, but try to find out what happened to it between his purchase of it and it turning up on the ground beside the garage."

"I have to tell you something about the garage." Tara took a deep breath. "There's a possibility the electrical system was tampered with." Paul just tilted his head, his eyebrows frowning, but a little smile at the corners of his mouth. She went on. "The electrician who restored the power said there were two wires missing from the electrical box in the garage. He said he couldn't understand it."

"Okay."

"Well, if there's a possibility the meter was tampered with, maybe that's what caused the fire in the garage. Not the wildfires, not blowing embers like Cameron said, but an electrical fire."

"When did Cameron say that?"

"That day when he and his father were looking at the fire damage."

"See? You're doing it already."

"Doing what?"

"Investigating and bringing me what you found. Well done. Keep it up." He stood and opened the door. "Tyler? Do you have that file?"

Tyler was standing beside the door and handed Paul a legal-size Manila folder. Paul opened it up on the coffee table in front of Tara. "You can't become a legal adviser or investigator just by calling yourself one—at least not in this state. So to give you some protection, I'll have to hire you."

"You're offering me a job?"

"Part-time and probationary." He pointed to the paper. Tara saw her name neatly typed near the top of a letter, under the bold heading "Notice of Offer."

"The pay isn't much, just enough to be accepted by the state bar association. But because I'm paying you, you're officially an employee of this firm, and that means you are entitled to ask certain questions. It also means that your discussions with the client are privileged, within limits."

"The client?"

"Nicole Fong and the estate of Alan DaSilva." He flipped over the letter of offer to reveal a check made out to her. She gasped when she saw the amount. *I guess "not much" means something different in California than Vermont.*

"That's a two-week advance. Keep your gas tank full and think about upgrading your mobile phone plan to unlimited voice and data. Do you have a computer?"

"Yes. It's a new one. My Dad bought it for me."

"Good." He moved the check, revealing a form. "Fill in your email and phone number. Oh, and sign the letter of offer."

"But what about my job at the winery?"

"You told me you haven't been paid."

"What do you want me to do?"

"Nicole is not my only client. And this situation is getting more complicated by the minute. For now, just keep doing what you have been doing. Keep an eye on Nicole. Be her friend. Call me immediately if she makes any more sudden decisions. And keep looking into things, and tell me whatever you find out."

"Look into things like what?"

"For starters, like whether your theory about Roberto and Nicole holds any water. But do it carefully."

The situation felt surreal. Tara found a pen in her hand. She scribbled her name on the letter and put the check into her wallet. Within minutes, she found herself at the side of her car.

Did that just happen? Did I just get a job at a law firm?

Something I can tell Mom and Dad that they could be proud of.

I need to open a bank account.

Back at Cyrano's's upstairs office, Tara fired up Skype. For a change, Ken Rezeck's face appeared on the screen first. "Tara! How are you?"

"I'm great, Dad. How is Roxanne?"

"She's having her nap right now. Hang on. I've answered you on the iPhone." The image on the screen blurred as Ken Rezeck carried the phone upstairs. Tara saw familiar, if dizzying, glimpses of her parents' home. "Ssshhh," she heard. The image steadied on a crib in a dim room.

There she is. Mom's right. What an angel.

Tara felt a real pain in her chest. She wiped away a tear. "I'm sorry I've been away so long. We'll be together soon. I promise," she whispered.

The image blurred again as Ken carried the phone out of the baby's room and closed the door. A few seconds later, she heard her mother's voice. "Is it Tara?"

"Yes. Let me put this in the stand," said her father.

The image steadied and both her parents' faces appeared, pressed together. "You two don't have to get so close to the phone, you know."

They backed up. "So, how are things?" Mom said.

"I got a job," she answered. She wiped her eyes again, hoping her parents did not notice. "For a lawyer."

Dad beamed. "Really? Wonderful! A job in your field, at last. Well done, Tara."

"That is wonderful news. Does it pay well?" Mom asked.

"Better than I ever expected. But I get the feeling that in California, it's still not going to be a lot."

"So you'll be leaving the winery? Have you found a new place to live?" Mom asked.

"Is it suitable for a baby?" asked Dad.

"Uhhh ... not exactly. I'm still at the winery. The owner has asked me to stay so she won't be alone. She's still freaked out over her husband's death. I've moved into her guest room. Just for a little while, until she feels stronger."

Dad looked concerned, Mom sympathetic. "How is that going to work?" he asked.

"Well, I guess I'll live here at the winery and work for the lawyer."

"Is the lawyer close to the winery?" Dad asked.

"Not far."

"And this ... Nicole is okay with this arrangement?"

"She ... look, I can't talk too much about it. Client privilege. But it's all cool. And yes, I promise I'll find a permanent place for me and Roxanne real soon. Look, I have to go back to work now. Love you."

The vineyard

Once she had finished organizing the DaSilvas' papers, Tara decided to do some work for Paul Rondeau. *He said to keep an eye open, so I'll look around.*

It's called "snooping." So I'll snoop.

She went past the winery, where she could hear Mark's and Amy's voices through the open door. Her eyes went to the place in the weeds where she had found the bracelet as she passed the remains of the garage. *Maybe I should advise Nicole to get someone to start taking this away, cleaning it up.*

Past the garage, to the open gate into the vineyard. *It's funny that I haven't gone into the vineyard since I arrived here. Not since that first time when Roberto showed me around.*

Maybe I could get him here to show me some more.

Focus, Tara. Keep your eyes open, and your attention on what you see. And hear.

Yes, conscience.

The sun shone hot on her right shoulder, but the air was not as hot as the day before. The radio weather reports promised rain in the next week, but still the fires burned in Napa and Sonoma.

I should have brought some water, though. It's still dry and hot.

200

She followed the dirt road traversing the slope. Here and there, water sprayed from the irrigation system. She avoided muddy spots on the road. Ruts would become deep puddles when the promised rain finally came.

Uphill of the road, the vines hung limp and dry. Tara saw no grapes on them. *That must be where the harvest is done. The chardonnay and sauvignon grapes.*

Down slope, though, dark purple clusters bent the vines. The leaves looked healthier. *I guess that Roberto is still irrigating them.*

She could see tire tracks in the dirt road. *Is that a clue? Could the police tell something by analyzing tire treads? Or is that just in TV shows?*

The road began to climb higher, even though it followed a more or less straight path ahead. As she approached a ridge, she saw a low wire fence with wooden posts, running between two parallel rows of gray-leaved trees. A closed gate crossed the dirt road, bearing a brightly painted sign that read "Harris Estates." Tire tracks led to the gate, and when she got closer she could see they continued beyond it.

No lock on the gate. I wonder how old those tire tracks are.

Maybe the same picking crew works on both estates, and the fence is more to show the boundary than to keep anyone out. Have to ask Roberto about that.

Beyond the gate, the land sloped down again, with more rows of grapevines. In the distance, Tara thought she could see a truck and people. A picking crew?

Closer, though, a large patch of the vineyard was dark grey. Black branches twisted along the ground like tortured skeletal fingers.

Tara turned and looked back along the road that curved gently between dry, but green, rows of vines. *It must be more than 200 yards between the burned part of the Harris vineyard to the other side of Rocky Creek's.*

How could burning embers blow all that way to set the garage on fire, but miss everything in between?

Something else to talk to Roberto about. In addition to why he lied about the bracelet.

She walked back toward the Rocky Creek Winery. On the ground in a row between the grapevines, halfway between the two fences, she saw something shine, reflecting the oppressive sunlight. She strode toward it.

So here's where the small truck's side mirror went. She crouched down to look closer.

Torn from its home on the side of the truck, the mirror looked strange, almost lost. The housing and the mirror were both cracked and wires hung from the housing. A piece of fabric hung from where a corner had jammed into one of the cracks.

Blue plaid. Why does every guy who thinks he's macho have to wear blue plaid?

Still, what does this mean? Alan drove the small truck into the vineyard to look for Toby and Gabriela, the missing pickers. Then he came back at some point. Did he hit something?

She looked at the road. Sure enough, deep, curving ruts showed where a truck had turned around.

Then, he negotiated his way through the gate, but smashes the truck into the corner of the garage?

Was the garage on fire already? Did that make him panic, leading to the crash?

Is that how he suffered blunt force trauma—hitting his head on the steering wheel or something? Then he managed to get out of the truck, but collapsed in front of the garage, catching fire? After taking out the tire iron?

Seems pretty far-fetched. And where did the cloth come from? It couldn't have been Alan's shirt.

She closed her eyes to try and picture Alan on the day of the evacuation. *What was he wearing?* She thought of him pacing in front of the winery, phone to his ear. *Was it a blue plaid shirt?*

She thought of him getting into the small truck. *No, not plaid. It was a yellow short-sleeve golf shirt. Yes, something cool on that hot day.*

So whose shirt is this? And how did it get stuck into a crack on the broken side mirror?

She walked back to the gate, looking at the tire tracks again. She could see where trucks turned between the gate and the garage. One curving rut looked deeper than most. *Would that be from the truck turning fast, maybe spinning its tires?*

Maybe that's why Alan crashed, trying to turn fast and he hit the garage?

As she passed the gate into the winery yard, she remembered where she had seen that pattern on the fabric stuck to the mirror.

Cameron Harris wore this shirt the first day I saw him.

The vagaries of making wine

The temperature started to moderate more than a week after the fires. Clouds were moving to the west, with a hint of rain. The hillsides looked weary, the leaves on trees wilted. Even the horsetails, the tall brown weeds that grew along the roadsides, seemed to droop.

Tara took a glass of ice water on her morning walk around the estate. *What should I be looking for? Am I still working for Nicole, now that Paul Rondeau, Attorney at Law is paying me?*

She strolled past the winery. Through the open door, she heard voices in argument: Roberto and Nicole.

"I'm telling you, Nicole, the chardonnay will be fine. We were mostly finished with that harvest," said Roberto, his voice insistent. "But half the grapes for the cabernet sauvignon are still on the vine, and we don't know what the smoke and ash will do to the quality of the wine. We have to test and take steps to minimize the damage."

"Rocky Creek Winery's reputation is based on our pinot noir," Nicole snapped. "You need to concentrate on that right now. It's our most profitable product line, and we need profits now. Finish picking it, get it into the vats and bottle it. And get going on shipping last year's chardonnay."

"You want to take the reserve and bottle it before it's ready! Alan would not have wanted that."

Tone it down, Roberto. That's your boss you're talking to.

"Alan's not here anymore. I am. Right now, we need cash. So I'm telling you to maximize the amount of chardonnay we can ship. And get another picker crew here to get those grapes in, wash them twice if you want to and start bottling."

Tara stalked closer to the wide-open garage door of the winery. Nicole stood just inside the door, out of the direct sunlight, her back to Tara. Nicole wore a light blue blouse, off-white pants and sensible, but stylish, shoes. Her hair was piled on top of her head again. At least she's dressed well, Tara thought. But those pants are a little tight.

Be kind, Tara. She's been through a lot.

Roberto stood deeper inside the winery, holding a clipboard. His heavy eyebrows were drawn close together, his stance aggressive. Behind Roberto, Mark and Amy stood beside a gleaming stainless steel vat. They looked from Roberto to Nicole, then at each other. Mark kept shifting his weight from one foot to the other. Amy fidgeted with a heavy elastic band.

"I'm telling you, you're taking a huge risk with the cabernet sauvignon and pinot," Roberto continued. "They're our biggest sellers by volume. But if they taste like ashes out of the bottle, we won't sell any of them. And what will that do to cash flow, then?"

Tone it down, buddy, Tara thought again.

"I'm not debating this with you, Roberto. Bottle the chardonnay reserve and get the others into the tanks. I have shippers coming in."

"What about next year's reserve?"

"What part of my being the sole owner now of this winery do you not understand, Roberto?"

Roberto opened his mouth, closed it, then opened it again. Finally, words came out. His voice was strained, clipped, his words bitten off. "Fine, Nicole. No reserve in two years."

"Good. I'm glad I've made myself clear." Nicole turned and strode out of the winery. "Tara! Good morning," she said, with forced cheer.

"Good morning. What's going on?"

"I'm running a winery is what's going on. Someone has to around here."

"Are you having a problem?"

"I was. But I solved it. Come with me. I have some more for you to do."

The intruder

The smell of smoke had faded from the Sonoma air, but the heat persisted, day and night. Tara lay on her back, staring at the ceiling. It was too hot for covers, even though the air conditioning hummed outside her window. Tara pulled the sheet up to her chin and continued staring at the ceiling, willing herself not to look at the clock.

Her mind wandered from her daughter to her daughter's father. Then Roberto.

Maybe it's me. Bobby didn't want to stay with me, even after we made a baby together. And Cameron is worse than Bobby, even if he is better in bed.

Was that a footstep? Listen hard.

Another creak. Then a slipping, slithering sound. *A snake? God, I hate snakes. Are there snakes in this part of California? What if it's a rattler?*

Aren't you supposed to shoot rattlesnakes? Does Nicole have a gun?

Wait—there's no rattling sound. Isn't that why they're called rattlesnakes?

The soft sound, then a bump. Like something hitting the wall. *Is that breathing?*

She glanced at the clock: 12:30 a.m.

Gently, careful not to make any sound herself, Tara slipped from the bed and padded to the open doorway of the guest bedroom, holding her arms outstretched to prevent bumping into anything in the dark.

A creak. *That's Nicole's bedroom door. Someone is sneaking into her room.*

If she has a gun, does she keep it in the bedroom?

Tara slowly leaned out of the doorway, until one eye could see down the hall to Nicole's room. She could just see that the door was open, barely wide enough for someone to slip through.

A rustle, the sound of bedclothes, lost in the susurrus of the air conditioning. Tara put one bare foot onto the hardwood floor of the hall, transferring her weight so, so carefully. Then another foot. Then another.

What if the intruder has a weapon? Remember your disarming techniques, Tara. You know them.

Shit. Where's my phone? I should be calling 911.

She reached the doorway and paused.

Whispers, then murmurs. Nicole's soft voice. "What are you doing here?"

"I miss you, Nicole," said a whisper. Man or woman? Too soft to tell. "It's been a long time since we've been together. I miss your touch. I miss making love to you."

"Get out. Now," Nicole murmured, but with force.

"Come on, Nicole. We love each other—"

This is it. The proof that Nicole was having an affair while Alan was alive. But who with?

"Cut the crap. That was a mistake. A long series of very big mistakes, but it's over. Now get out before I scream and Tara comes in here to beat the crap out of you."

"What?" It was a man's voice, talking low now, not whispering. Tara heard a chuckle. "That little thing?"

"She knows karate or something. Don't kid yourself."

Where is Charlie? Why isn't he barking?

The only reason could be that Charlie knows this man. If only dogs could talk.

"I'm not afraid of Tara," said the man.

"Then you'd better be afraid of me." Nicole's voice rose to another level. If she had been still sleeping, Tara would have woken at that sound.

Or the next one, the sound of a drawer opening. Then a scrape and rustling of the bedclothes and an unmistakable click of a gun's safety. "Get the hell out of here now."

"Okay, okay," the man whispered. Tara heard more rustling, then a soft footfall. "Take it easy, Nicole. Do you even know how to use that?"

From somewhere in the room, Charlie whined.

"Shut up and get out. Quietly. No one else has to know you were here, but I'll use this if I have to."

"You don't have to, Nicole. I'm going. You're breaking my heart, but I'll go."

"Oh, skip the bullshit. You don't have a heart."

Nicole's bedroom door creaked, and the shadow beyond it deepened. As quickly as she could without making a sound, Tara went back to her room, ducking behind the wall.

A tall, slim shadow crept by her door. As he crossed in front of her door, Tara could see a familiar, handsome profile.

Cameron? Nicole's been fucking Cameron Harris?

The bastard. I'll kill him.

Wait—I don't need to. I'll let Nicole do it.

Nicole followed, a gun in her outstretched hand.

Tara leaned against the door frame again, just far enough to watch Nicole follow Cameron down the hall. She then padded after, pressing against the corner to see them go into the kitchen.

"Go," Nicole repeated. Tara heard the back door open, the squeal of the screen door. "And if you ever come back, I will use this. Comprende?"

"No need to be dramatic, Nicole. I get it. Now put that away before you hurt yourself."

"I should shoot you right now just for that condescending comment. Get the fuck out and don't come back."

The door closed. Tara heard clicks as Nicole secured the deadbolt and then the extra chain lock. Then she hightailed it back to her room and threw herself—quietly—into her bed before Nicole returned.

But Nicole did not return. Tara waited long enough to let her pulse slow down, then taking care to make some noise, got out of bed again and walked to the kitchen.

She blinked in the glare of the light over the stove. Nicole sat at the kitchen table, staring at a semi-automatic handgun on the table in front of her. Charlie, curled up on the floor at her feet, looked up at Tara. His tail began to wag.

"Nicole?" Tara said gently. "Are you all right?"

Nicole looked up quickly, eyes wide. Her hand went to her throat. "Oh, Tara. I'm sorry for waking you."

"It's all right. I thought I heard the door. Was someone here?"

Nicole looked down at the gun again. "I thought I heard someone," she mumbled.

Tara heard a cricket outside. "Did someone try to get in?"

"No."

Tara sat at the table and put her hand on Nicole's. "Do you want to talk about it?"

"No."

"Do you know how to use that?"

"Of course I do."

"Maybe you should put it away now."

Nicole sighed. She stood, picked up the gun and returned to her bedroom.

Tara followed, pausing at the bedroom door. Nicole turned on the light on her nightstand, and Tara saw her put the handgun into the drawer and push it shut.

Cameron Harris. She was having an affair with Cameron Harris.

This changes everything.

Tara thought she would never get to sleep that night, but she was startled to see light filtering through her curtains. The clock on the nightstand showed 8:30.

She peeked into Nicole's bedroom, and saw that Nicole had left her bed unmade. She tiptoed to the nightstand and Tara slid the drawer open, hoping it would not squeak. *Did it squeak last night? I don't remember.*

The gun was still there. Glancing over her shoulder in case Nicole came back, Tara slid the drawer gently closed.

Wearing pajamas and a housecoat, Nicole sat at the kitchen table, reading a newspaper. A mug steamed near her hand.

"Good morning, Tara," she said without looking up. "I made coffee." She flipped the page.

"Good morning," Tara answered. She poured herself a cup and sat across the table from Nicole. "Are you okay?"

"Why wouldn't I be?"

That newspaper story must be really fascinating. "Because of last night. Did you get much sleep?"

Nicole shrugged. "Sure."

Should I tell her I know there was someone in her bedroom? No. I need to find out more.

"What are we going to do today?" Tara asked as she stood. She found cereal.

"Maybe you could go into town and buy some groceries. There's not much left here, and almost no coffee. I'm going to talk with customers."

Is that where she's been going every day?

She wasn't sneaking off with Roberto. She was sneaking off with Cameron Harris. How much younger than her is he?

I have to tell Paul about this.

Unanswered questions

Tara waited until Nicole had gone into the winery. Then she got into her Civic and headed for Sebastopol. She called Rondeau once she reached the highway to tell him she'd be there.

Tyler had hot coffee ready, just the way she liked, when she arrived. She sat down across the coffee table from Rondeau and launched into it.

"I can confirm that Nicole was having an affair while Alan was alive. But she's ended it."

Paul did not say anything. He just tilted his head to one side and looked into Tara's eyes.

Tara took a breath. "Nicole wants me to sleep in the house. So I moved into the guest room, pretty much from the second night after we came back to the house. Last night, someone broke into the house in the middle of the night. Snuck into Nicole's bedroom. They knew each other. She recognized him and drew a gun."

"That Sig Sauer in her nightstand drawer?"

"Yeah. She kicked him out. Told him never to come back."

"So—did you see who it was?"

"It was dark. He was tall with broad shoulders and wavy hair."

"Tall, broad shoulders, wavy hair."

Tara took a deep breath. "At first, I thought it was Roberto."

Rondeau sat back, eyes narrowed. "You thought?"

"It was Cameron."

Paul blinked, sat forward and frowned. "Cameron ... *Harris*?"

"That's the one."

He slumped back in his chair. "Well. I always thought Cameron was gay."

"I can confirm he's definitely not gay."

Paul's eyes narrowed again. "Oh? How do you know?"

Oh, damn. "Be-because he was in Nicole's bedroom. He talked about how much he missed her. He said he missed making love to her." Tara realized she was talking very quickly. "So, he was sleeping with Nicole. Which means he's heterosexual. Not gay."

Paul held up a hand. "Tara, it's okay. I don't need to know about your personal life. Okay, so Cameron is not gay. Not all the time, anyway. One other thing: you told me once that you can usually tell when someone is lying. But you are a terrible liar yourself."

Paul pretended not to notice Tara's blush. "I need you to keep looking around. Nicole seems to be recovering from her shock, but PTSD is a long-term problem. Keep an eye on her. Remember, our job is to look after her best interests.

"And while we now know that she was having an affair with Cameron, and *not* Roberto, we still need to figure out what Roberto's secrets are."

"Roberto's secrets?"

"You told me he has secrets. And he's actually close to becoming owner, if the stars align. What has he been up to? And who did he buy that bracelet for?"

"But he's leaving for another job."

"That's according to Steven Harris. That doesn't mean it's true. Roberto is still at the winery every day, isn't he?"

"You're right—there are still a lot of unanswered questions."

"That's what I'm paying you for, Tara: to find the answers to baffling questions."

She stood. "All right. My new target: Roberto Gonsalves." She saluted.

Paul laughed.

She left.

Following Roberto

Where is it you go, Mr. Gonsalves? Tonight is the night to find out.

Tara stood on the mansion's veranda, where Roberto would not see her as he left the winery.

He's really working late. Mark and Amy left hours ago. He's dedicated to this place, even though Nicole's been doing her best to make him miserable.

Maybe he plans to marry Nicole to get his hands on the winery. Good luck with that plan, after that little toss-up in the winery yesterday.

The sun had set by the time Tara heard the sound of a vehicle door slam and the engine start. She pressed herself against the wall, hoping to find deeper shadows, as Roberto's pickup drove past the restaurant. As it turned onto the road toward the highway, she ran for her own Civic, which she had left facing out, in the parking spot closest to the road.

This is going to be tricky now that it's dark.

Her plan had been to let Roberto get far enough down the road that he would not notice another set of headlights coming out of the lot. But she could barely see a set of taillights ahead of her in the twilight, let alone verify that it was Roberto's truck.

She pressed on the accelerator, gratified as the taillights ahead grew larger. *I think that's him. I didn't see another truck come onto the road.*

The highway was still another mile ahead when she convinced herself she was indeed following Roberto. She turned on the radio, set to a pop music station.

Roberto turned south on the highway. Tara accelerated again so that she would not lose sight of him in the heavier traffic.

He got off again at the next exit, and Tara let the space between them increase, following him into a town called Roseland.

Damn. He's just going home.

She followed from what she hoped was a discreet distance into a development of new homes, and she stopped when the truck pulled into a driveway. She killed the lights, watching Roberto unlock the side door of a small bungalow.

I could have just looked in the employee files to see where he lived.

She stared at the house, trying to memorize as many details as she could in the dark: the porch in front of the door, the potted plants on the sides of the steps. Two double-hung windows to the right of the front door, a large tree in the front yard, its branches drooping toward the eaves of the house. At the corner of the yard, near the street, a street lamp that illuminated a big Ford pickup.

Why does that truck look so familiar?

She got out of her car, closing the door as quietly as she could. She crept closer until she could see it was a four-door F-350. She memorized the license number and crept back to her car.

She backed away from Roberto's house to the end of the block before turning around and driving home, trying to remember where she had seen that F-350 before.

I am such an idiot. I rode in that truck a few days ago.

Cameron Harris' truck.

The next day, Tara sat on the verandah, bored. All of Alan's papers were in order. The restaurant was closed, the house clean. Nicole was making a pest of herself in the winery, as usual. There was nothing for her to do but "keep an eye on Nicole," as Paul Rondeau had instructed.

The winery door opened and Roberto came out. He stopped to tap on the screen of his phone, then shoved it into his pocket before walking around the winery into the vineyard.

Tara got up and went after him. *Let's see what you're up to all day, instead of following you home at night.*

I should have thought of this yesterday. I would have saved some gas, at least.

The weather had started to cool. Though the day was bright, clouds to the west hinted at rain.

Tara paused to peek around the corner of the winery. She glimpsed Roberto striding down the dirt road. Slowly, she followed.

What do I do if he sees me?

Tell him the truth. You were bored with nothing to do and went to walk in the vineyard. It's nice here, now that the weather is a bit cooler.

Roberto was walking fast, so Tara picked up her pace. She froze, heart pounding, when Roberto stopped suddenly. He half turned, making Tara wonder whether she should look for a place to hide.

But he did not see her. Instead, he went between two rows of grapevines.

Tara continued ahead, hoping she was right about which row he'd disappeared into. She stopped before she got to it and turned into the row before it, hoping to parallel Roberto's progress without being found.

Soon she heard the sound of cloth brushing against plants. She slowed.

Voices. "About time you got here," said a man's voice.

That sounds familiar. Where have I heard it?

She closed her eyes, listening.

Roberto: "Sorry. Nikki's driving me crazy."

The other man: "Don't let her get to you, man. I tell you, you should find another job. I'm sure my dad would hire you."

"I don't know. I still feel like I owe it to Alan to finish this year's crush, at least."

More rustling sounds. Footfalls, the sound of a hand moving across cloth. Then a smack followed by a sigh.

That can't be a kiss.

More rustling. "The problem is, Nicole keeps getting in the way of doing my job," Roberto said.

"Well, she *is* the owner," said the other man.

Tara refused to admit that she recognized the voice.

"She doesn't know what she's doing. She's insisting on producing the cab-sauv and pinot."

"That does sound pretty stupid. Just sayin'." The sound of a long zipper opening.

"Whadja bring?" Roberto asked.

"Our very best," said the other man, and Tara heard glass clinking. "Along with real glasses."

"Is there any other kind?" Roberto laughed.

One of them grunted. She heard a cork pop, then liquid being poured. "Oh, that's good. Cold, too."

"Like I said."

A tremor, a wisp of a memory teased Tara's mind. She closed her eyes again to listen. Rustling of paper. "This is your sandwich. I put avocados on it, the way you like. This other one has no avocado." She pictured ... darkness. Her bedroom in the guest house.

"Thanks, man," said Roberto. "I cannot understand how anyone could not like avocado."

"You're so Mexican," the other man teased.

That laugh. Please don't let it be who it sounds like.

"'Sides, avocados aren't even that great this year. It's a low year for avocado trees."

"Even when they're not that great, they're still good." Crunch, crunch. "Is that bacon?"

"Yeah. I overcooked it a bit. Sorry."

"It's all good, bro."

Maybe it's his brother.

Right—he came for a romantic picnic in a vineyard with his brother.

"Y'know," Roberto said, his voice muffled by food, "We should get Tara to make some food for us."

"She's a bitch."

Now there's no question who that is.

"Hey, come on. She's nice. And she's really been helping Nicole a lot."

"Another bitch."

Roberto sighed. "Guess I can't argue with you there. But Tara really *is* a good cook."

"Maybe you should marry her." Roberto laughed, deep and long.

More clinking, more sound of liquid pouring. Then silence. Tara was getting warm. The sun pricked the back of her neck. *I should have brought sunblock. Who knew the sun could be this strong in October in California?*

A moan. Rustling of cloth.

I can't stand this anymore. Tara lay on the ground and pushed through the grapevine until she could see Roberto. She froze, not daring to breath.

Between the leaves, she could see Roberto in profile, his thick dark hair tousled, kissing another man. Roberto's face blocked the other man's, but she could see some of his curly, reddish-blond hair. His thick, muscled, athletic arms wrapped around Roberto's shoulders.

Still holding her breath, Tara drew back from the grapevine. Moving slowly to avoid making noise, she crawled backward until she felt she could turn and crouch-walk to the dirt road, where she rose and walked as quickly as she dared.

Now at least I know why I couldn't get into his pants. Why didn't I pick up on this before?

I am such an idiot. I should have let Nicole shoot Cameron fucking Harris.

Truth

Tara paced the restaurant the rest of the afternoon, hoping Nicole would not come home early, looking toward the winery every few minutes and wishing Mark and Amy would leave for their own homes soon. She made coffee, then forgot about the cup on the counter until it was cold.

The sun was low before the two winery employees left. As their cars pulled onto the main road, Tara crossed the lot to the winery. A rising anger sped her steps. *It's time for some truth, Mr. Gonsalves.*

Roberto was sitting at the desk, tapping on the computer keyboard. He didn't look away from the screen, but said, "What can I do for you this evening, Tara?"

"When are you planning to leave Rocky Creek?"

"What are you talking about?"

She decided to hit as hard as she could. "Steven Harris told Nicole that he has it on good authority you have decided to move on."

Roberto's face paled. "Where did he get that?"

"You tell me. Are you planning to leave?"

Roberto's eyes darted around the office. "No. Of course not. I—I've had offers, of course, but, but ..."

"I don't believe you." She slammed the bracelet on the desk. Startled, he stared at it for a long moment, then up at Tara.

"Why did you lie about this bracelet?"

"I don't understand. I told you I didn't know anything about it."

"Stop fucking with me. I found out where it was sold and talked to the store owner. She looked up the credit card records. Sold last February to a certain 'R. Gonsalves.' Why did you lie about it?"

"I, uh, I bought it for ... a friend."

"Which friend?"

"What difference does that make? A friend, okay? A romantic liaison. I'm allowed to have those, aren't I?"

"If you gave it to a romantic partner, what was it doing here, in the dirt, after the fire?"

Roberto's mouth hung open. He looked away, then back at Tara. "What do you mean? You found it here?"

"Who did you give it to, Roberto?"

His eyes flashed. "None of your damn business, Tara. Now give me the bracelet, so I can return it to its rightful owner."

"Sorry, lover boy, but I can't do that."

"Why the hell not?"

"Because it's evidence." *Yes, you liar, chew on that for a while.* "In a murder investigation."

Oops, maybe I shouldn't have said that.

Roberto's eyes grew wide. He fell back into his chair and croaked "Murder? What murder? Alan was murdered?"

He's a good actor.

"Look, Roberto, I can help you, but you have to come clean. You have to tell me who you gave this bracelet to."

"Are the police investigating Alan's death as a murder?"

Be smart, Tara. "It's a possibility. I hope it's not true, but ..."

"Wait a minute. How come you're asking questions? You're not a cop ... are you?"

"You should be smart and tell me what's going on. Who did you give the bracelet to?"

"Maybe I should get a lawyer."

"You want to lawyer up? Okay. I'll just go to the cops right now, with the bracelet, and tell them where I found it and when. Then you'll *need* a lawyer."

Roberto closed his eyes and took a deep breath. "I'm going to tell you something in confidence. You're not a cop, so you don't have to reveal this. Whatever you do, don't let this get back to my Mama. It would just kill her."

"I know you're doing Cameron Harris. What I want to know is how this bracelet ended up on the ground by the burned-out garage the day after we found Alan's burned body."

"I am not 'doing' him. We're in a relationship. We've been seeing each other for a year now."

How do I tell him the truth? "So you gave the bracelet to Cameron?"

"For Valentine's Day."

"When did he lose it?"

"I don't know." Roberto's eyes were still closed. "I didn't know he lost it. He couldn't wear it all the time. His parents don't know he's ... gay. Steven wouldn't like it. He's pretty religious. I haven't come out yet either."

Cameron hasn't come out because he's not really gay. He's just a whore.

Tell him, Tara. Tell him the truth. He told you the truth.

She took a breath and sat down in the guest chair. "Roberto, look at me. There's something I have to tell you."

Roberto's chocolate brown eyes gazed deep into hers. *Damn, why did he have to be gay?* "Cameron ... hasn't been faithful to you." *Should I be telling him this? Too late now.*

"What are you talking about?"

"Cameron has another lover. A woman." *Just tell him, Tara!*

"You know, you'd think I'd be used to all the homophobic bullshit by now. But I certainly didn't expect it from you."

"Homophobic?"

"It's an old story. 'He can't be gay because he's fucking a woman.' A self-defense mechanism in the straight community. No one's really gay; they're just between heterosexual partners. It's bullshit. I expected better of you, Tara."

Tara's face felt hot. "It's true Cameron is fucking Nicole! He has been for months. Open your eyes, Roberto!"

Roberto's face was pale. He coughed again, his body wracked in a fit. Finally, he wiped tears from his eyes.

"Nicole?"

"You know it's true," she repeated.

"Even now?"

"No. I've hardly let her out of my sight since ... since the fire. " *Plus, she drew a gun the last time she saw him. But I'm not going to tell you this now. Not when this is going to go to trial.*

"Wow. I just ...wow. So this is what it feels like to be cheated on."

"Is that all you can think about? How your boyfriend cheated on you? This is not about you, Roberto. Think of the bigger picture."

"Bigger picture?"

"Why was Cameron sleeping with Nicole DaSilva?"

Roberto opened and closed his mouth several times. "I think— it was something he needed."

"What are you talking about?"

"I guess ... he's bisexual. He needs sex with ... a woman. Sometimes."

"That's it? That's all you get out of this? He 'needs' sex with a woman? You men. You can't see past the end of your dicks.

Cameron was sleeping with her as part of his family's plan to break her down so they could buy Rocky Creek."

Saying that sent her mind flying ahead, tracing the last part of the path that had been before her the whole time. She sat still, not seeing the office as she became more and more certain.

"What are you talking about now?" Roberto said.

"Cameron killed Alan."

Roberto reeled back, eyes wide, mouth sputtering. "Alan died in the fire. It was an accident."

She spoke the words faster than the logic connected. She felt like she was turning the dial on a dimmer switch, increasing the light and seeing more connections, more facts. "A fire isolated from all the other fires by at least a mile. A fire to just one building in the winery. How did the fire spread from the Harris Estates all the way to this one building without burning anything else?"

"It was the winds. Fires are unpredictable. You've seen the stories on the news. One house left intact in a whole burned neighborhood ..."

"Oh, come on, Roberto. That's too much of a stretch. Then there's the other evidence. The blunt force trauma on Alan's head."

"What blunt force trauma? I never heard anything about that."

Shit. I should not have said that. Get it together, Tara.

"And then there's the bracelet. I found it here, near the garage. And now you tell me you bought it for Cameron."

"That doesn't mean anything. Cameron's here all the time."

"Yes, all the time. And there's the history of sabotage all over the winery. Pumps breaking, filters getting clogged over and over, hoses rupturing, the computer system failing."

"Things like that happen all the time in a winery."

"Then the Harrises make a lowball offer to buy the winery." *It all fits. Oh, my god.* "It was Cameron. Sneaking over here at night to sabotage the place, then fuck Nicole. And then having romantic picnics with you during lunchtime."

"How did you know about that?"

"Oh, my god, Roberto? How could you not see this? Cameron comes over here all the time, wrecks things, and bangs the owner's wife and business partner. He was trying to break up the marriage so they'd also want to dissolve the business partnership and sell. And he was sabotaging the place to reduce the sales value. It was a business venture.

"Then wildfires break out all over Sonoma County," Tara continued, talking more to herself than to Roberto. "Cameron gets a bright idea to burn down one of Rocky Creek's buildings, or maybe all of it, because no one would suspect arson in the middle of wildfires. He didn't think Alan would still be here, and Alan found him. So Cameron killed him with a blow to the head with a blunt object. He sets fire to the garage and the body to obscure evidence."

"That's crazy. Cameron's not like that."

"Oh no? Why do you think he decided on the garage? Because he wanted a functioning winery to remain on the property."

Roberto stared at her. "That can't be possible," he whispered.

"When the cops get here, they're going to find Cameron's fingerprints all over the winery. And I bet they find all sorts of trace evidence in the garage, too. Along with signs of accelerant. Face it, Roberto—your boyfriend is going to be investigated for this. And you are, too. So, yes, you'd better start looking for a good lawyer."

"You're overreacting."

"Overreacting? Is that what you're going to tell Sheriff Doyle? That she's overreacting?"

Roberto opened his mouth, but nothing came out. He looked out at the winery, then stood fast.

"Where are you going?"

"To talk to Cameron."

"That's not a good idea. Not now, Roberto. Not when you're upset."

Roberto ran out of the winery and into the vineyard.

Damn. He's going to the Harris estate.

She ran after him as the last sunlight gilded the grapevines.

She didn't notice Nicole standing just outside the winery door, Charlie sitting at her heels.

Wild fire

The gate between the two vineyards hung open when Tara reached it. She paused to dial 911, directing police to the Harris winery. Then she forced her feet to start running again.

I have to start running or exercising or something. When things settle down. And I have Roxanne with me.

She jumped as a fuzzy brown blur swept past her. Charlie the dog raced into the vineyard, quickly closing the distance from Roberto.

What the hell?

The sun was gone. She could no longer see Roberto, nor Charlie, ahead of her in the twilight. She continued jogging across the Harris vineyard until she could see the end of the rows of grapevines. And standing just beyond it, two men.

They're almost exactly the same height, the same build. She could hear their voices, loud and angry, but could not yet make out the words. Roberto was waving his arms, pacing back and forth. Cameron had his hands up as if he were surrendering. Charlie jumped back and forth between them, yapping.

"I thought we had something!" she heard Roberto shout as she got closer. "I thought we *were* something."

"I never lied to you," Cameron said. "I never said we were exclusive. Come on, man, you know us queers are sluts."

"I'm not. I was faithful to you. I haven't seen anyone else since we hooked up. I certainly haven't slept with anyone else."

"What makes you think I—"

"Tara told me."

"Tara? What does that bitch know?"

"She saw you, you idiot. In Nicole's bedroom. And everyone knows Nikki was cheating on Alan. So put two and two together."

"That doesn't prove anything."

"Then what about this?" Roberto flung the bracelet at Cameron. It bounced off his chest and fell to the ground. "Tara found it on the ground beside the garage, right after the fire. How did it get there, Cam?"

Charlie nosed the bracelet, then looked up at Cameron and growled.

Tara reached the end of the vineyard. A gravel road led downhill toward a large house, its windows filled with light. "Roberto, take it easy," she puffed.

Cameron rolled his eyes. "Oh, great. The bitch herself. You're responsible for this fairy tale? What are you going to tell us next, pizza gate?"

"I've called the police. They're on their way," Tara said.

Roberto looked pained, but Cameron's eyes went wide and his mouth fell open. "Why?"

Tara had to catch her breath. "Just settle down, both of you. You can tell your stories to them."

"You called the police because I was sleeping around?"

"I called the police because I was worried that Roberto was going to pound your face in, Cameron."

Cameron shook his head, closing his eyes. "Don't be ridiculous. Roberto couldn't take me."

"I've been taking you for a year, Cam. But Tara called the cops because she thinks you killed Alan DaSilva."

Cameron's eyes went wide again. "Killed Alan?" He started to shake. "What the fuck?"

The gravel road lit up. They turned to see a car driving up the slope, fast. Nicole's RAV4 skidded to a halt only yards from Roberto. Charlie ran to it, barking, his tail wagging as Nicole opened the door.

She jumped out, leaving the door wide open as she strode toward Cameron. Her hair was wild, her face twisted in rage. "You son of a bitch!" she screamed. "You cheating, lying son of a bitch."

"Cheating?" Cameron came back. "You're the one who's married. I was just fucking you."

"And fucking Roberto at the same time!"

"I'm not married."

Tara put her hand on Nicole's arm. That earned her a growl from Charlie. "Nicole, calm down. Let's go. It's over now."

Nicole threw Tara's hand off her arm, but stayed focused on Cameron. "You killed my husband! You animal! You sick, depraved—" Her words slipped into an inarticulate scream, and she took a long step toward Cameron.

How did she figure that out?

He backed away, looking left and right. "I didn't kill anyone."

Charlie dashed between them, teeth bared at Cameron. He growled continually.

"I know all about it, Cameron. I know about you and Roberto. And I know about the bracelet he bought you."

Charlie barked as if to underscore the statement.

She figured it out the same way I did.

Nicole pulled a gun out of the duffel bag, aiming it at Cameron. He blanched.

"Nicole, don't!" Roberto yelled.

Shit. That's the SIG Sauer from her nightstand. I knew I should have gotten rid of it.

Even Charlie looked confused. His growl became a whimper.

"Get away from him," Nicole ordered. She motioned with the gun. "Move, unless you want me to shoot you, too."

Roberto stepped to the side. "Farther, you jackass. Go stand beside Tara."

"Don't do this," Roberto said, but he complied, walking in a wide circle around Nicole, never taking his eyes from the gun.

Nicole aimed the gun at Cameron's chest. "You burned my husband to death. You burned him, you bastard. He *suffered.*"

"No, Nikki. You've got it all wrong," Cameron babbled, backing away.

The Sig banged and Cameron hit the ground. Roberto yelled and ran to him, but Charlie got there first.

Tara jumped to grab Nicole by the wrist, but Nicole pulled away and pointed the gun at her. "Get away from me, you meddling little bitch."

Roberto helped Cameron to his feet, both of them looking shocked."You didn't hit him. Thank God."

Charlie seized Cameron's pant leg in his teeth and pulled, growling renewed.

"Nicole, drop the gun before you kill someone," Tara said. "You don't need to do this. The police are on their way."

Nicole did not move the gun from pointing directly at Tara's head. "How long have you known?"

"I just found out today about Roberto and Cameron."

Cameron kicked savagely, and Charlie flew through the air, crashing into a grapevine. Cameron ran into the vineyard, making three steps before Nicole whirled to fire at him. He screamed as he stumbled to one knee, his hand on his thigh. He tried to rise, screamed again and collapsed. Charlie dashed toward him at the same time as Roberto sprang forward.

Nicole fired a third time. Roberto fell, rolled once and did not move again. Charlie grabbed Cameron's pants again and leaned back, his feet digging into the soil.

Nicole strode toward Cameron, keeping the gun on him, and put the duffel bag down at the end of a row of vines.

Tara dashed to Roberto. Blood spread across his shirt and pooled on the dry ground. She put two fingers to his throat and felt a weak, racing pulse. Gurgling sounds came from his mouth. She ripped his shirt open to see blood running freely from the wound in his chest.

Nicole was standing over Cameron. "You burned my husband and I'm going to burn you."

Charlie released Cameron's pants and looked at her. He whined as if he understood her words.

Tara bunched up Roberto's shirttail to press it against his wound, then pulled his head onto her knees, hoping to keep his airway open. Blood came from his mouth.

"Wake up, Roberto," she said, slapping his cheek. "Keep breathing. Hold on."

"He suffered," Nicole repeated. "Alan suffered like you cannot imagine. You're going to suffer like him."

"No, Nikki, no," Cameron whined. "He didn't suffer. He died instantly."

"*What?*" Tara yelped.

"I was at the garage. I admit it. I torched it. I didn't mean to hurt anyone. I thought the fire would spread, and everyone would think it was because of the wildfires."

"It *was* you doing all the sabotage, wasn't it?" Tara yelled. "You plugged the filters. You cut the lines and set the garage on fire."

"Yes," Cameron nodded. "Yes. We were trying to get you to give up so we could buy the vineyard at a better price. But I didn't burn Alan, Nikki. Please believe me."

Nicole took a container from the duffel bag and began splashing liquid on the grapevines and the ground around Cameron.

What is she doing? "Nicole?" Tara called. "We have to get Roberto medical help. His lung is punctured."

"I thought everyone had evacuated," Cameron continued whining. "I started the fire at the garage. It was hard to get it going. I started by shorting out the electrical meter. Then Alan came flying up in his truck. He clipped me with the side mirror—that's how I hurt my arm. Then he came at me with a crowbar. I fought back. I pushed him against the garage and he hit his head on the corner, hard. He fell and didn't get up."

"Why the hell didn't you help him, then?" Tara yelled.

"He was dead. He wasn't breathing, had no pulse. Plus, the garage was already on fire. His clothes caught fire. Then my—my shirt caught, and I had to run. I had to save myself."

"Coward," Tara snarled.

Nicole ignored her, continuing to pour liquid on vines. Tara smelled gasoline. She heard a distant siren, then a second. Then pounding footsteps.

Steven Harris ran up the path, carrying a rifle. "Nicole? What the hell is going on? *Cameron!*"

Nicole faced him, expressionless. "He killed Alan. He burned my husband to death. Now he's going to suffer the same."

"No, no," Cameron whined. "He didn't suffer."

"Killed Alan?" Steven exclaimed.

"He didn't suffer," Cameron went on. "He died instantly. From the blow to the head."

"Put the gun down, Nicole," Steven said, raising his rifle.

Nicole dropped the gun. She raised her other hand, and a flame ignited from the lighter she held.

"Don't!" Tara screamed, and Charlie yelped, jumping up at Nicole's hand.

Nicole bent to touch the flame to fuel-soaked leaves.

The rifle in Steven's hands cracked. Nicole flew back, her body twisting. Flames leapt up from the ground, surrounding Cameron and flying up the vines.

Cameron screamed, struggling to drag himself up the path. His father dropped the rifle as Charlie leaped at him. He managed to throw the dog into the vines again, then tried to pull his son out of the vineyard. That spread the flames further. Harris uselessly swatted at the burning clothes until his clothes caught fire, too.

Tara got her arms under Roberto's and dragged him down the path. *If I can get him out of the vineyard, he'll be safe. I can call an ambulance.*

But it was impossible to keep the wadded shirttail pressed against the wound. Tara watched blood run freely down Roberto's chest and stomach, falling onto the ground. "Hang on, Roberto. Hang on."

Cameron's screams reached a new high, and then they were joined by more. Vines blazed bright yellow and orange. On the path between, two men rolled over and over, trying to extinguish their burning clothes, but all they succeeded in doing was to spread the fire to more vines.

Tara dug her feet into the ground to pull faster. *Come on, come on. How much farther is it?*

Cameron stopped screaming as Tara reached the edge of the vineyard and the gravel road that led to the Harrises' home. The sirens were close now, louder than Steven Harris' screams.

She put Roberto down and pressed the shirt against the wound. One more look back showed her the Harrises had ceased moving.

But something else moved. *Charlie.* Looking into the vineyard to where Nicole's body lay on the path, clothes blazing, he backed away reluctantly from the growing fire.

Abandoning reason, Tara took a deep breath and ran into the vineyard, grabbing Charlie's collar before he noticed her. She hefted the dog and ran for the end of the vineyard, depositing Charlie beside Roberto. From the road beyond the Harrises' house, she could see blue and red lights flashing. She heard cars stop and seconds later two Sonoma deputies ran up.

"There are two men and a woman on fire in there," she said.

One cop spoke into the microphone pinned to his shoulder while the other knelt down beside Roberto. Charlie, fur singed and blackened, licked his face. "And this man has a gunshot wound to the chest."

"Come on, man," said the first cop, and they dashed into the vineyard.

Holding the shirt against Roberto's wound with her knee, Tara tilted his head back, pinched his nose and put her mouth against his. She exhaled hard and felt his chest rise a little.

Good.

She came up to let him exhale, then blew again.

Funny how much I thought about his lips meeting mine before, but the first time they do is after I know I'll never kiss him.

One cop emerged from the vineyard, dragging Steven Harris. Smoke rose from his clothes. The cop put him down and began artificial respiration beside Tara.

The other cop came out with Cameron and dumped him on his back before straddling his body and starting to push on his chest. Tara watched him alternate between chest compressions and leaning forward to breathe into his mouth.

From where she knelt beside Roberto, Tara could not see Cameron. *Maybe it's a good thing that I can't. I've seen enough burned bodies.*

She rose from Roberto's face. "There's a woman in there, too."

The cop on Cameron said, "We didn't see her." The flames refracted in the sweat on his soot-streaked face.

"Steven! Oh, my god, Cameron!" Janet Oakley ran up from the house.

"Please stay back, ma'am," said the cop working to revive Cameron, not ceasing his chest compressions.

"Nicole's in the vineyard!" Tara said.

"Do not go in there, ma'am," said the cop. "There's no point endangering another person." He paused to feel Cameron's throat, then began pushing on his chest again.

Janet fell to her knees, touching the young man's face. "Oh, Cameron." She sobbed.

Tara tried to shut it all out, focusing on breathing for Roberto. Breathe, up, breathe, up. At some point, she felt him breathe in himself, but she kept going.

She had no idea how long it took for ambulances to arrive. At some point, firm, gentle hands pulled her away from Roberto. Someone in white replaced Roberto's blood-soaked shirttail with a bandage. Two men put him on a stretcher and loaded him onto an ambulance beside two other stretchers. One of the paramedics helped her climb up beside him.

Only after the doors closed did Tara register the sound of more sirens. Men in yellow raincoats leaped from red trucks. She realized one of the paramedics was talking to her. "Can you hear me? Are you hurt?"

She looked down and saw her clothes were blood-soaked, too.

The paramedic repeated his question. He held a mask over Steven Harris' face, squeezing a rubber bottle rhythmically.

"No, no, I'm not hurt."

Steven's clothes were charred, both pant legs gone below the knee. The skin on his legs and hands was black. Soot smeared most of his face, but it did not look burned.

She did not look at Cameron.

Family

The coffee from the machine was too hot to drink, so Tara put the cup on the worn vinyl upholstery of the seat next to her. She rubbed her eyes, wondering briefly about the bright spots behind her eyelids, starting up again when she felt herself toppling over.

She picked up the coffee and sipped. *Cold, already. Damn. How long was I asleep?*

She looked around at the other tired people waiting for news of loved ones, or waiting to see a doctor, their bandages and splints varied, but most were still white.

"Tara!" said a voice that Tara knew she should recognize. Then Paul Rondeau was crouching in front of her, his hands on her shoulders. "My god, you're covered in blood."

She shook her head. *God, I'm so tired.* "It's not mine. It's Roberto's."

"Roberto? Where is he?"

"He's in surgery now."

"What the hell happened?"

Tara sighed and looked at the floor. *I don't know if I even have the strength left to tell him.* "He was shot."

Rondeau pulled back, eyes wide. "What? Shot? What—"

"Nicole shot him."

Paul had to sit down on the chair next to Tara. "That's ... that's not possible. That's crazy. Why ... where is she? Why didn't she call me?"

Tara had no more emotion to express. "She's dead." She could not bear to look at Paul, but she knew he was waiting for an explanation. Staring at the floor, she told him what had happened. "Nicole found out that Cameron killed Alan. She found him in the vineyard tonight and shot him. Roberto tried to stop her. So did Steven Harris."

"Oh, my god. Where is Cameron? And Steven?" He looked wildly around the waiting room. "Is Janet here?" He pulled out his phone and checked for messages.

Tara managed to raise the cup to her lips and took a gulp of cold, disgusting coffee. She took a deep breath and slumped back in the chair to tell Paul Rondeau the whole story.

Rondeau took Tara to a hotel in Santa Rosa, stopping at a small store on the way. She was too tired to do more than wait in the car, willing her hands not to shake, until he returned, throwing a bag into the back seat. "I hope I'm right about the size. I tried to err on the larger side, just so they'll be comfortable. But you can't stay in those bloody clothes, and you can't go into the DaSilva house for a few days, at least."

In the hotel room, Paul put his hands on Tara's shoulders and looked intently into her eyes. "Don't go anywhere. I'll get you some food, and then I have a lot of work to do. I'll try to hold off the cops as long as I can, but eventually you'll have to make a statement. In the meantime, you know my private cell number if you need anything at all."

Tara gasped. "Charlie!"

Paul turned. "Who?"

"Alan and Nicole's dog, Charlie. He was there, at the Harrises'. I had to pull him out of the fire. He must have stayed behind when I got into the ambulance. Oh, please, find him. I hate to think he's been outside by himself all night long."

Paul looked at Tara for a long beat. "All right. I'll find him."

He left. Tara pulled off her bloodstained clothes, dropping them into the hotel room wastebasket. When she emerged from the hottest shower she could tolerate, steam billowed through the bathroom. Every surface was slippery with steam.

She was glad she could not see her reflection.

Wrapping a towel around herself, she flopped onto the bed and hit a speed dial number on her phone.

"Dad? I'm not at the hospital anymore. I'm at the Holiday Inn in Santa Rosa."

The next day, Tara opened the door and a voice more familiar to her than her own said, "Oh, Tara. We were so worried." Hands were around her shoulders, the touch she had known her entire life, and her head was under her mother's chin, hair tickling her nose, scent filling it. She closed her eyes and returned to her mother's kitchen, the warm embrace of the home around her. Eyes closed, she could see morning sun streaming through the windows, and she forgot the smell of wood smoke and sterile hotel room.

Tara opened her eyes again when she heard Roxanne call "Mama!" The baby scrambled up into her arms, locking her little arms around her.

"Oh, Roxanne, baby," Tara said, rocking her child. "I've missed you so much."

"We got on a plane as soon as we could," Dad said, stepping in from the hall and putting down a suitcase and a bright green diaper bag to wrap his arms around Tara and Roxanne. He squeezed too tight, like he always did, making Roxanne whine. "The first thing you said when you called was 'I'm at the hospital.' You just about stopped my heart. Are you sure you're all right?"

"I'm fine, really."

Dad released his daughter and granddaughter to look around the hotel room. Mom was inspecting the bathroom. She did not look as though she approved. "It seems like a nice hotel," she said, finally. "A little small. Too small for a crib, let alone the two of us. Why are you here?"

"Paul Rondeau is paying for it."

"Why? And why aren't you in the guest house at the winery?" Mom asked.

"It's complicated."

"I'm sure it is," Dad said as he sat in the room's single upholstered chair. "First, though, I want to know why you were in the hospital."

"I went with the winery manager, Roberto Gonsalves. He'd been shot."

"Shot!" Mom and Dad said together, in the same tone of voice. Mom came close, touching Tara's shoulder, while Dad looked her up and down as if examining her.

"I told you, I'm fine. I wasn't hurt at all. Well, except for a little smoke inhalation."

"And this ... Roberto? Did he make it?"

"He'll recover. He's still in the hospital, of course. It was a pretty serious wound in the abdomen."

"Jesus," Dad whispered.

"You'd better tell us everything that happened," Mom said. "We were worried sick all the way here."

"Tell us at a restaurant," Dad said, rising again. "I'm starving. Damned airline food is disgusting."

They found a pizza place within walking distance of the hotel. Dad fed Roxanne digestive cookies as they waited for their order, and Mom interrupted repeatedly with questions as Tara tried to summarize the events since she had evacuated the winery with Roberto and the other employees.

"This is terrible," Mom kept saying. "What happened to Nicole DaSilva?"

"The firefighters found her body in the morning. It took them that long to put out the fire. The Harrises must have lost half their vines."

"And that boy?" Dad asked, looking away from Roxanne long enough for her to yelp for another cookie. "What did you say his name was? Calvin?"

"Cameron," Tara said. "He died before the paramedics got there. He'd been shot twice and set on fire. His father's in the burn unit now. He was badly burned."

Mom shook her head. "That poor family."

"So, you haven't explained who this man is who's paying for your hotel room?" Dad asked, his eyebrows high. He broke a cookie in half before giving one piece to Roxanne. "Don't spoil your supper, sweetie."

"Cookie," Roxanne said softly, holding the piece in both hands. "Want eat."

"Stop worrying, Dad," Tara said, ruffling Roxanne's fine, short hair, soft as feathers. She touched her nose to the baby's cheek. I can't believe how good that feels. "Paul Rondeau is—was—the DaSilvas' lawyer. He's also my boss. He hired me last week to look around the winery after Alan died, and to keep an eye on Nicole, too."

"Wait—that's the work you're doing for the law firm?" Dad asked. "You're a legal investigator?"

"I never thought of it that way ... yeah, I guess so." She didn't know how to describe the feeling welling up in her chest. *Legal investigator. Sounds good.*

"Oh good, here's our pizza," Mom said. "I'm famished."

Epilogue

Roxanne on her hip, Tara led her parents into Paul Rondeau's law office. Tyler Patel's face lit up at the sight of the baby. He almost ran up to hold the door until Ken and Marie Rezeck had entered, Dad holding the diaper bag.

Paul emerged from his office. "Very pleased to meet you, Mr. and Mrs. Rezeck." Paul smiled brightly at Roxanne. "And you, too, Miss Rezeck. It's too bad we don't have any baby toys in this law office."

"May I hold her?" Tyler asked. Tara gave Roxanne to him. He hugged her and tickled her, and she squealed in delight. "Hey, baby. I know things we can play with." He sat cross-legged on the floor and put Roxanne beside him. He reached up to his desk for his tablet computer and put it on the floor. Tara watched as he opened an app that showed colorful cartoon animals. "Do you see a cow?"

Roxanne tapped the screen and laughed when the cow mooed.

"It looks like she's entertained for now," Tara said.

"If your folks wouldn't mind waiting, we need to talk for a few minutes?" Paul asked.

Tara looked at her parents. Mom shook her head at the first question, while Dad nodded fast at the second.

Paul led the way into his private office, motioning to the chair in front of his desk as he went behind it. *Oh, oh. He's putting the desk between us. This is not going to be good.*

"You realize I have some criticism of how you handled this," Paul said. "You're a private investigator, not a police officer or first responder. There is no way you should have gone to confront Cameron Harris like that."

"I went with Roberto. I was worried what he might do."

"You should have just called the police."

"I did call the police. Right away. Roberto got there first. He's only next door."

"*Was* only next door. But you still put yourself into a dangerous position. And Roberto is not the kind of man to have done anything violent."

"Anyone can be violent. Did you think Cameron was capable of murder?"

Paul shook his head sadly. "No. Which makes it even worse. I've just lost two good friends in Nicole and Alan DaSilva, and while I can't say he was a friend, Steven Harris is still in critical condition. And his son is dead. I don't want to lose an employee in the same horrible week."

"How is Mr. Harris?"

"He has second-degree burns on his legs and arms, but the doctors say he'll recover. But I can't imagine how he and Janet are going to get over Cameron's death."

"Not to mention finding out he's a murderer. *Was* a murderer. What's going to happen to the Rocky Creek Winery with both co-owners dead?"

"Alan and Nicole had no children, so under the terms of their wills, the ownership goes to their respective parents. They don't have any experience running a winery. And as you know, the Wappo Tribe now has the right to purchase the winery. I doubt they will, as they decided not to after Alan passed away. But in the event they do, they'll keep Roberto as general manager—if he wants to stay. Again, that's not certain. I can understand how he would want to find a different job.

"I don't know what to do about the restaurant. I'm trying to find a buyer, but the market is now understandably spooked by its history."

"Why not … let me keep running it?" Tara asked.

Paul smiled. "Tara, I like you, and you're smart, but you don't have any experience managing a restaurant. I know you're a good cook, maybe even a chef, but operating a high-end restaurant like that requires a lot of experience. Besides, you're going to be busy with your day job."

"Day job?" Tara thought over his words. Then things clicked into place. "You said 'employee?' You're hiring me?"

"See that? I said you were smart." Paul laughed a little. "Yes. You're a good investigator, Tara. And you have excellent credentials from a high-falutin' eastern law school. So I'm offering you full-time employment. You'll be probationary for six months. That's standard policy. Tyler, there," he motioned toward the door to the waiting room. "just finished his probationary period."

"He's only been here six months? He seems like a fixture."

"He knows where everything is and can put his finger on it whenever needed. That's what makes him such a good legal secretary."

"So, full-time. Like, nine to five?"

"I like to start at eight, but I guess I can be flexible. If you're dependable. But there's going to be overtime. Investigations don't normally follow office hours. And there's an online course and exam you have to pass by California law."

"Okay. I guess I can do that."

"There's a private investigator that I use on a contract basis pretty regularly. He can be a good resource."

"Really? Won't I be replacing him?"

"Not necessarily. But yes, one reason I'm hiring a full-time investigator is because I'm spending a lot more than your salary on contractors."

"Is there really that much crime in Sonoma?"

Paul shrugged, playing with an expensive pen. "No more than any other wealthy county in California with a huge disparity between rich and poor, I suppose. But don't think that every investigation is going to involve glamorous wineries and mysterious murders. Most of it is pretty dull, insurance-related stuff."

"Fraud?"

"Not always. Sometimes the insurance companies just need some details clarified. But sometimes people are trying to make a claim they're not entitled to."

"So … will the pay be the same as that first check you gave me?"

Paul laughed. "I was going to say no because that was a short-term contract, and I needed you on the job immediately. So I told myself I was giving you a bonus. But I like you, and you have such a pretty daughter. I'll tell you what." He leaned on his arms on the desk. "When you pass the exam, I'll raise your salary to that level. Deal?"

"Wow! Thank you." She stood. "I guess I better start looking for an apartment."

"Not so fast—you haven't said 'yes,' yet."

"Oh. Yes! Yes, I'll take the job." She reached across the desk to shake Paul's hand.

Tyler came in then, Roxanne holding his hand. In his other hand, he held a leash, at the end of which Charlie trotted. His eyes were fixed on Tara, his mouth open. He strained against the leash until he could get his head under her hand. She petted him, pulling her hand away when his tongue wrapped around it.

"Doggy!" Roxanne squealed and grabbed Charlie's tail. He danced out of the way, pressing his shaggy body against Tara's legs.

Tyler transferred Roxanne's hand to Tara's, then pulled a green, legal-size folder from under his arm and put it on the desk.

Tara picked up her daughter and bent to rub Charlie's ears. "What's this all about?"

"Consider it your signing bonus. I found him back at the DaSilvas'." His voice hitched, and he coughed to try to mask it. "Anyway, I had him shampooed and groomed and checked out by a vet."

Tara realized then how clean and soft the dog's fur was, and how it was so badly singed and sooty the last time she had seen him. "So ... you want me to take him?"

Paul smiled. "He seems to love you more than me. Besides, I already have a dog. Princess was good about letting Charlie into her home for a couple of days, but I think she's had enough competition."

He scanned the pages in the folder, then turned one paper around so Tara could read it. He gave her a pen. "Sign here. Then you can give Tyler your banking information. We use direct deposit here."

Tara signed, and turned to see her parents standing at the office door. "Congratulations, dear," Mom said.

"Tyler told us," said Dad. To Paul, he said, "Can I take you and Tyler here to a family lunch?"

"Sure," Paul answered. "I know a good restaurant that has a place where they'll give Charlie water and a treat."

FIN

Dear Reader:

Thank you very much for reading *Wildfire*. I anticipate this to be the first volume in a series of Wine Country mystery novels, so I hope you liked it.

If you did, I'd really appreciate it if you could write a review on the e-tailer where you bought it.

A couple of notes about some elements in the story. First, I know there is no such place as Barnestown, California. While places like Sonoma, Monte Rio and Sebastopol are real, I found it necessary to make up a town close enough to the entirely fictional Rocky Creek Winery on Rocky Creek Road. There is a Rocky Creek Road in California, about sixty miles from where I imagined the setting of this book, so if I offended anyone by usurping the name, I apologize.

There is also a Rocky Creek Winery in Cowichan, British Columbia. Thanks to them for allowing me to use their name and featuring this book in their establishment.

I have a lot of people to thank for helping in the writing, editing and publishing process. First of all, my wife Roxanne, who first suggested I write a book about the wildfires in California during our visit there in the autumn of 2017. She also said the protagonist should be a woman, and there should be a dog.

Thanks to Elsa Hainzelin for owning the real Charlie the terrier-mix.

Thanks to my beta readers for their insight and excellent suggestions that have done so much to make this story better: Ann and Thane Brown, Dana Griffin, Diana Geraldizo, Peter Forsyth, Jeanne Hughes, Laura Gwen, Karin Carlson, Marilyn Hiliau, Kenneth Lingenfelter and Laura Broussard.

A side note to Thane: I know that the work-around for the electrical panel is not something a real electrician would do. But sometimes you have to take a little license to make the story work. You have to admit, there is a lot of wiring out there that doesn't quite meet code.

Thanks to Cheryl Sirkus of Sonoma Art Works for letting me use her name and products as a clue in this story.

Thanks to Cyrano's restaurant for allowing them to be featured in the book. A few words about Cyrano's. First, it's not in Sonoma, but rather in Ottawa. It's the favorite restaurant of my wife and me. Second, the owner/chef is not Gordon Bailey, but the excellent Giovanni Baccala, who has further graced these pages with his recipe, below. I also want to thank Cyrano's manager, the very gracious Joe Guidone.

Thanks to my awesome editor, Gary Henry—who may not be the Fire Marshall of Sonoma County, but he easily could be. And thanks also to my excellent proofreader, the eagle-eyed Joy Lorton.

Also, thanks to the Lei Crime Kindle World authors who attended the Russian River writers' retreat last October, many of whom are now characters in this book—whether they like it or not: Toby Neal, Erin Finigan, Shawn McGuire, Janet Oakley and Amy Allen. Ron Logan and Corinne O'Flynn, the only reason you did not make it into this book is that you're already characters in *Echoes* and *Torn Roots*, respectively.

Thanks to my late uncle, Paul Rondeau, for inadvertently forming the character for the lawyer in this book.

Finally, thanks again to all the readers and reviewers for their thoughts, comments and ideas. Keep them coming, because they're all grist for the mill for the next story.

Cyrano's Grilled Eggplant Salad

1 Italian eggplant
2 ounces goat cheese
1 red Bell pepper, roasted, peeled and sliced
Extra virgin olive oil
Balsamic vinegar
Fresh basil

Using a vegetable peeler or a sharp knife, peel eggplant lengthwise in equally spaced strips leaving half the skin on.

Cut eggplant into 6–8 slices.

Place slices of eggplant onto hot grill. Mark and cook evenly on both sides.

Brush with olive oil.

Once the eggplant is soft, place a few slices of the roasted red pepper and a small amount of goat cheese on each slice.

Drizzle balsamic over each slice and allow to cook another couple of minutes while the flavors of the red pepper and goat cheese soak in.

Remove from grill and plate.

Drizzle olive oil and balsamic over each piece and top with fresh basil ,salt and pepper.

Thanks to Megan from Cyrano's restaurant in Ottawa.

About the author

After a 30-year career as a journalist and editor, Scott Bury turned to writing fiction with a children's story, Sam, the Strawb Part, and a story that bridged the genres of paranormal occult fiction and espionage thriller: Dark Clouds. Since then, he has published 12 novels and novellas without regard to staying in any one genre.

He lives in Ottawa, capital of Canada, with two mighty sons, two pesky cats and a loving wife who really tolerates a lot.

Find out more about Scott and his writing on his website, ScottBuryAuthor.com.

Books by Scott Bury

If you liked *Wildfire*, you'll love these other books by Scott Bury.

The Hawaiian Storm series

Hawai'i mysteries featuring FBI Special Agent Vanessa Storm

 *Torn Roots:* FBI Special Agent Vanessa Storm's first case in Hawaii is to find a kidnapped woman. When she gets to Maui's jungled south coast, she finds the kidnapped woman is also suspected of arson. Throw in a dispute between resort developers and a loud environmentalist, a taciturn geologist, a laid-back local police lieutenant and a rogue Homeland Security agent, Vanessa has to find her way through this labyrinth without triggering an international incident.

 *Palm Trees & Snowflakes:* In Honolulu, where the palm trees are strung with lights for the holidays, FBI Special Agents Vanessa Storm and Alan Terakawa have their hands full trying to stop the deadly flow of snowflake, the newest designer drug. Faulty intel brings the agents into a deadly firefight, which yields even more puzzles.

Dead Man Lying: With lush rain forests, black sand beaches, and a laid-back lifestyle, Maui offers the perfect retirement location for once-famous country singer Steven Sangster … until he ends up dead.

As the killer, or killers, strike again and again, FBI Special Agent Vanessa Storm must untangle the lies spun by the singer's associates, friends, family — and the singer himself before the music dies.

Echoes: The Kahuna—"wizard" in old Hawai'ian—was the only one who could surprise Vanessa Storm when she was a teenager. When she's an FBI Special Agent, though, things are different. She's no longer a girl impressed with small-town bad boys.

But the echo of a crime pulls the Kahuna back into Vanessa's life.

Action-thrillers featuring Van and LeBrun

Stealth: How can anyone sneak a gun onto an airplane these days? A seemingly unemployed surfer with no apparent training in counter-intelligence pulls a retired Mossad agent into his campaign against an international criminal cartel. Maya, the agent, only wants to start a quiet life, but there's something about this clumsy and dedicated man she cannot say "no" to.

This novel combines breakneck pacing and non-stop action with wry humor.

The Wife Line: Human traffickers are selling young women from eastern Europe as sex slaves and killing them when they become inconvenient. Taylor job is only to protect her client, until a mysterious, aggravating and irresistible young crusader pulls her and Blue on a far more dangerous path: taking down the whole slaving ring.

The Three Way: How is Daesh, the Islamic State, funding its  war of oppression in the Middle East? Van and LeBrun are determined to find out.

Van Freeman, the socialist secret agent, takes his electromagnetic gun and his hunter-killer drones on a harrowing trip through Daesh-occupied territory, blowing stuff up in his inimitable style, to unravel a three-way deal that feeds the 21st century's most evil regime.

Historical magic realism

The Bones of the Earth: The late sixth century, the darkest era  of the Dark Age, when barbarians have destroyed the Western Roman Empire. Volcanoes, rising seas and new plagues threaten the Eastern Byzantine Empire. A young Sklavenic man named Javor searches for answers: what is the link between his great-grandfather's heirlooms, his lover and his enemies? And why has the Earth decided to wipe out human civilization?

The Eastern Front trilogy

Army of Worn Soles: A Canadian is drafted into the Soviet Red Army just in time to be thrown against Nazi Germany's invasion in 1941. Caught between Nazi and Communist forces, Lieutenant Maurice Bury keeps his men alive as they retreat from the German juggernaut. But will they escape from the hell of the POW camp before they starve to death?

Under the Nazi Heel: For Ukrainians in 1942, the occupying Germans were not the only enemy.

Maurice Bury is deep in the resistance, fighting to protect their country against enemies on all sides.

Experience this seldom seen phase of World War 2 through the eyes of a man who fought and survived Under the Nazi Heel.

Walking Out of War: The Soviets draft every remaining Ukrainian man for their final push on Germany. Maurice Bury, Canadian citizen, is thrust once again into the death struggle between Hitler's Germany and Stalin's USSR. Maurice's has to survive until Nazi Germany dies, to return home to Canada. But to do that, he'll have to elude Stalin's dreaded secret police.

Other works

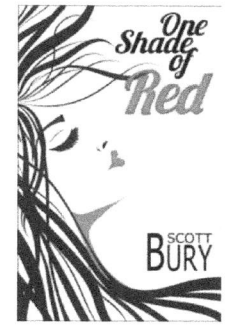

One Shade of Red: Women want the perfect man, so they can change him. But when university student Damian Serr discovers a rich, beautiful woman who's voracious about sex, he doesn't try to improve on perfection. It's all that he can do to hold on for the ride.

Over the summer, Alexis gives Damian an intense education. Day after day, she pushes him to his sexual limits. The only question he has is: will she break them?

Sam, the Strawb Part: What happens when a thin boy dresses as a pirate, attaches a jolly roger to his bicycle and starts to hijack strawberries?

The evil fruit monopoly doesn't take kindly to pirates. They hire the notorious pirate-killer, Commodore Tiberius J. Swinkill, to hunt Sam down.

This swashbuckling tale of fury and fruit is for children, parents and everyone who loves strawberries, children or pirates.

Dark Clouds: The Witch Queen's Son, Part 1: Matt always knew when his mother was on the way: the wind would swirl from all directions at once and dark clouds would mass in the sky.

Matt and his pretty wife, Teri, try to get out of the way, but as the Witch's Son, Matt is drawn into a spider's web. Only he can stop the Witch Queen's plans—but the price for that is to be paid in blood.